Praise for Scott Gibson's previous novels

A YEAR IN STUCKER'S REACH

"Gibson brings a small Colorado town to life without sentimental-ity or condescension... There is nothing cutesy or quirky about these characters, yet their nuanced decency is undeniably powerful."
—Kirkus Discoveries

STOPPING BY EARTH

"Gibson is a talented storyteller whose prose reflects a quiet sensibil-ity and humor. For example, the author's omniscient narrator reflects on Michy's sixteen-year-old acquaintance: 'Peter was one of those in-dividuals who had inherited just the correct combination of features from both parents to prove he was indeed their offspring, and that perhaps they should have thought twice about reproducing.'"
—Robin Farrell Edmunds, ForeWord Clarion Review

All the Colors of You

Scott Gibson

PINECONE BOOK COMPANY

ISBN 978-1-949053-06-7

Pinecone Book Company
P.O. Box 65 | Evergreen, Colorado 80437

PineconeBookCo@gmail.com

To Ann Davis

For 45+ years of friendship and wonderful memories.
Which is ridiculous, since neither of us is that old.

Crawl inside this body—
find me where I am most ruined,
*love me **there**.*

Rune Lazuli

A Note from Alberta Before We Begin

A couple of things, if you're serious about reading this book.

You're about to meet a lot of people, and I do mean a *lot*. I come from a big family, and most of them have their own families on top of that. Don't worry about keeping track of everybody. Trace is the person you're going to spend the most time with; let everyone else fall where they may. Oh, except for me. Modesty aside, I'm pretty important, too.

Also, while he's my brother and I love him and all that crap, take most of what he says with a grain of salt. He's had a head injury, plus the doctors went poking around in his brain, so you know… if things start to get a little crazy in here… consider yourself warned.

Finally, there's a kicker coming near the end. It'll be our little secret.

Chapter One

Bertie's funeral was set for February 14th.

Trace wondered if, in their grief, his parents hadn't taken into consideration that the fourteenth was also Valentine's Day, a day when most people's thoughts would be focused on other things. He contemplated saying something, but what could that be, after all? That his folks should pick another time so as not to forever link the tradition of giving flowers and exchanging cards with unfortunate memories of his sister's death for all the years to come?

So he didn't. And, after all, the conflict didn't impact him very much, not the way it would his siblings, the ones with kids of their own: Having to tell them that, instead of enjoying pink-frosted cupcakes and candy hearts with their classmates, they would be putting on their best dresses or suits and ties to go and sit in a pew at St. Paul's for a somber ritual in observance of an event they didn't entirely understand.

"Glad I don't have to try to explain it to anyone," he muttered, looping one end of his necktie through the knot and smoothing it down the front of his shirt.

"What are you talking about?" Marla called through the open doorway of the bathroom. She had just finished applying mascara, and was standing sideways in front of the mirror, viewing the results from different angles.

"Nothing. Just talking to myself."

Marla appeared in the open doorway, surveying him as he stood in front of the dresser. She sighed.

"Here, let me do that for you."

There was an amused, resigned tone to her voice. Trace turned at her approach, dropping his arms to his sides so she could undo the haphazard knot and start all over again. He lifted his chin as she turned up his collar and pulled the necktie free, smoothing the fabric before looping it around his neck once more.

"I can do it," he protested weakly.

"I know you can," she agreed, her eyes focused on his Adam's apple as she deftly constructed a Windsor knot. "But we have to be at the church in thirty minutes. There!" she concluded, patting his chest with satisfaction.

He could tie a necktie, but just barely. His brother Cord had shown him how, on some now-forgotten occasion when they were younger. But even nowadays it was an iffy proposition, requiring several attempts before the front part of the tie was longer than the back part and both pieces descended precisely down the center of his shirt. Thank goodness he didn't have to wear one on a daily basis. Or maybe it would be better if he did; he'd probably be better at it by now, in that case.

It was midday, so traffic was lighter than during the usual weekday commute, and they reached St. Paul's sooner than expected. Even so, the parking lot behind the austere yellow brick structure was already full, and he had to circle the block and then widen his radius until he could find an available space.

"Who all's here this early?" he muttered with irritation, slamming the car door and locking it. "The service doesn't start for an hour and fifteen minutes."

Marla shrugged. Neither of them were regular churchgoers, and they'd never been inside St. Paul's before. It had been suggested by the mortuary handling Bertie's remains.

"Some people just like to be early, probably," she said, then added, "Out of respect."

The clarification came almost too quickly, and Trace had the suspicion that she'd been about to say, "To get good seats," instead. That was probably a more accurate assessment.

As they crossed the street, they saw Aria and her husband Peter approaching from the other end of the block, and paused at the bottom of the steps to wait for them.

"Can you believe this?" his sister demanded. "We're family, and we have to park on the street? They couldn't reserve space for us in their parking lot?"

"We were thinking the same thing," Marla said in that commiserating tone of voice she was good at adopting. She hugged Aria and then squeezed Peter's arm. "How're you two doing?"

"Oh, you know," Aria shrugged. "Dreading the next few hours, mostly. You?"

"The same," Trace replied. "Hi, Pete." He shook hands with his brother-in-law, but did not move to embrace his sister. Bannerlys, for the most part, weren't the demonstrative sort. He glanced over their shoulders, then went ahead and asked, "Where are the kids?"

His sister gave him an incredulous look. "In school. They're six and eight, for God's sake. They don't need to be here for this."

"Plus, it's Valentine's Day," Pete added.

"Cord and Sky and I talked last night," Aria said over her shoulder as they ascended the steps. "We all decided—especially under the circumstances—that, except for Zeke, none of the kids should attend."

"Oh. Sure." Trace nodded, feeling slightly vindicated. He was glad to know he wasn't the only one who'd been comparing the weight of funerals to that of chocolate-themed holidays.

Inside the heavy doors, they were met by a somber man in a dark suit with thick dark eyebrows to match.

"I'm sorry," he greeted them. "We aren't seating anyone in the sanctuary just yet. Not for another thirty minutes."

"We're family. It's our sister's service," Trace told him.

The other man's scowl deepened.

"Relatives of the deceased usually enter through the side door. From the parking area."

To his right, Trace heard his sister's indignant intake of breath.

"Well, we didn't know that, obviously," she snapped. "And anyway, the lot's already full. You would think—"

Trace opted to cut her off at that point.

"—You aren't going to make us go out and go around, are you?"

Their greeter appeared to be considering this for a second or so before he finally acquiesced and held open the door leading into the sanctuary.

"There's a door toward the front by the organ. See? Go through there and down the corridor. The mourning room is to your right."

They walked through the opening and moved single-file down the aisle, passing rows of dark wooden pews fitted with burgundy cushions. Though the high-ceilinged sacristy was laden with sprays of floral arrangements, Trace was aware only of the smell of furniture polish and stale air. The latter came, he supposed, from the enormous empty space overhead, bereft of circulation, at least in the winter months. He was still gazing upward when he felt Marla's hand tighten on his upper arm.

"What?" he started to say, but then followed her gaze. Their path to the massive organ with its row of escalating brass pipes had brought them within feet of the coffin, reposing to one side. Pete and Aria, ahead of him, kept moving, unaware that he'd stopped in his tracks. A second later, they had vanished through the doorway tucked back in the alcove.

"Oh," he said, more an expulsion of air than a comment.

This chrome-plated, brass-handled *thing*, this gigantic box that now held Bertie, would be the resting place for her earthly remains for the rest of eternity.

Why, she could roll over in it, shift into whatever position was most comfortable, he thought dazedly. Even draw her knees up to her chest, if she so desired.

"Trace?" Marla whispered softly. "Honey?"

"To your right!" came a booming voice from far behind them. Apparently the man who had ushered them through the doors had been watching all along, tracking their progress. "The door to the mourning room is on your right!"

"We know that!" Marla hurled angrily over her shoulder. "Just leave us alone, will you?"

"I'm fine," Trace assured her. "I just… I didn't expect…"

"Me either," she said.

She kept her hand on his arm as they moved across the heavy carpet into the shadowed recess and deserted hallway. Aria and Pete were nowhere to be seen, evidently having assumed that Marla and Trace were still right behind them. But there were voices, lots of them, booming from an open door some distance ahead.

Mourning room, Trace thought with bemusement as they stepped across the threshold. Within, there were half a dozen conversations, all of them lively, flying between several groupings of people. It sounded more like a party. Aria and Pete were already absorbed into the crowd, talking to Aunt Ivy and one of the cousins. His brother Cord stood by a row of folding chairs, nodding and listening to Ivy's husband Nick, who sat with his cane resting across his knees. Cord's wife Leslie and their other sister, Sky, were some distance away with Trace's mother. Quince, youngest of the siblings, leaned against the wall, propped on his elbow, chatting with Sky's husband Matt.

His father, catching sight of them, detached himself from another group and came forward.

"Hey, son," he said, shifting a tall cardboard cup of steaming coffee from one hand to the other in order to touch Trace's shoulder. "Good morning. Marla, you look lovely." He brushed his lips to her cheek.

"Hi, Frank," she returned. "How are you doing?"

He twisted up one corner of his mouth and glanced around the room as he gave the question some consideration. Then, nodding vaguely, he delivered his response. "Oh, well. You know." He pointed to a table in the corner and said, "There's coffee, if you want some." He hoisted his cup. "I stopped and got my own on the way. I didn't know there'd be any."

"I'm good for right now," Marla said, then looked at Trace. He shook his head.

"No thanks, Pop."

A man in dark slacks and a dark shirt was moving through the clusters of people. He held a small spiral notepad in one hand.

"That's Father Bradley," his dad explained. "He'll get to the two of you in just a bit. He's checking to see who might want to stand and say a little something about your sister during the service. Do you think you have anything to say?"

"You… You mean, like a eulogy, or something?" Trace blinked a few times.

His father's shoulders rose and fell in another shrug. "Well, that. Or just a little anecdote, or something. It doesn't have to be anything fancy."

"Oh. I… I don't think so. I mean, unless…"

"No. No, that's fine." Frank dismissed the notion with a casual wave. "I think that's asking a lot of family members, actually, to get up and speak in front of everybody. He says he's going to open it up to all the mourners as well, once things are under way. But he wanted to check with us first. Marla? How about you?"

The question seemed to catch her off guard. "Uh, no, Frank. I guess not. But thank you for asking."

He nodded. "Just tell the Father, then, when he gets around to you." Leaning in, he added in a lower tone, "Frankly, I don't see the point of dragging things on for too long, anyway."

"They could have given us a little more notice, you'd think," Trace said. "To give it some thought; maybe write something down." But already his father was drifting off, hoisting his cup for a gulp of coffee as he approached another group.

"Write what down?" his brother Quince asked, stepping up behind them.

"Are you going to stand up and say something?"

Quince grimaced, shaking his head. "Hell—I mean *heck*—no." He glanced around sheepishly, remembering their surroundings. "I mean, it's not from a lack of caring. But I just don't know what it would be."

"Hello, I'm Stuart Bradley." Trace found himself staring down at a hand that had seemingly appeared from nowhere. His gaze moved from the outstretched fingers to the black shirt cuff, up the sleeve and to the face of the priest who had sidled up from somewhere behind and was now standing between Quince and Marla, smiling at him sympathetically. "And you're Trace, I gather? The last of the siblings. And your wife, Marla? I've met everyone else, I think." His hand, Trace noticed as he shook it, was smooth and cold, like marble.

"I'm sorry we didn't get to meet before now," Father Bradley continued. "I visited with your parents the other night, but today is the first time I've had the opportunity to meet any of the rest of Alberta's family."

Trace glanced at Quince and then looked back at the priest. "Uh, yeah. Yes, I mean. It's nice to meet you, Father."

"It's Stuart, please." Eyes lowered, the priest was flipping through the pages of the small spiral notebook in his hand. "I have the impression that none of you got my message about having the opportunity to stand up and say a few words during this morning's service. If you would like to, that is."

"Um, no. I mean, no, I hadn't gotten that message, anyway." Again, Trace glanced at his brother, who raised one quizzical eyebrow and shrugged.

"Well, I know that it's last-minute now, but I still wanted to extend the courtesy." Stuart found an empty page in his notebook and reached to lift a pen from his shirt pocket.

Trace was shaking his head and about to utter a polite refusal, when the priest added, "Your mother thought that you, especially, might like the opportunity."

And on the far side of the room, over Father Bradley's shoulder, Trace saw his mother turn from a conversation with his Aunt Ivy to beam at him. She raised one hand and wiggled her fingers in a perky little wave that held him transfixed for another second.

"Uh..." Finally he was able to transfer his gaze back to Stuart. "No. No, thank you. I'd just as soon not."

To his relief, the priest did not cajole or look disappointed. He merely nodded, re-pocketed his pen, and closed the notebook. "Of course," he said agreeably. "Well, if you will excuse me, then, I should go and get into my robes. You will all stay in here until the other guests are seated in the sanctuary. Then one of the ushers will be in to escort you to your places just before the service gets underway."

He shook their hands in turn, then wheeled and disappeared through the open doorway.

"I wondered," Quince said, after he was gone, "if he was going to conduct this service dressed like that. In just the black shirt and tie. I don't know how Episcopalians do these things."

"He's awfully young, don't you think?" Marla observed, still looking at the doorway through which Stuart had departed. "Not that it matters, of course. But I wonder if he's even as old as Bertie." She put her hand on Trace's wrist. "Or you, I guess I mean."

Trace turned to his brother. "Did you know that he'd been to visit Mom and Pop earlier?"

Quince shook his head. "Nope. But that's what men of the cloth do, right? If they're going to officiate at a funeral, they pretty much would have to talk to the deceased's relatives, don't you suppose?"

"Yeah," Trace said. "I just... I..." But then he didn't say anything more, even though Marla and his brother looked at him expectantly for another second or so.

TRACE WAS SURPRISED to find the pews nearly full when the family filed into the sanctuary for the service. Who were all these people? He recognized faces here and there, scattered among the much larger number he didn't know. Friends of Bertie's? Was she acquainted with this many people? He'd heard that there were such things as folks who made funeral-going a kind of habit, showing up for services whether they knew the departed or not. Was that who some of these were? Yet, surely there couldn't be so many individuals at such loose ends that they had nothing better to do than to come here to St. Paul's in the middle of the day, a work day for most, for someone they'd never even met.

"We are here to honor the life of Alberta Bannerly, and to cherish the time spent with her…"

Father Bradley's voice was sepulchral and commanding, much different than the soft, effacing tone he'd used when talking with the family earlier. It was the acoustics of the high-ceilinged sanctuary, Trace supposed, designed to carry sermons effortlessly to every single listener. The robes helped, he thought. Slipping into heavy, dark garments so formal and important-looking just naturally gave a weight and gravitas to anything a person might say.

"…not to mourn so much as to celebrate her passage into something more glorious and fulfilling…"

A shaky sob escaped someone's throat from a pew behind him. He started to look, then thought better of it. It hadn't been from anyone in the immediate family, all of whom were seated to his side or in the row ahead. As the eulogy continued, he was aware of more gasps and strangled little chokes coming from one direction or another. As discreetly as he could manage, Trace turned his head in either direction. To his left, Marla clutched a handful of tissues, but her eyes were dry. Quince was seated next to her and beyond him Uncle Nick, Aunt Ivy, and their daughter Estelle. Sitting to Trace's right were his sister Sky and her husband Matt. In front of them were his parents. His father's arm was draped across his mother's shoulder. They were flanked on one side by Aria and Peter and on the other by his brother Cord, wife Leslie, and their son Zeke, the oldest of the grandchildren, and the only one in attendance. Everyone held identical postures, shoulders back, heads bowed to the same slight degree. Not a one seemed overtaken by outward emotion.

Who, then, he wondered, was doing all the crying?

When the time came for people to come forward and offer reminiscences, his cousin Estelle was the only family member to participate. She recounted a handful of misadventures she and Bertie had shared, including the time when they were thirteen and had succeeded in getting to a rock concert by convincing each set of parents they were staying overnight at the other one's house instead. This elicited a few wan smiles.

After Estelle, a few non-family members spoke: a childhood friend or two, one of the neighbors, a junior-high teacher. Everyone recounted experiences from years earlier, when Bertie was six, ten, thirteen or thereabouts, all except for the last person, a lanky, somewhat emaciated-looking man with a shaved head who made his way from one of the last rows, clumping down the aisle in heavy-soled boots.

"Oh, God," Trace heard Sky murmur under her breath as the man stalked past their pew. Like Trace, she'd caught sight of the intricate tattoo that wound its way from the back of his neck, up over his right ear, ending in the hollow of his jaw. At first, Trace had thought it was a scar or some unfortunate disfigurement, but no. It was a dragon.

The man mounted the carpeted steps at the front of the sanctuary to stand behind the podium as the other speakers had done, and turned to face the crowd. Black jeans were tucked into his boots, but from the waist up, his attire was more formal: a white button-down shirt and navy-blue necktie. Tied, Trace reflected, more neatly than any he himself would have been able to manage without Marla's help.

The young man's appearance was so unexpected, so startling, that the quiet room had grown even quieter. It seemed as though the entire congregation was holding its collective breath, waiting. He stared back at his audience, fingers gripping the edge of the podium. His expression, under dark brows, seemed fierce, but after a few seconds, Trace realized he was nervous and attempting to summon the courage to speak.

"Um…" he said finally. "…Um, so… Albie, she… She was all right. I didn't know her for very long, but I liked hanging out with her. She wasn't like, you know… some people. She was cool, you know?"

He glanced uncertainly in Father Bradley's direction. The priest smiled encouragingly, evidently not at all alarmed by the intimidating appearance of this last speaker, or at least practiced at concealing it if he was. The tattooed fellow did not return his smile, but only nodded.

"I'll miss her," he concluded simply. He stepped around the podium and made his way back up the aisle. Next to the pews containing the family, he paused.

"Thanks," he said, his gaze sweeping over all of them. "For, you know... having her."

As one, they stared back at him, at a loss for words. He shrugged in a no-hard-feelings sort of way.

And clumped to the back of the church.

Trace watched his mother turn to his father and mouth the word, "Albie?" His father shook his head blankly.

"Maybe he's confused. Maybe he's in the wrong church," he murmured.

TRACE WAS FLOPPED ACROSS the bed diagonally, arms flung out to either side. He studied the ceiling, which was swaying slightly, an effect of the alcohol he had consumed over the past several hours. Marla was in the bathroom, this time removing her mascara and the rest of her makeup, in between taking sips of wine from a glass perched next to the sink. Neither of them had said anything for several minutes. It had been an arduous day, the funeral followed by a trek to the cemetery for another prayer over the coffin before it was lowered into the ground. Afterward, some of the group adjourned to his sister Sky's house for a meal and still more condolences from well-wishers.

Marla flicked off the bathroom light and came into the bedroom, carrying her glass. Her face was pink and shiny from being freshly scrubbed as well as from her wine.

"Scootch a little," she ordered, setting her glass on the nightstand and sliding her way onto the bed. Trace wriggled a few inches to one side so that they were lying side by side, both gazing overhead. Marla had changed into a nightshirt. All he had managed to do was remove his jacket, loosen his tie, and kick off his shoes.

"It seems unreal and real, at the same time," she said after a few minutes.

"Yeah. I guess."

She turned her head to look at his profile. After a few seconds, she faced forward again.

"Like when my uncle died a few years ago. I hardly ever saw him, so it wasn't like his being gone affected my day-to-day life. But still… there's the knowing."

Marla sought out his hand and threaded her fingers through his.

"That's not the same, I know. Bertie was your sister. And a lot younger than my uncle."

Trace could tell she was waiting for him to say something in return, anything at all, probably. But he was sifting through images, like a kind of mental nickelodeon with picture after picture flickering past his mind's eye.

"Albie," he said at last.

"Oh, yeah!" she rolled onto her side, resting her head on the crook of her elbow as she faced him. "Wasn't that bizarre? That guy, I mean? With that wicked-looking tat and everything."

But Trace was recalling the perplexed look that had passed between his parents.

"It's short for *Alberta*," he explained. "Just like *Bertie* is."

"Oh, sure," Marla responded vaguely. "It's just that none of you ever called her that."

"No, but somebody obviously did. We should *know* it. My *parents* should."

There was an annoyed tone to his voice that made her look more closely at him.

"Oh. Well, I'm sure they do. It just may have taken them a little longer to—"

"—They didn't!" Trace insisted. "They just chalked it up to him being some weirdo or druggie off the street, walking up to the front of the church and rambling a little bit."

He flung the back of one hand across his eyes and sighed heavily. Marla studied him with concern.

"Well, but, does it really matter all that much?" she ventured tentatively after a few seconds. "I mean, he just said a few random things. He wasn't even there when we all walked out of the church afterward. He didn't show up at the cemetery. So, yeah, he was talking about Bertie and he actually knew her. But, do you really think we're ever going to see him again?"

"No, but—"

"—Is it really that big a deal if your poor folks thought he was talking about somebody else altogether? Does it change anything at this stage of the game?"

Trace lifted his hand from his face and began unknotting his tie.

"No," he agreed. "It doesn't. I just think it's interesting that some guy with a shaved head and black jeans acted more genuinely bereaved about my sister's death than anybody in her actual family did."

He sat up to slide the necktie free from his collar in one snapping motion. He tossed it over the side of the bed and began to unbutton his shirt and cuffs. Marla, amazed, continued to rest her head on her elbow, watching him.

"You're kidding, right?"

Trace didn't answer. He was occupied with tugging his shirttails out of his pants. He wriggled out of the garment, turning the sleeves inside out in the process, then slid off the bed to stand and unfasten his belt and drop his trousers.

"Trace?"

"Forget it," he instructed, peeling off one sock and then the other before collapsing back on the bed in his boxers. "I'm drunk, is all."

He had been, but the inebriation was slipping away. What remained, however, was a collection of stray moments recalled from this day now ending: His mother's coy little wave at him from across the mourning room. His father brandishing a cup of gourmet coffee that he'd stopped to buy on his way to the church. The sight of Bertie's massive coffin standing alone and unattended in the sanctuary while all the rest of her family was across the hall chatting up a storm. The service itself, punctuated by the sound of sniffles and weeping, none of it coming from them. No, the Bannerlys weren't precisely the shining example of a bereaved family.

"Your mother thought you, especially, might want to say something," Father Bradley had told Trace. Because he was just a little bit closer to Bertie than the rest of them were. Because, nearly twenty-nine years ago, they had arrived on this planet at the same time, fellow travelers in the womb.

"I'm sorry, sweetie," he said, nuzzling his face against his wife's before tugging back the covers and sliding into the cool, welcoming sheets. "It's just been a day, that's all."

He turned away from her, closing his eyes and pulling the covers up to his chin. His eyes were stinging from staring at the overhead light for so long. Nothing else.

Chapter Two

The Bannerly gene was an alpha, it seemed, running roughshod over any unwary recessive ones it happened to encounter. It was borne out in the fact that Trace and his siblings shared an overabundance of similar features: brown hair and golden-brown eyes; crooked grins that sloped to one side; pinched, sharp noses, better-looking on the girls than the boys; large hands with thick fingers, not particularly good-looking on any of them.

Even diluted a generation later, its influence was unmistakable. From behind the counter, Trace watched his nephew Zeke take packages of permanent markers out of a cardboard box and hang them on display hooks. The boy's forehead was wrinkled in concentration over standard-issue Bannerly eyebrows, and his mouth was pursed in an expression of complete focus. At fifteen, he was nearly a replica of his father, moving with the calculated motion of a disenfranchised adolescent trying to extend the task as long as he could manage. And that was fine; sometimes it was exhausting finding enough tasks for him to do during his two-hour after-school shift. If he wanted to drag this one out, Trace had no objections.

He'd hired Zeke as a favor to his brother Cord, not from any burning need to have someone sweep the floor or restock the shelves at glacial speed, but to keep Zeke occupied for the two hours between the end of school and when his parents got home each evening. Unsupervised, he'd been putting his time to a variety of uses they were finding increasingly alarming.

"Will this package reach my niece by Tuesday?" the woman facing Trace inquired. "Tuesday's her birthday, you know."

He didn't know that, of course, but he continued to smile confidently. "It will," he assured her. "Since this is Wednesday, it may well reach her by the end of the week. Shouldn't be a problem at all."

"Oh." She considered this. "Well, but, I'm not sure I want it there that quickly. Her birthday's not until Tuesday," she reiterated. If she heard Zeke's snort from behind her, she gave no indication. "I don't want Claudia—Claudia's my niece, you see—I don't want her thinking I don't even know when her birthday is. Isn't there some way I can make absolutely certain that it arrives Tuesday?"

Aware that Zeke had stopped unpacking markers and was now watching with undisguised interest, Trace managed to maintain a sympathetic, professional expression while pointedly not looking in his nephew's direction. "Well, yes, there is. But only by shipping it on Monday for priority overnight delivery, and that's going to cost quite a bit more."

"Oh." The woman looked crestfallen. She looked down a moment longer at the tidily addressed box sitting on the counter between them.

"How about this?" Trace suggested when it appeared the woman was hoping for a more satisfactory resolution to her dilemma. "Why don't you go ahead and ship it today? And you can call your niece on Tuesday to wish her a happy birthday. That way, even if the package gets there sooner, she'll still know you remembered the exact day."

"Old people are weird," Zeke pronounced a few moments later, when no customers were left in the store. "If it was me, if I were her niece, I'd just be happy to get the present. I wouldn't ever wonder if she remembered the right day or not."

"That's because you're fifteen and the world revolves around you alone. Teenagers are greedy little bastards without much thought for what other people might like to see happen." This observation came from Mikayla, the gaunt woman sitting with her back to them at a desk behind the counter. She continued entering figures on a spreadsheet that flickered on the screen in front of her without missing a beat or turning to see the effect her words might have on him.

Zeke didn't seem to register any offense at this. He finished hanging the rest of the markers and carried the empty box to the counter.

"I don't see why you didn't just let her send the package overnight," he said to Trace. "That'd be more money for the store, right? Isn't that what you want?"

"Well, yes, sort of." Over his shoulder, he could hear Mikayla's fingers clattering on the keyboard at a brisk pace, though he was sure she was waiting with interest to hear what else he might be about to say. "But…" and there he paused, wondering just how much of a lecture he wanted to give, or that Zeke would be willing to hear, in any event.

"But we'd like her to be a repeat customer," he added finally. "And she might not be, if she associates us with a large fee to send a gift."

"'Specially if the charge is more than the gift itself cost," Mikayla contributed.

Zeke scrutinized Trace for a moment, weighing the validity of that answer. He was at the age where he tended to question most things adults told him, just on general principle. Finally, though, he picked up his cardboard box once more and headed toward the back room.

"Oh, I forgot," he said a second later, leaning through the open doorway. "I was supposed to ask if you could give me a lift home tonight. Dad's got a late meeting, and Mom's picking up Lisa from ballet." He ducked back into the storage area without waiting for a response.

There was a snort from Mikayla's direction that may or may not have been related to that revelation. Though she had nothing against Zeke personally, she'd always viewed his employment here as an indulgent response to a problem with more practical solutions elsewhere.

"Sure," Trace called after him, because what else was he going to say?

"Mm-hm," Mikayla said, not quite under her breath.

A BRISK, WARM BREEZE sent leaves and a fast-food bag skittering across the parking lot and ruffled their clothing as Trace and Zeke got into the car. The restless air carried on it a promise of spring, but it was instead the start of a cold front threatening more snow. It was still February, after all.

"Next Monday's an in-service day at school," Zeke told his uncle as they pulled out into traffic. "So no classes. Me and Sean and some others thought we might go snowboarding."

Though it didn't sound like it, Trace realized this was being framed as an inquiry.

"So, you're wondering if you could have Monday off," he said.

His nephew shifted in his seat, carefully avoiding eye contact. "Only if you think you wouldn't need me. And…"

"…And if I could maybe mention that to your folks," Trace finished for him.

In the dim light of the car's interior, he could see Zeke's sheepish grin. "But only if it's okay with you," he reiterated.

Taking his uncle's laugh as a tacit yes, Zeke settled back against the seat. They rode in silence for several blocks. Then, seemingly out of nowhere, he inquired:

"Do you believe in a heaven?"

It wasn't the unexpectedness of the question that jolted Trace as much as it was that his own thoughts just then were about Bertie and last week's funeral.

"I don't know," he said finally. "I want to believe there is. A lot of people who've had near-death experiences have talked about seeing a bright light and having an overwhelming sense of calm and joy in those few seconds before they were resuscitated, or whatever. They seem to think that was a glimpse into whatever awaits us after this life."

Zeke chewed his lower lip for a moment. "I don't think there is. I don't think there's much of anything. Isn't that what Jewish people think? That this is all we get? This one life?"

"I… I believe it's something like that," Trace answered slowly. He didn't feel knowledgeable enough to offer more than that.

"It's a good idea," Zeke acknowledged. "Floating the idea of a heaven out there. So that we try to be good, try not to fuck up too much. Just in case, you know? But I don't really think there is."

Trace nodded. "I guess we all have to figure out a philosophy that works best for each of us. Given the lack of conclusive evidence. Still…

try not to fuck up too much, all right?"

Zeke glanced at him and they both laughed. "Okay," he agreed.

A car was turning left at the intersection just ahead, and they turned as well, following it down the residential street. It pulled into the same driveway Trace had been aiming for, and as he pulled in behind it, the doors on either side opened. In the glow of his headlights, his sister-in-law Leslie and his niece Lisa emerged, both shielding their eyes to see who had followed them. Trace cut the engine, leaving them standing in semidarkness. Zeke was already bolting from the passenger seat.

"Oh, it's you," Leslie called. "Playing chauffeur? Thanks!"

"Hey, Trace!" ten-year-old Lisa greeted him. All the nieces and nephews had dispensed with the "uncle" and "aunt" designations and addressed everyone by their first names. Even Trace's parents were referred to as "Gram Karen" and "Gramp Frank," a practice of unclear origin to him.

"Hi, sport! Looking good," Trace returned, gesturing to her leotard-clad legs protruding from beneath her jacket. In response, she executed some sort of twirling maneuver presumably newly learned in ballet class, then launched herself into his arms, sending him staggering back a step or two. Regaining his balance, he rolled her to one side and tucked her, squealing, under his arm like a squirming, multi-limbed book.

"Lise, come on," her mother admonished helplessly. She shrugged at Trace, smiling apologetically. "Your uncle is not a set of monkey bars, you know."

"I didn't do *anything!*" Lisa protested. Her voice was muffled, coming through the hair that had fallen across her face. "He's the one doing it!"

Zeke, in the meantime, had strolled up the driveway without acknowledging either his mother or his sister, and had gone inside.

"Well, if you're going to carry around some dead weight, why don't you give me a hand with the groceries, instead?" Leslie appealed to Trace. To the wriggling mass of arms and legs along his side, she added, "And you can carry in some bags, too."

Both he and Lisa followed her mother into the house, shouldering sacks of groceries.

"Anywhere's fine," Leslie directed when they reached the kitchen, dropping her own bags on the counter. "Stay for dinner? It's nothing fancy, but there's plenty."

"Yes! Stay!" Lisa insisted. "It's takeout from the grocery deli. Chicken and mashed potatoes and pistachio and marshmallow salad!"

Leslie grimaced. "I'm all about serving well-balanced meals, as you can see."

"I understand," Trace laughed. "And I love a good pistachio and marshmallow salad."

"You'll stay, then?"

He shook his head. "Marla's at home. I need to get going."

"Call her," Leslie suggested. "Have her join us, too."

"Yes, call!" Lisa chimed in.

"Another time. I'm sure she's already started fixing something."

Lisa slumped against the counter. "You hardly ever come for dinner anymore. Ever since you got married. And you're my favorite uncle, too."

The adults laughed. "You can say that because Quince isn't here," Trace pointed out.

Rather than deny it, she tugged her jacket's zipper up and down petulantly. "Well, you're in the top two. Sometimes you're the top one. You'd be the top one now, if you'd eat with us."

"I guess I'll have to settle for being the runner-up tonight, then," he told her, summoning a mournful expression.

"Enough guilt-tripping," Leslie instructed her daughter. "Hang up your coat and go change out of your dance things. Shower now, or after dinner, your choice.

"You and Marla should come for dinner one of these nights," she added once Lisa had left the room. "I figure you've got another year, maybe two, tops, before Lise follows Zeke into that awful adolescent stage of not wanting to associate with any of us. Right now, her dad's little brothers are the coolest people she knows. That's going to change."

"That'll be kind of a relief. It's been exhausting, living up to all the hype, anyway."

She swatted his shoulder playfully and walked him to the door.

"By the way," he said, affecting an offhanded tone. "I don't think we need Zeke at the store on Monday. We're pretty much caught up on chores. Would that be all right?"

"Yeah, I guess. I don't have anywhere I have to be that day," Leslie said after a moment's thought. She allowed just enough time for Trace to feel smug and then she smirked. "So, you know about the in-service day, then? And he wants to be able to tell his dad and me that he has the whole day off? No school *or* work?" She laughed at his guilty expression. "Don't be telling me you aren't still vying for the favorite uncle designation."

"Fine!" he conceded. He pulled the door closed so that they were both standing on the front porch, out of Zeke's earshot. "He wants to go snowboarding with some buddies."

"Who does? Zeke?" Trace's brother Cord was strolling up the front walk, emerging from the darkness into the circle of light from the porch.

"Well, yeah," Trace was caught off guard. "On Monday."

Cord stood on the step below, the wind ruffling his hair and coat as he glanced back and forth between them.

"Instead of working," he said.

"Uh..."

Cord set his bag on the walk and placed one hand on the wrought iron step railing. The other he rested on his hip. "Trace," he began in that vaguely lecturing tone Trace knew so well from their shared youth. "When we asked if you could help out, could keep him occupied for a couple of hours after school each day..."

"He doesn't have school on Monday."

"That isn't the point. The point is, he hasn't worked at your store for a full month yet, and he's already asking for days off."

"A day. *One day.*"

"Would another employer, one who wasn't related to him, give him a day off so soon after starting a new job?"

Trace had a momentary, uncomfortable vision of Mikayla seated at her desk, arms folded in front of her, scowling as Zeke prepared to make such a request of her.

"I can't answer that, Cord. It would depend on the circumstances, I guess."

His brother sighed and raised both hands in an exasperated gesture. "And who's going to supervise? Who'll take him, or them, however many are going?"

"Well, there's the ski bus," Leslie put in. "They could ride up and back on that. Or I suppose that I could do it…"

"I was planning on taking them," Trace heard himself say. Ignoring the astonished looks on their faces, he plunged ahead. "When I heard he didn't have classes, I figured, why not? I haven't been up all season myself, so why not go now?"

"So… you're not going to work that day, either." Cord studied him through narrowed eyes.

"It's my store. I'm the manager. I get to do stuff like that. Look," he concluded, edging his way down the steps and around his brother, "If you don't want him to go, if you want him to work that day, fine. I just thought it would be a good excuse to snag a vacation day of my own."

Now Cord and Leslie were looking at each other, weighing the offer.

"Think about it," Trace urged. "Tell Zeke what you decide, and he can let me know tomorrow afternoon when he comes in. I need to get home. I haven't called Marla, and she probably wonders what's holding me up." He turned and walked across the grass to open his door and climb into the driver's seat.

All the way home, he stared distractedly over the steering wheel, trying to decide just how he'd gotten himself into all of this.

"So, why are we doing this, again?" Quince asked.

Zeke and his two buddies had just piled out of the back seat and were barreling across the snow-packed parking lot, boards in hand, yelling at the top of their lungs. Trace and his brother faced one another over the top of Trace's car. The air was frigid, and tiny ice crystals stung their faces. Last week's front had brought snow and colder temperatures to the city, and even more to the ski resorts.

"Just for the hell of it," Trace told him through puffs of frosty air. "When's the last time you and I got up to the mountains together?"

"Fine. And why *them?*" Quince tilted his head in the direction the boys had gone as he pulled his knitted ski mask down over his face, leaving just his eyes and mouth exposed.

"All right. You want me to admit it? I cornered myself into taking them and then panicked," Trace said grimly. He released one of the clasps holding his skis to the roof of the car. "I didn't really want to do it alone. Not with three of them."

"Now, was that so difficult? Did you think I'd turn down the invitation if I'd known they'd be coming along?" Quince crossed behind the car to pull his board from the trunk.

"Would you?"

"Possibly." He watched his brother lift his skis to the ground. "So, you're not boarding?"

"Last time, I nearly broke my neck. I need more connection with the ground than just a single piece of fiberglass."

"But if you're on skis, you won't be able to…" Quince paused in the act of pulling on his gloves. Even with most of his face obscured by his ski mask, the change of expression was obvious. It shifted from realization to dismay to indignation. "I am not spending the day babysitting those kids just because we're all on snowboards and you're off skiing!"

"Nobody's asking you to." Trace moved around to the rear of the car to retrieve his own boots from the trunk. "Just, you know, make sure they stay on the trails."

"How is that not looking after them?"

"Just Zeke, then. We don't really have much stake in what happens to the other two. You got everything?" Trace waited a second for a response, then aimed his key fob at the vehicle, locking the doors, ignoring his brother's stony glare. "Let's meet at the chalet at one. Lunch is on me. Tell the kids when you see them."

If he'd thought the slopes would be less populated on a Monday, the theory was quickly disproved. Though he already had his ticket, the lines for the lifts were depressingly long. It would have been more fun to wait with Quince and ride up the hill together. He hadn't deliberately plotted to foist the boys on him, though he couldn't help but be amused by how things had turned out.

In their youth, they'd often hit the trails together. Though Quince was the youngest in the family, barely fourteen months separated the two of them. He was their parents' surprise, the unexpected coda to their child-producing days.

His arrival had evidently so overwhelmed them that they abandoned all but the most perfunctory parenting skills, and those had been fairly minimal to begin with. So when it became apparent early on that Quince had attached himself to his older brother, they'd been only too happy to allow Trace to shoulder some of the responsibility of looking after him. Together, the boys stumbled through adolescence, bonding and fighting with equal fervor. Trace had with Quince the bond he'd never quite established with his twin, Bertie.

Today was the first time he'd been to the slopes all winter, despite having purchased a season pass in September. Stepping off the chair lift and gliding down the short dismounting slope, he experienced a rush of exhilaration. He paused to adjust his goggles and to take an appreciative scan of the white hill descending in front of him, and then he was off.

He completed his first run with caution, moving at moderate speed as he relearned the skills that had lain dormant the past year. Then, confidence renewed, he chose a black-diamond trail for his second descent, moving faster and executing sharper turns. His nose was running and his eyes stinging from the rush of air, but he felt great, and he was reluctant to stop for lunch. The others had been waiting for fifteen minutes when he finally arrived.

It had been an exhilarating morning for everybody, though, and no one was upset. Quince even seemed to have overcome his initial reluctance to be saddled with the boys.

"They were pretty lousy at first," he informed Trace just loudly enough so the kids, seated at the next table, could hear. "But they kept their eyes on me, and after a couple of hours, they'd picked up enough technique to not embarrass themselves too badly."

This prompted jeers and laughs, not just from Zeke, but from his buddies, who'd now spent enough time alongside Quince to feel comfortable razzing him the way his nephew did.

"Oh, you wish!"

"Yeah, we learned what *not* to do!"

"He spent more time wiping out than the rest of us put together!" Sean informed Trace.

"Put away those skis, old man, and come with us this afternoon," Quince urged his brother. "You can rent a board."

Trace refused to be goaded. "I'm fine where I am. Let's meet at the car at four. And don't let the boys get too crazy." He'd heard a few harrowing tales from the next table over lunch. Most of them were likely just testosterone-fueled boasts, but he remembered from his own morning on the slopes that as a sense of complacency grew, so did the impulse to try riskier stunts.

A light snow had begun to fall while they were eating. By the time he'd ridden to the summit and was getting off the lift once more, clouds had socked in the mountains just below timberline, and the flakes were thicker and falling with greater urgency.

Leaning on his poles, Trace winced. His calves and the muscles on the backs of his arms had stiffened somewhat during lunch, and he realized with dismay that this afternoon's skiing wasn't going to be quite as much fun as the first half of the day.

"Just one last run," he decided, adjusting his goggles and launching himself into space.

He'd selected one of the intermediate runs again. It wasn't as populated as it had been in the morning, perhaps because the inexperienced skiers were intimidated by the increased snowfall, or maybe just because it was growing late in the day. He moved in slow, easy arcs, listening to the hiss of his skis across the white ground. Gradually the soreness began to leave his limbs and he breathed deeply, savoring the scent of pine and moist air as he swept downward. He rounded a bend in the trail and, for a moment, the field was deserted, the slope entirely his. He crouched, tucking his poles under his arms, preparing to gather one last burst on the open trail.

He'd only begun to pick up speed when another skier appeared from nowhere, shooting out from a cluster of trees barely fifteen feet in front of him. Trace swerved sharply to the right, only to encounter a second person emerging from the same spot. Nearly atop him, Trace veered again, managing to avoid a collision, but passing so closely that their poles made contact, throwing him off balance.

"Hey!" he heard the other man yell indignantly from over his shoulder.

And then Trace was on his back, pinwheeling downhill as his skis went flying. He skidded off the trail and away from the packed snow after a few seconds, sloughing into the uncleared powder and undergrowth. It slowed him considerably, but his shoulder still met the trunk of the medium-sized tree with enough force to ricochet him back toward the slope. He was dizzily aware that he was momentarily airborne and thought, "Well, at least it happened now, instead of first thing this morning when it would have ruined the whole day." And then there was a peculiar knocking sound that seemed to come from far away. Only much later did he figure out it was the sound of his skull making contact with a rock.

WHEN HE OPENED HIS eyes, he thought he was gazing into a mirror, and wondered why his ski mask was pushed up over his forehead, making his hair stick out in wild tufts. He was looking at himself with an expression of grave concern.

"Are you all right?" his reflection asked, and then he realized that he was actually gazing up at his brother, hovering over him.

"These... These guys came out of nowhere," he rasped. "I don't think I ran into them, but I fell down..."

Quince was nodding vigorously. "You hit your head. You've been unconscious for awhile. How do you feel?"

Trace considered this for a moment. He attempted to wiggle his fingers and shift his feet.

"I can't move."

"They've got you strapped to a board. You're in the ambulance. They're taking you to the hospital."

For the first time, Trace took in more of his surroundings. He could not move his head, but he shifted his eyes in either direction. He could hear the squawk of a two-way radio and was aware that someone else, a man in a drab gray jacket, was crouched alongside him, doing something to his arm.

"I'm going to follow the ambulance down," Quince was saying. "I'll drop the boys at Cord's place and meet you at the hospital."

"All right," Trace mumbled. Now he was experiencing a sensation of falling backward. "But, one thing first..."

"Yeah?"

"...Are... Are you dead, too?"

He had a fleeting image of Quince's astonished face before his eyes fluttered closed. He was aware there was an increased burst of activity around him then: his brother's panicked babble and someone else telling him he needed to get out of the ambulance, now. Then that same voice directed toward him. "Sir? Sir? What's his name again? ...Trace? Trace, listen to me. I need you to stay awake. I know you want to fall back asleep, but you can't, understand? I need you to stay with me."

"All right," Trace said agreeably without opening his eyes.

"What smells so bad?" he demanded in what seemed like just a moment later.

"You've vomited a couple of times, remember?" the paramedic reminded him.

"...Oh. Yeah. Was that today?" It seemed like quite a long time ago that the two people riding with him in the back of the ambulance had tilted his board to one side to keep him from choking as Trace began to puke. "Jeez, I'm sorry."

"It's common with head injuries. Don't worry about it."

"We've seen it before. A lot," the other paramedic said consolingly.

Trace faded in and out of consciousness, with the men on either side of him prodding him back to wakefulness with questions any time he began to drift away.

"What do you do for a living?" "I see you're wearing a wedding ring. What's your wife's name? Where did you meet?"

The inquiries buzzed around his head like annoying little gnats. It wasn't that they were difficult to answer, just that it seemed to require so much effort. Finally, he asked one of his own.

"How bad is it? Is... Is the back of my head split open, or something?"

He sensed, rather than saw, the two medics exchanging a glance over his restrained form.

"Well, you're still with us, aren't you?" one of them said after a moment.

With effort, and squinting through what seemed to be an extraordinarily bright overhead light, Trace looked as far as he could in either direction. An assortment of medical devices hung on the walls: Coils of tubing. A small green tank with what looked like a compressor. A white metal box with the standard-issue red-plus first-aid symbol on it. The man on his left had a shaved head and an earring. The one on his right had removed his gray jacket and was leaning forward, resting his elbows on his knees. He had a close-cropped dark beard and moustache, but even so, looked young. Younger than Quince, even.

That was it. It was just the three of them riding in the back of the

---

ambulance now.

"Funny," Trace said.

"What? What's funny?"

Trace shook his head feebly before realizing that even that small motion sent spirals of pain down his neck. A fresh wave of nausea swept over him, and in another minute, the paramedics were tilting the board once more as he vomited into the dark void alongside his gurney.

What he'd decided not to tell them was the same thing he didn't tell Quince just before they'd made his brother get out of the ambulance.

For a moment, as plain as day and as real to him as the rest of them, Trace had seen his sister Bertie hovering just over Quince's shoulder and watching Trace every bit as intently.

Chapter Three

They kept him in the hospital overnight, mostly for observation and to keep waking him at brief intervals, just to be sure he wouldn't slip into a coma or anything. His skull hadn't been split open; there was just one small gash. There was, though, an impressive-sized bump, and Trace was released with the admonition that he was not to do anything but go home and stay there for the next four or five days, moving around as little as possible.

He'd readily agreed, but in reality intended to give it just a day or so before going back to the store. However, vertigo kicked in as Marla was helping him across the parking garage below their apartment building. Even the gentle rising sensation of the elevator had him reeling and clawing the walls in an effort to keep his balance. He barely took notice of the wide-eyed expressions of their fellow passengers, but as the doors opened and he lurched against Marla before they stepped out on their floor, she called back apologetically, "He's got a concussion." With the thumb of the hand she'd wrapped around his waist, she gestured up to the bandage on the back of Trace's scalp.

"Ashamed to be seen with a drunk husband at eleven o'clock in the morning?" he muttered dryly as she fitted her key into the door of their apartment.

"Something like that. Plus, well, you don't smell all that great. A drunk husband is one thing. But they might've thought I'd picked up a vagrant somewhere, and was bringing him back for a tryst." Trace's fifteen-hour stay in the hospital had not included a bath.

"Fair enough," he said, raising his arm from around her shoulder and taking the next few steps on his own. "I want a half-dozen extra-strength aspirins, and then I'm going to brush my teeth and take a shower."

"You'll take a bath," she corrected him firmly. "The last thing we need is for you to lose your balance and fall through the shower door. I'll run the water while you brush your teeth, and then we'll get you undressed and into the tub."

"I don't like baths," he complained. "How about you get in the shower with me? That would work, wouldn't it? I'll even scrub your back for you."

Marla studied him impassively for a moment, then she turned and left the room. A moment later, he heard the water running in the bathtub. "Damn," he muttered to himself.

NEITHER ASPIRINS NOR ANYTHING else alleviated the dull throbbing that set in behind his eyes and stayed. Even the simple act of running a toothbrush around the inside of his mouth, no matter how slowly or carefully he attempted it, sent his head spinning, and he had to clutch the edge of the bathroom counter with his free hand to keep from staggering. "It's like having a marathon hangover," he complained to his sister Sky when she stopped by one morning for a visit. Marla had stayed home from work that first day; now various family members were taking turns checking on him. At first, he resisted the near-constant attention. But when he realized that watching television or studying a computer screen only increased the pain and added nausea to the mix, he became grateful for a distraction that didn't add to his discomfort.

"Well, you should be familiar with the sensations," Sky quipped, handing him a glass of lemonade before settling herself on the opposite end of the couch, shifting sideways so she could prop her chin in the palm of her hand to study him. "If I remember correctly, you spent most of your college years wasted, didn't you?"

"Nothing like this," he said, closing his eyes and savoring the first cold gulp. "And anyway, I was younger then. I had more brain cells to spare."

"I doubt that." She leaned forward to scrutinize him. "Nice to see your pupils looking normal-sized again. That night in the hospital, they were the size of pie plates. It was like staring into two black holes."

"You were there? You came to see me?"

"Oh, nice," she retorted acidly. "Most of us did. You don't remember? Guess I didn't need to bother, then."

"I barely remember that I was there. Everything else was just white noise. You know, the way you always are to me." Sky was his next-oldest sibling and the only one besides Quince with whom he could joke. Too many years separated him from Cord and Aria, both of whom had always taken a sort of parental attitude toward the younger kids. And now that they were genuine parents themselves, they seemed more humorless than ever.

Almost unconsciously, Sky had raised his legs off the cushions and was resting them across her lap. She began massaging his bare feet, something she would never have done any other time in their lives.

"You scared the hell out of us, you know. First, when Quince called from the road and told me what had happened. Then later, even after the doctors said that it looked like you were going to recover all right, you looked so awful. No color in your face, and like I said, those eyes, all big and black. You seemed to recognize us and everything, but you also seemed to be having conversations with people who weren't there."

Trace lowered his glass. "I did? With who?"

"Not a clue. You'd be talking to us, and then you'd pause for a few seconds and you'd say something that didn't track. As if you were answering a question that somebody the rest of us couldn't see had asked."

"Huh," he said, and took another swallow from his glass. "What kinds of things did I say?"

Sky considered this for a moment. "Random stuff, mostly. It was pretty unsettling. But the nurse was in the room during some of that, and she said that sometimes people who've bumped their heads have a kind of delayed response, and you might have been answering questions that somebody had asked minutes ago, or even further back than that, from before we even walked in." She looked down at the foot she was holding. "You have hairy toes, you know that? Weird. Matt doesn't have hair on his toes. He doesn't have a whole lot of body hair at all, actually."

Trace withdrew his legs from her lap, pulling his knees up to his chest. "I don't want to know about your husband's toes, or any other part of him, for that matter. At least I had the excuse of a concussion when I was saying unsettling things. What's yours?"

"Oh, relax." She slapped the cuff of his jeans before getting to her feet. "It's nearly noon. I'll fix you some lunch before I take off. Marla said she was going to try to leave work early, but Quince is swinging by at about three, anyway. Will you be okay until then?"

"I'll be fine. And you don't need to fix anything. I had a big cinnamon roll just before you got here, so I'm not hungry."

"Maybe some tuna salad," Sky mused meditatively, as if he hadn't said anything. "I'll go see if Marla's got a can of tuna anywhere."

"I don't want any tuna salad," Trace called after her as she disappeared into the kitchen, but he knew it was a lost cause.

EVERY EVENING, HE RETIRED to bed determined that in the morning, he would get up and go to work. And each daybreak, he awoke feeling as if the bed were spinning. It would slow gradually, the sensation replaced with the feeling of a pair of giant hands pressed against his temples and squeezing mercilessly. It was all he could do to make his way to the bathroom to pee, a journey that seemed to take forever. Going any further than that was clearly an impossibility.

"IT'S AWFUL, I KNOW," the doctor agreed sympathetically at Trace's follow-up visit on Thursday. "But it's a normal response. Yours was a pretty serious injury, but everything is looking good, and this will go away." Then, allowing a second to pass, he added, "But if it doesn't in another week or so, come back and see me."

Despite that less-than-heartening diagnosis, Trace was aware that the sensations were gradually lessening in severity. He was supposed to keep the pressure off the back of his head as much as possible, but he found sleeping on his stomach to be impossible, and even when he drifted off while lying on his side, more often than not he would awake in the mornings fully on his back once more. No wonder recovery was taking so long.

And so the parade of visiting relatives continued into the weekend. Saturday morning, it was his sister-in-law Leslie's turn, with Lisa and Zeke in tow. It was the first time the children had seen him since before the accident.

"You don't *look* hurt," Lisa said, eyeing him critically. The disappointment in her tone was evident. Trace obligingly ducked his head so she could see the point of impact, but that did little to assuage her. The swelling was nearly gone. "There's just a teeny white spot where they shaved your head," she complained.

"Well, I'll try to do better next time," he promised her solemnly, which at least made her laugh.

"No, don't do that," she conceded. "I want you to be okay, honest."

Zeke was morose and lethargic, like always, but there was a new discontent behind it.

"Mikayla busts my ass at work all the time," he complained. "She made me straighten up the storage room, *and* she makes me wait on customers. I'm not sure it's even legal for me to do that."

"And I guess she expects you to be polite to them, too," Trace said.

His nephew was not fooled, however. "Quit it," he ordered, though he couldn't help grinning. "I want you to come back to the store."

"I'll bet you do. Two whole hours every afternoon of backbreaking labor. Thank God you'll be an adult soon, and you won't ever have to do anything like that again." He realized abruptly that there was a heretofore unseen positive outcome of tumbling down a hillside and planting his head on a rock. Perhaps Mikayla should always be in charge of handling Zeke.

Marla was still out grocery shopping when Leslie and the kids left, and Trace decided to take advantage of her absence and shower for the first time since his accident.

He moved with inordinate care, not just because he had no desire to lose his balance and further injure himself, but also because he did not want to face the grim expression on his wife's face as she bit back the urge to say *I told you so* if she should happen to come home and find him sprawled across the bathroom tile, perhaps bleeding copiously from falling through the shower door.

The blast of warm water against his skin felt like a godsend, and he soaped his arms and torso leisurely, his feet planted some distance apart to give him maximum balance. Even after he was finished rinsing off, he stood under the hot spray for several more minutes. This, more than anything else he had tried all week long, made him feel almost normal once more. He stood with his eyes closed, inhaling great lungsfull of steam and finally, with reluctance, shut off the tap and opened the shower door.

The entire bathroom was shrouded in mist, the vanity and toilet just hazy images a mere three feet away. Trace reached for a thick towel, pulling it from the rack and using it to dab his forehead and face before unfolding it and running it up and down his back and chest. It was as he was sliding the towel back and forth across his butt that he caught a glimpse of something through the dissipating steam. Not something: someone. A figure standing against the closed bathroom door, watching him. She raised a hand and gestured with one finger toward his feet.

"Sky's right," she said. "You do have hairy toes."

Trace stopped drying himself. His astonishment might well have sent him sprawling, but instead, he numbly reached behind him to lower the toilet seat lid, and he sank down upon it, resting on his towel.

"I saw you before," he said. "A couple of times. You really were there, weren't you? It wasn't an hallucination." Then, aware of his current appearance, he lifted the corners of the towel and folded them discreetly across his lap.

"You needn't bother," Bertie said, smiling slightly. "We spent nine months together naked, in a very confined space. I know what you look like."

"I thought I was dead, or dying, the first time I saw you. In the ambulance. I figured that's why you were there."

"To escort you to the afterlife?" Bertie laughed. "That's what you thought?"

"I don't know what I thought. A lot of things go through your mind when your dead sister shows up out of nowhere."

"Was one of them that you were going crazy? Because that might be it."

"It was you I was talking to in the hospital the other night, wasn't it? I'm starting to remember now."

Bertie shrugged.

"Nobody else can see you or hear you, right?" he continued. "It's just me. Is it because of the concussion?"

"I guess. That's the logical explanation, isn't it?"

"So, you're not really here."

She looked down at her hands. "Well, it feels like I am."

"But why?" Trace checked himself. "I don't mean… I mean, I'm glad to see you again. Oh, God, yes. Real or not. I have so many questions."

"Okay." She tucked her hands into the pockets of her jeans and tossed her head to flick the bangs out of her eyes, a gesture so familiar that his knees might have buckled if he wasn't already seated. "Go ahead," she instructed.

"Can… Can I touch you? I mean, could I feel you, if I tried?"

She stepped away from the door. "Let's find out." But she did not remove either hand from its pocket, and Trace, trying to keep his towel in place with one of his, was forced to stand and reach toward her.

He took the fabric of her sleeve between his thumb and forefinger, sliding it back and forth softly. It felt as real, as authentic, as the tiles beneath his bare feet. And then he touched the flesh of her upper arm, just inside the sleeve. Not cold and hard like marble, as he almost assumed it would feel, but soft and pliable and warm, like anybody else's.

Bertie was watching his fingers on her arm while he looked at her. He had a sudden urge to take her in an embrace and squeeze tightly. But as if she realized this, she glanced up sharply, and he sensed she would recoil if he tried. Plus, he was naked just now, which made it seem even less appropriate, dead or not.

"Trace?" he heard Marla call from somewhere in the apartment. "Trace, where are you?"

He glanced at the closed door, then back at Bertie, who regarded him without expression.

"I..." he said hesitantly, and then raised his voice. "In here!" he called. "The bathroom!" Then, in a softer voice again, he asked, "Do you have to go now?"

She shrugged. "Your call."

"Maybe... Maybe you'd better."

Then Marla was opening the door. She looked at him, at the fogged mirror over the sink and at the trails of water down the open shower door. "Oh, honey," she sighed. "Really? I mean, I know that's what you've been wanting, but I wish you'd waited until I was here. Just in case."

"I was feeling better. No vertigo all day," Trace assured her. "I think a shower is just what I needed."

Marla nodded. But the way her eyes again swept the room before lingering on him for a final searching instant made the color rise on his neck and face, although this may not have been noticeable in the moisture-filled air.

"Now, I WANT YOU to understand something," Mikayla informed Trace upon his return to the store the following Monday. "I've worked hard on making some changes while you were lying on your ass all last week, and I don't want you undermining them now that you're back."

He grinned as he hung his jacket inside the back door. "Yeah, Zeke told me you've been riding him pretty mercilessly. And that's fine. He needs to know he can't skate just because I'm his uncle."

"There's that," she agreed. "Hell, if I'd known you were taking on charity cases as employees, I'd have suggested my granddaughter. She at least makes a big show of looking busy, whether she does anything or not."

"Well, maybe around Mother's Day when things get busy, we could take on another—"

"—But there's one or two other things I've been itching to try, and with you out from underfoot the last several days, it seemed like a good time to give them a whirl."

Not only did she make it sound as if his regular presence here was a hindrance, but there was the slight implication that he had been away somewhere enjoying himself. As he pondered how to respond to this, his attention was drawn to the formica-topped island now dominating the area by the front windows.

Following his gaze, Mikayla said, "I relocated the wrapping station up front, instead of by the registers. Got rid of the bottleneck where people who brought in pre-labeled packages or who just wanted to buy a roll of tape or something had to fight their way around the ones who take half an hour to get their stuff boxed up and addressed." Clearly it wasn't just Zeke she thought needed some whipping into shape. "Plus, up there, they can stand on both sides of the table. Twice as much working space."

"But where are the—"

"—We put the copy machines by the registers. Seems like we spend half our time fixing paper jams or showing people how to make double-sided copies. Now, we don't have to walk so far to do it."

"But, Mikayla, we have service agreements on those machines. We're not allowed to move them without—"

"—The technician was in on Wednesday to do regular maintenance. I had him move them. Relax. We didn't violate the warranty."

She stood watching Trace as if anticipating further objections. But under her cool, defiant gaze, he couldn't think of any. Actually, what she'd done made a lot of sense.

"Well, good," he said. "When word of this gets out, they'll want you running this place."

She chose to ignore that. "So, that was some bust-up you had, huh? Zeke said he watched them bring you down the hill on one of those sled-stretchers. Had you bundled up like a mummy, he said."

"Yeah, I guess. I don't remember any of that."

Mikayla produced a cloth from the shelf beneath the cash register and began to wipe the counter with vigor. "Those head injuries, those can mess you up all kinds of ways. That's one reason—one of a whole bunch—why you won't catch me up there risking my life on the side of a mountain."

"Yeah," he said. "I'm leaning that way too, now."

She transferred her efforts to the display shelves, lifting each item to give it an efficient flick of the cloth, then swiped the shelf beneath it. No dust motes flew into the air, no doubt due to the fact that she kept as on top of this task as she did indolent teenagers who had less than a stellar work ethic.

"My cousin Eddie, for example," she said after a moment. "Fell out a second-story window when he was seventeen or so. Well, jumped, sort of. A hasty exit from his girlfriend's bedroom when her father caught them unexpectedly. Wasn't far—twelve feet maybe—but banged his skull on a drain spout or something on the way down. Wasn't ever the same afterwards."

"A drain spout?"

"Or something. The point is, changed his whole personality." She paused in her cleaning efforts to squint at Trace from around a display of indelible markers as if waiting for him to do something peculiar.

"Changed him how?" he asked, feeling uncomfortable under her gaze.

She shrugged. "He got a whole lot quieter, for one thing. Became a preacher. Not right away, that is. That happened quite awhile later."

"But you think there was some sort of connection?"

Another shrug. "Hard to say. His mother said she thought that was when he started to hear the voice of God, though."

"Really?" He considered this. "He thinks God talks to him?"

"I said that's what his mother thinks." Mikayla gave the edge of the shelf a particularly vehement swat of her dust rag.

"And you?"

Now a customer was entering, attempting to wedge a large box through the doorway ahead of her with some difficulty. Trace went to offer assistance. As he did, he heard Mikayla, behind him, say:

"I think he's just an idiot who fell out of a window."

"YOUR MOM SENT HER customary valentines," Marla reported when Trace walked in that evening. "A couple of weeks late, but that's under-standable with everything that's happened lately." She was standing at the kitchen counter slicing onions and peppers into strips, but tilted her head to receive his kiss. She turned back to her task, but he'd caught the mirthful look in her eyes. This tradition of his mother's amused her no end. He took a soft drink from the refrigerator and sat at the table on the other side of the low partition that divided the kitchen from their dining area. He spent a moment looking through the rest of the mail stacked there, then pulled the manila envelope toward him. It was creased and lumpy, and the exterior had been adorned with a variety of heart and Cupid stickers around the address. Taking hold of two corners, he lifted it and shook out the contents. Two boxes of sugar candy hearts, the kinds with little sayings on them, rattled into view. There were two pink envelopes, as well, one with his name and one with Marla's printed on it.

"You haven't looked at your card yet?" he asked, sliding his finger beneath the seal of his own.

She shook her head. "Haven't even dived into my candy, either," she declared without a trace of facetiousness. "I wanted to wait for you."

The valentines were the kind purchased in boxes of a dozen or more, silly little single-sheet depictions of cartoonish animals, trucks, and trains. Trace's was a circus cat perched atop a star-ringed cylinder, and the caption read, *"I'd be lion if I said I didn't want you for my Valen-*

tine." On the back, in a familiar scrawl, was written, *"That's right, you'll never be too old to be my special sweetheart. XXXOOO, Mom."*

"What's it say?" Marla asked. After he read both sides to her, she said, "Now open mine and read it. My hands are all smelly."

Trace dutifully tore open the other envelope and extracted the card. Scanning it, he laughed and said, "Well, the picture is of a big pink flower that looks really happy. It has a face on it, I mean. And it's saying, *'I don't su-posey you'd like to be my Valentine, would you?'* On the back, Mom's written, *'Just so you know, you don't get any choice in the matter.'* Then there's a bunch of 'x's and 'o's, so apparently she's sending along a lot of kisses and hugs for you, too."

"That's sweet." Marla tilted the cutting board and slid the onions and peppers cascading into a wok, where they began to hiss and send up a cloud of yellowish steam. "I like how she gives us each our own separate card instead of just addressing one to the both of us."

"Our own boxes of candy, too," he reminded her, brandishing one of them. Then he looked at it more closely. "I guess we all must have eaten these as kids," he said dubiously. "But even back then, I don't remember liking the taste very much."

Marla was rinsing her hands under the tap. "I suppose she sends those because they travel through the mail better. They don't melt or get old very fast."

"My folks live thirty minutes from here. She could hand-deliver valentines. And bring chocolates, instead. Something I'd actually enjoy."

"Listen to you, you ungrateful child," she scolded. "It's supposed to be the thought that counts. She's just reminding you that she loves you."

"I know. I know she does," he said, even if he didn't sound entirely convinced.

Trace, Aria, and Sky met the following Sunday to collect Bertie's things from the last place she had been living. They had intended to do it a week earlier, but Trace's mishap had derailed those plans. So now, at ten a.m., the three of them stood on the sidewalk in front of a row of repurposed storefronts staring at a nondescript door sandwiched between a cellular-phone store and a pawn shop. Aria had pressed the buzzer twice so far without response. After another few seconds, she took a step back and gazed at the second-floor windows.

"The roommate said she'd be here. Specifically asked me to come by before eleven, because that's when she would have to leave for work," she said.

Sky was studying the weathered door that appeared to have been shedding its pistachio-colored paint for quite some time. There were several nicks and gouges in the wood, suggesting that unlawful entry had probably been attempted a time or two. "How long had she been living here? Does anybody know?"

Aria ignored the question, and Trace shrugged. Since her late teens, Bertie had flitted in and out of their lives, resurfacing at random intervals to report she was living someplace different, working at some new job, seeing some new guy. The only consistency to any of it was that they all seemed like questionable choices. So far as Trace knew, nobody from the immediate family had ever visited her at any of them. Nor had she ever extended an invitation.

"Oh, come *on*," Aria muttered, stepping forward and grinding her thumb into the buzzer one more time. She moved back to the edge of the curb, cupped her hands to either side of her mouth, and shouted at the row of overhead windows, "Hello? Anybody up there? Anybody going to answer the door?"

Sky and Trace exchanged bemused, slightly embarrassed smiles. This was Aria, after all, never anything less than self-possessed and more concerned about her own rights than those of anybody who might be trying to sleep in on a Sunday morning.

They were all still looking upward when at last a crackling sound came through the intercom next to the door and a logy male voice responded thickly, "Yeah? What is it?"

Aria shouldered her bag and stepped forward. "I'm Aria Evans," she said, leaning into the speaker. "I'm here with my sister and brother to collect our sister Bertie Bannerly's things."

There followed a few seconds of ponderous silence. Then the voice responded, "I don't know who that is. Bert… Bertie-somebody, you say?"

"Bannerly. Bertie Bannerly," Trace repeated, feeling as though he ought to contribute something.

"Uh… hold on." And then the static was gone, leaving them looking at each other and wondering whether anybody would be back.

"At least we're not standing here in a driving snow," Sky rationalized. But it was chilly, and she dug her hands into her coat pockets. Though he didn't say anything, Trace was wondering just how many trips they were going to have to make up and down the stairs, carrying out Bertie's things.

They heard feet pounding on steps on the other side of the pistachio-shaded door, followed by the click of a bolt sliding, and they stepped back to avoid the door as it swung open toward them. A girl of nineteen or twenty with the whitest blonde hair Trace had ever seen greeted them.

"Hey. Come on up," she invited, and without waiting, turned and clopped up the stairs on bright red heels. They crossed the threshold in single file and followed. She turned and waited for them at the top of the staircase.

"I'm Katie," she said. "I was blow-drying my hair and didn't hear you buzz. So, anyway, through here."

She led them into an apartment much brighter than the stairwell and hallway, where the three of them clustered in the center of the room, glancing around curiously. The place matched the eclectic appearance of the young woman now closing the door, and suggested the transitory nature of a dorm room, its few pieces of furniture clashing in both style and era. Decorations consisted of one painting and nearly a dozen t-shirts thumb-tacked to the wallpaper, all bearing the names and dates of recent concerts. Katie herself wore a red miniskirt partially concealed by a gauzy black outer wrap that reached almost to the floor. This was topped by a wide gold belt, a scoop-necked t-shirt and a black jacket with gold trim. Her whiteish-blonde hair was trimmed into a pixie cut, and she peered at them through a pair of wide round lenses set in thick lavender frames. Thus attired at ten-twenty on a Sunday morning, it would seem she was just home after a lively Saturday evening on the town, but she'd just finished blow-drying her hair, after all. Plus, she'd told Aria she had to work this morning. So apparently this was her job attire.

She was, Trace reflected, a very attractive woman, under all of that. And several years younger than Bertie. How had they become roommates? he wondered.

Now Katie was gesturing to a couch against the far wall.

"Albie's stuff is right there. Oh, and I'm really sorry, by the way. For your loss, and all."

Their eyes followed her pointing hand to a cardboard box and a stack of clothing at one corner of the sofa.

Aria moved across the sagging floor to peer down at the items. "This is it? That's all of her things? Are… Are you sure?"

"I think so." Katie followed her across the room and perched on the arm at the other end of the couch, resting her hands on her knees. "Jillie and Cassie—those are my roommates—anyway, Jillie and Cassie and I looked around pretty good, and that's all we came up with. There were one or two things in the bathroom that we weren't sure were hers, but they didn't belong to any of us, so I put them in there too. They're in a plastic bag. You can just throw them out if you don't think they were your sister's."

Aria had been fingering one of the pieces of clothing. She let it drop, straightened, and faced Katie with narrowed eyes.

"Now, let me get this straight…" she began.

She was, Trace recognized, ready to launch into an accusation that this young woman was keeping some of Bertie's things for herself, but his attention had been drawn to something Katie had said, and he intervened.

"Wait. You say that Jillie and Cassie are your roommates?"

Katie nodded.

"But not Bertie? She didn't actually live here?"

Katie shook her head. "No. She'd just been crashing here for, I don't know, maybe three weeks or so. I knew her a little bit from around. *You* know," she added, although they obviously didn't. "Then, a month or so ago, she was hanging around the café for, like, three days in a row. I asked her what was up, and she said she'd had a fight with her boyfriend and he'd ditched her and she didn't have anywhere to go. So I offered her our couch until she could get it together again. She was here most nights after that. Not all of them. Until… Until a couple of days before she… Before we heard what happened." Katie shifted uncomfortably.

"The boyfriend," Sky asked after they'd all spent a few seconds absorbing this information in silence. "Do you know where he lives? His name?"

"Beau, I think. Albie used to talk about somebody named Beau. Usually called him either *Pisshead Beau* or *That Fucker Beau*. So that's probably him. I never saw him or talked to him. I don't have any idea where he lives."

They fell into silence once more. Aria, it appeared, had decided to forego her accusations.

"Well…" Katie said at last, and started to rise.

"How was she?" Trace demanded suddenly, surprising himself as much as the others. "During that time, those few weeks… Did you and she talk much?"

"Not much." Katie settled back onto the arm of the couch. "I work the six-to-two shift on weekdays, and she was always sacked out when I'd leave in the mornings. Sometimes we'd hang a bit if she was still around when I'd come home in the afternoons. She seemed fine, I guess. Mad as hell at Beau, but otherwise okay. She talked a little about applying for some jobs."

For the first time since their arrival, their hostess looked slightly uncomfortable. "I don't know if she ever did, though. She didn't seem to want anything that was, you know, practical. And, to tell the truth, we were getting ready to kick her out." She looked at each of them, the owlish glasses highlighting her already enormous eyes. "We didn't, though. I want you to know that. We hadn't even said anything to her before... But, you know, it was starting to seem like maybe she was just going to be on this couch forever."

As one, Trace and his sisters nodded. That idea didn't seem at all far-fetched.

"So, anyway..." Katie was getting up again, and they recognized this as a cue. "I wish I could have met you all, you know... a different way."

As they descended the steps, Trace carrying the box and his sisters having divided the clothing between them, he recalled with a twinge of guilt his concern about just how many times they might have to be going up and down this flight of stairs with Bertie's things. Just one, it turned out.

Her mind running along similar lines, Aria said, "I figured we'd be at this for a couple of hours, at least. I've got the whole day ahead of me, now."

Katie, who had closed the apartment door and was following them out into the street, said, "Well, if you'd like, you could come have breakfast where I work. I'm the hostess. It's just a couple of blocks over. It's called The Grease Trap. Horrible name, I know, but the food's really good. I'd comp your meals if I could, but I can at least get you my ten percent employee discount."

"Thanks. Another time," Sky said, answering for all of them. They stood a moment, watching the girl clatter down the uneven sidewalk on her inch-tall heels before they turned the opposite direction.

"I would be up for a bite to eat, actually," Sky added as they walked to their cars. Then she shuddered slightly. "But someplace else. Even a Denny's or something."

"Sounds good to me," Trace agreed.

They slid into a curved booth at a restaurant some blocks away. It wasn't a Denny's, though the architecture and generous arrangement of plastic flora poked into planters behind each booth suggested it might have been that, or another chain restaurant, at some point in its past. Now it was an independent establishment, clinging to some of the appurtenances of the better-known franchises as it began a slow descent into something else. For now, though, it appeared safe and clean, if somewhat faded, and they agreed it would probably be just fine for breakfast, anyway.

As she studied her laminated menu, Aria sighed.

"Until she could get it together again. Did either of you catch that?" She pressed the heel of her hand to her forehead for a second. "Bertie was staying with those… those *teenagers,* practically, until she could get it together again." Sighing more heavily this time, she dropped her hand and reached for her glass of ice water. Trace and Sky knew the unfinished part of that statement: Bertie's entire life, it seemed, had been spent getting it together again.

"So, what do we do with her things, now that we've got them?" Sky asked. "And do we try to track down this *Beau* to get the rest of her stuff?"

"Why bother? How important could any of it be if she managed to live the last three or four weeks without it? Plus, if what she told that girl Katie was true and Beau kicked her out, he probably trashed anything of hers she left behind. Or peed on them, or jacked off on them, or worse."

Sky stared at Aria in horror. "What could be worse than… No, don't even answer that." She stared resolutely at her menu. "Now, what am I supposed to order after a mental image like that?"

"Anything but eggs," Trace suggested dryly. He closed his menu. "Blueberry pancakes for me."

"I suppose one—or all—of us should go through her stuff. From the look of things, it shouldn't take more than about five minutes." Aria wrinkled her nose. "Fumigate anything we might want to keep, and just pitch the rest."

"Should we show them to Mom? Or Pop?"

Trace and Aria shook their heads in unison.

"Well, shouldn't we at least ask if they want to see them?"

"No. They'd have brought it up by now if they had any interest," Aria replied firmly. "They don't. I can keep the stuff, or one of you can, if you want. Just put it away somewhere, and if either of them asks, you can let them take a look at what's there. But we don't say anything until then."

Ordinarily, Trace resented his eldest sister's proprietary attitude toward their parents, but in this case, he found himself agreeing with her. By all appearances, the folks were eager for the few lingering ripples caused by Bertie's passing to subside without further comment or observation. Perhaps they all were.

"Weird, isn't it," he interjected. "Today's the second time we've heard somebody call her 'Albie' instead of 'Bertie.' There was a whole other version of our sister that we didn't know anything about. It's as if she had another identity away from us."

"Well, she kind of did, didn't she?" Sky pointed out. "I'd go months without seeing or hearing from her—there was even that whole year she just vanished. None of us knew where she'd gone, or what the hell had happened to her. Then, when she finally did turn up, she wouldn't say a thing about it."

"She probably figured you were prying, or something," Aria speculated. "Trying to find out whether she was using again."

Sky studied the salt shaker she was turning back and forth between her fingers. "I didn't get that impression," she said. "It was more the feeling that there was just too much to get into and she didn't have the energy. And maybe... Maybe we just weren't worth it."

"Oh, well that's silly," Aria began, but she was interrupted by the approach of their waitress, and once their orders had been taken, she seemed to have lost her steam to keep going on the topic.

"Do you suppose," she asked instead, dumping a packet of sugar into her coffee, "that the strange guy who showed up at the service, the one with the shaved head and the body art, was Beau?"

Her siblings considered this. "Could be," Sky said. "Except, he seemed… well, nice, I guess. Not particularly eloquent, but apparently he liked her, judging by what he said."

"That could've just been remorse," Trace suggested. "Feeling guilty for having dumped her." He leaned back in the booth.

"Well, look," he added after some consideration. "I'll take the stuff, unless one of you really wants it. We can go through it first, if you like, but I'll find a place to keep it."

"Fine with me," Sky said. She looked at Aria. "I don't think I need to see what's there, but if you do…?"

But their sister merely shook her head and lifted the cup of coffee to her lips.

And, as simply as that, they had relinquished their final claims on Bertie. Or so it seemed to Trace.

Chapter Four

In April, Trace and Marla flew to Charleston to spend a week with her folks. Kaye and Meacham, her mother and stepfather, lived on Wappoo Creek, a channel of leisurely moving water that ferried its contents to the ocean several hundred yards below their home.

There was a curious kind of days-gone-by feel to the area, even though their house, shrouded among thick vegetation, was as modern as anything Trace had ever seen. The newest amenity, added since the last time they had visited, was a system of lamps and lights controlled by spoken command.

"Isn't that just the most ridiculous thing?" Kaye appealed to them just after Meacham had proudly given them a demonstration. "He points it out to everyone who sets foot in the place. Telling people you have voice-controlled lights is basically just confessing that you're too lazy to get up and walk halfway across a room to flick a switch."

Trace had always liked Kaye. She was resolutely energetic, quick to laugh, and even quicker to laugh at herself. At sixty, she seemed not years, but decades younger than his own mother. Meacham was equally engaging. A retired banker, he displayed unquenchable interest in people, gadgets, and life in general. In stark contrast to the slow-moving blue-green water flowing past their door, Marla's folks moved with what appeared to be an endless supply of energy.

They encouraged Trace to relax and take it easy, and to sleep in as late as he liked every day—but that was hampered by the guilt of hearing their hosts bustling around by seven each morning. Trace would totter out onto the porch, cup of coffee in hand, to be greeted by Kaye as she dragged a canoe ashore.

"Did I wake you?" she'd pant, red-faced with exertion, pulling two large bags out of the boat. "I hope I didn't wake you."

"You didn't wake me," he assured her. Leaving his cup on the railing, he stepped off the porch and through the coarse grass to take the sacks out of his mother-in-law's arms. And it was true; he'd been awakened much earlier by the voices of Meacham and Dana, Marla's sister, playing badminton in the side yard just outside his window.

"I decided to paddle down to the store and pick up a few things," Kaye said, following him to the steps. "Careful, darlin'. You shouldn't go barefoot in this grass. It can cut up your feet something fierce, plus there's chiggers," she cautioned in a soft, rounded drawl the rest of her family had lost, if they'd ever had it to begin with. The girls referred to it as an affectation, but Trace found it charming and somewhat hypnotic.

"That's fine; I'll take them from here," she instructed, scooping the canvas bags from him once they'd climbed to the porch. "You take your coffee on over to the side veranda. I'll be out in a minute with some fruit and cinnamon rolls."

"There you are," Marla greeted him as he rounded the corner. She was stretched out on a chaise lounge in a t-shirt and shorts, reading a magazine. Perched on her head was a huge straw hat he'd never seen before. Its wide brim seemed to undulate outward from her head in waves.

"Where did you get that ridiculous thing?" he grinned, dropping onto the chair alongside her. "I can't kiss you good morning while you have that on. I can't even get within three feet of your head."

"It was hanging just inside the screen door. Presumably it's Mom's. If it's Dad's, then he's got some explaining to do." She folded back a generous flap of brim in order to let his lips reach hers. "Have you seen him since you got up?"

He shook his head. "I've heard him, though. He and your sister are playing badminton on the other side of the house."

Marla grimaced. "I know. They're waiting for you to get up so they can challenge us to a doubles match. Try to keep your voice down and maybe we can have a few moments of peace, first."

Trace used the toes of one foot to scratch an insect bite on the ankle of his other. He hoped it wasn't one of those chiggers Kaye had warned him about. "Why do they play this early?" he asked.

"The humidity will make it too miserable in another couple of hours."

Not that this meant there would be a period of inactivity as the sun crept higher in the sky. He knew from their previous visits that there weren't enough hours in the day to accommodate all the events his in-laws would have planned for them. For all Kaye's disclaimers that they were to relax and take things easy, those were inevitably the two things left off that list.

And, as if to underscore that fact, the thundering of footsteps across the wooden planks preceded the appearance of Meacham and Dana, swinging their badminton racquets, foreheads shiny with sweat.

"I knew you couldn't still be asleep!" Dana crowed, dropping down on the chaise lounge by Marla's feet. "Not with all the noise we were deliberately making!"

She grinned at him with a smile that perfectly matched her sister's. Her hair, gathered into a high ponytail, was darker than Marla's, and though five years younger, she stood two to three inches taller, a characteristic inherited from her father. Meacham was a lanky six-foot-four, and could—and probably did—present an intimidating figure to the girls' suitors, at least in their teenage years, though he'd never been anything other than warm and welcoming to Trace.

Meacham stood over him now, grinning as he twirled the racquet in his hand. "We'll let you finish your coffee and get some shoes on, son, before we have a game or two. Then I thought we'd get the boat out. Head up the channel and do some fishing, or maybe down for a picnic on the beach. You have a preference?"

"Oh, honestly, Daddy!" Marla let her magazine drop to the wooden planks alongside the chaise. "We're here all week. We don't have to cram everything into one day."

"There's a place down the coast that offers parasailing," he continued, as if she hadn't said anything. "I've wanted to give that a try, but Kaye said I had to wait until you kids were here. She said if she was going to be widowed, she wanted her children around her when it happened."

"I'm in," Dana declared. She nudged Marla's legs to one side unceremoniously to claim more of the cushion. "We can do it in tandem. All four of us can go: two and two!"

"And leave me widowed *and* childless?" Kaye interjected as she came through the open sliding door bearing a tray of breakfast items. She set it on the glass table with a firm *plonk* for added effect. "Or just as bad, nurse all four of you back to health after you go *splat* on the sand?"

"You can relax, Mom," Marla assured her. "I have no intention of being towed behind a boat while two hundred feet off the ground."

"You are such a baby!" Dana jeered, nudging her roughly with her elbow. Marla responded by raising one knee in order to plant her foot squarely in her sister's back.

"You finally graduate law school in another month. At least wait until you've got a job and health insurance before risking life and limb!"

"Chicken!"

"Brat!"

Trace observed this banter, intrigued. His own family had this same kind of informality to their interactions, yet something was distinctly different in the way Marla and her kin treated one another. And though he had been a part of the fold a relatively short while and he only saw his in-laws once or twice a year, they treated him with the same kind of irreverence and intimacy.

Meacham had married Marla's mother when Marla was three, but she called him *Dad* or *Daddy,* and it was clear he loved her precisely as much as he did Dana, the biological daughter who'd arrived two years later. And though Marla lived halfway across the country from them, they were all resolutely connected, in touch with one another's lives. Something Trace and his family, all living in the same city, had not quite achieved.

They never got around to parasailing that week, either singly or in doubles, to Trace's secret relief, as well as Kaye's. He felt he'd pushed his luck far enough for one year with the skiing accident. But there was no shortage of activities to take its place: fishing, boating, volley-ball, swimming, and more. On one of the last days of their visit, he extricated himself from a proposed biking expedition and remained behind with Kaye, who was planning another trip down the channel to pick up groceries.

"You're welcome to come along," she said, tucking her canvas shop-ping bags in the bottom of the canoe. "But I imagine you're looking forward to a little quiet time, finally."

To his surprise, however, he found himself struggling out of the hammock mere minutes after having climbed in with a beer and his phone. "Sure," he said.

He helped her nudge the unwieldy fiberglass frame off the bank and leapt into the rear of the craft, teetering perilously for a few sec-onds before collapsing on the seat. His mother-in-law seated herself far more gracefully and picked up her oar.

"Okay, now I really should be the one in back," she spoke to him over her shoulder. "But you're heavier, so you're going to be doing the steering. The current will carry us, so we won't have to do a lot of pad-dling until the return trip." At this, she shifted on her seat to look at him with a critical eye.

"We'll have the weight of the groceries to counterbalance us then, so we might be able to switch positions coming back. Either way, it'll be more of a workout. Just so you know."

Trace nodded.

"We'll keep to the right, same as if we were in a car. You'll mostly drag your oar. I'll tell you when to pull left or pull right or hold it straight. Got it?"

"Got it."

And they were off, gliding across the water without effort and barely disturbing its docile surface. Even so, they moved at breathtak-ing speed. Trees, bushes, and dwellings flew past. At first, Trace was slightly alarmed. It appeared they had surrendered to the river's mercy and wouldn't stop until they had rocketed out of the channel's mouth into the ocean. But Kaye seemed unperturbed, mostly sitting with her own oar across her lap as she called out an occasional instruction, and gradually he began to relax.

There was an intoxicating scent in the air over the water, sweet and light, with none of the dank fishy smell it held closer to the banks, and even close to the house. Kaye raised her oar in greeting to boats heading up the channel and to people standing on docks and on the shoreline. Invariably, everyone waved back. Something about living on the banks of rivers engendered friendliness, it seemed. He found himself smiling and waving as well.

"Pull left!" Kaye commanded finally, and dipped her own paddle into the water, guiding them to a row of slips next to a stone wall just below a row of buildings. A moment later, they were alongside a bobbing dock and she was securing the canoe to the cleat with a length of braided rope.

"You don't have to come into the store if you'd rather not," she said as they climbed the steps to the street above. "I shouldn't be more than fifteen minutes or so, if you want to just look around some."

So he took her at her word, and they parted company in front of the market. He joined the flow of people wandering up and down the wide cobblestone street, which was lined with a variety of umbrella-topped carts selling food items and souvenirs. Small metal tables and chairs with swooping curlicue wire legs stood on the far side of the road, next to the sea wall, affording people the opportunity to eat their hot dogs and snow cones while gazing out across the waves.

More than half the tables were empty. It was early still, and most of the carts were draped in canvas tarps. One or two were open, the ones selling morning items like coffee and bagels. The heady smell of warm cinnamon rolls reached him, and he drifted over for a look.

A woman with two children stood at the head of the line, and she seemed to be having a difficult time coaxing an answer from either of them about what they wanted to eat.

"Orange or apple juice, sweetie? And do you want a muffin or a sweet roll? *Now,* Carla. We don't have all day."

But evidently they did, because Carla gazed around indifferently, one finger lodged in the corner of her mouth. Her brother was squatting by one corner of the cart and attempting to turn one of its wheels with his fingers.

The man behind them, who had a newspaper wedged under his arm, turned around to roll his eyes at Trace and shake his head in mild annoyance. Trace smiled and walked away. He really didn't need a pastry, anyway.

The wind was gusting over the sea wall. A teenaged girl stood with her back to him, arms folded on the top of the stones, hair streaming behind her as she looked into the distance. Nearby, an elderly couple walked a small, energetic terrier that barked enthusiastically at nothing at all, just announcing his happiness at being out and having a walk.

Trace continued to stroll, following the gentle curve of the walkway for another hundred yards where the stone wall ended, butting up against a far less romantic series of concrete blocks. The path likewise changed from cobblestone to asphalt, and a sign announced public parking for the beach.

He turned and began retracing his steps. Some distance along, he impulsively hoisted himself onto the broad stone wall and swung his legs across, dangling them on the ocean side. He studied the bank of clouds climbing over the horizon, more a part of the water than the sky.

He wasn't aware of how long he'd been watching this when someone said:

"You're not supposed to sit there; don't you know that?"

He turned his head to see a young woman standing some distance to his left. She was pointing to a sign that read *Keep off the sea wall.*

Embarrassed, he raised his knees and swiveled back across, lowering himself to the ground, aware of how clumsy his descent looked. He scraped the side of one leg in the process.

"I didn't see it," he explained, landing on the cobblestones and steadying himself with one hand on the wall. "Even though I walked right by it before."

The girl pointed to his leg. "Looks like you hurt yourself a little bit."

"It's nothing. I'm fine." He bent to examine the wound and to brush away any debris from the rocks. It was a small gouge, showing red, and it throbbed slightly.

"Boys always say that," she announced in a dismissive tone reminiscent of his sisters' smug pronouncements when they were about this same age. He realized now that she was the teenager he'd noticed earlier, the one standing on the far side of the street from the breakfast cart.

She followed him up the walkway, and when he sat at one of the tables, she pulled out the chair opposite his. He inspected his scrape one more time, then tugged up his socks carefully. He found her continued scrutiny a little unsettling.

"I really am okay," he assured her. "Or did you need something?"

One corner of her mouth twisted into a grin, and Trace leaned forward, looking at her closely for the first time. The brown hair, the golden brown eyes. The freckles across the bridge of the nose. His own eyes widened.

"I wondered how long it would take you," Bertie laughed. "Did you think I wouldn't show up again?"

It was the first time she'd appeared since the day he'd seen her in the bathroom nearly two months ago. Trace shook his head.

"I thought you might be there at that apartment when we went to get your things," he said. "Or later, while I was sorting through them back at home. I expected to look up and see you watching me."

She shrugged and pulled a wisp of hair away from her face.

"Why has it been so long, and how come you look the way you do right now?" he asked.

"What's wrong with the way I look?"

"I didn't say there was anything wrong. But you're twenty-eight. You *were*, anyway, when you… But today, you look about fifteen."

She leaned back in her seat, stretching her feet in front of her and splaying her toes in her sandals.

"I'd forgotten all about these," she declared. "These shoes. They're pretty nice. For once, something that wasn't a hand-me-down from Aria or Sky." She gave him a sidelong glance. "You must have remembered them, though. Since I'm wearing them now."

"What does *that* m—"

"—When I died, right? That's what you started to say a second ago, and then didn't. Wasn't it? I was twenty-eight when I died?"

He didn't answer, and she drew back her legs.

"If it's my feelings you're trying to spare, don't bother." She nudged his knee with hers under the table. "I already know I'm dead. And if you're just trying to be delicate for other people's sakes, or for yourself, for some silly reason, well, don't. That little pause before you don't say *died* makes it worse than if you did. It makes me seem like some sort of waif-like creature who was too sensitive for this world. Just tell people I'm dead, and be done with it."

A small bird hopped along the wall, stopping to peck at something between the stones.

"I'm sorry," he said finally. And before she could say anything, he added, "That I didn't do *something*. Didn't try harder."

"What?" she asked earnestly. "What would you have done?"

He worked his lower jaw back and forth. "I would have made more of an effort. Stayed in touch. Called more often. *Something*. I don't know."

"But I could have done that, too, right? If that's what I really wanted." She folded her arms in front of her, smiling as she studied the rockwork.

"That's what I told myself," Trace acknowledged. "Because it was easier. Because, sometimes, your problems seemed so big. As big as..."

He considered the waves churning up onto the beach on the other side of the wall.

"And you had problems of your own. Challenges, anyway," she offered in his defense. "You thought there'd be more time. Once you got your own shit sorted out. Or maybe, by then, I would have started to pull it together on my own."

"Why?" he demanded, his voice rising sharply. Startled, the bird on the wall took flight. "Why all the drugs, the distance? Why, when you'd start to get clean, come so close sometimes, would you fall back? Again and again. It was just so damn frustrating."

For a minute, he didn't think she was going to answer him. Finally, she unfolded her arms and pulled herself up in her chair. "I didn't like what I saw; don't you suppose that was it? At first, I would think, *I can do this. It's not so hard.* And it wasn't. But then, things would start to come into focus. Like when you walk into a dark room. First, you can't make out anything at all. Then, as your eyes adjust, you see vague shapes. If you stay long enough, you can finally see everything." Bertie faced him, her smile gone. "I decided the dark was so much easier to take, that's all."

"Sometimes I feel as if you picked all of it—the drugs, the isolation, the flaky boyfriends—over us," he told her.

"I can't help how you feel, Trace. And if you're looking to make me feel guilty, I'm well past that."

"That's not what I want," he said, but he wasn't altogether sure it was the truth.

"And don't you feel guilty, either," she ordered.

"Is that what you've come to tell me? That none of us should feel bad? Is that what these visits are all about?"

Another voice hailed him from over his shoulder. He swiveled in his chair to see Kaye standing just outside the market, waving at him.

"I don't know why I'm here," Bertie muttered. "I just am."

Now Kaye was walking their direction. Trace got to his feet. "Tell me this, at least: Was it an accident, or was it on purpose?"

He spoke quietly, though his mother-in-law was still much too far away to hear anything.

Bertie lifted her chin and met his gaze squarely.

"Don't you get it, Tracey?" she said.

"No. What?" he hissed, taking a step back and preparing to cross and meet Kaye before she could reach the table.

"I can't tell you anything you don't already know."

He stared at his sister in frustration, clenching and unclenching his hands, then wheeled and strode away. Midway across the cobblestones, he reached to take one of the bags from Kaye's arms. He forced a smile.

"We don't have to leave right away, if you aren't ready," she said, leaning slightly to peer around his shoulder at the table behind him.

"No, that's fine. I'm ready," he assured her. He wondered what she was looking at, but he didn't turn his head. They retraced their path to the steps leading down to the dock.

They tucked the groceries under the rear seat of the canoe, and Trace climbed into the front.

"Alternate your strokes," Kaye instructed him. "One left, one right, and so on."

He nodded, untying the rope from the cleat and using his oar to push them away from the dock. They paddled to the far side of the channel and then turned upstream.

He fell into an easy rhythm, watching the front of the canoe slice the current as he drew his paddle from one side to the other and back again. His arms began to tingle and his fingers ached, but he could hear Kaye's even strokes in the water behind him, so he kept at it without comment, letting his thoughts drift.

Tracey: The nickname, so long abandoned, and sprung from a name that was ridiculous to begin with. Only Bertie had perpetuated it beyond middle school, and only because she knew it bothered him. It had been a hard-won battle, following bloody schoolyard skirmishes, to earn the right to be called *Trace,* not *Tracey,* and in sisterly fashion, she had delighted in taking it away from him now and then.

Not that *Trace* itself was such a great name. Or *Bertie,* either, for that matter. The lot of them, in fact: *Cord. Aria. Sky. Trace. Alberta.* And *Quince.* A ridiculous, whimsical list.

"We took turns naming you," his mother had informed him once. "I got to pick first, and then your father the next one. Oh, and it was such fun when we knew you were going to be twins. I had named Sky, so it was your dad's turn next, but then, since there were two of you, I got to have another pick right away."

The delight in her tone as she explained this was dismaying. He didn't ask which of them had chosen *Trace*. It was less complicated to blame both of them equally. Clearly, neither of them should have been selecting names in the first place. Not for children. Pets, maybe.

Bertie's complaint had been a different one, however.

"I hate the way you always lump us together," she'd announced one afternoon when their mother got off the telephone after chatting with a friend. "We have names, you know."

Their mother had looked thoroughly bewildered. "What are you talking about?"

"You did it just now. Saying, *'With Sky off to college, it's just the twins and Quince around the house now.'* It's always that way, haven't you noticed?" She turned to Trace, who was sitting on the couch eating a bowl of cereal in front of the television. "You get it, right? It bothers you, too, doesn't it?"

He'd paused, a spoonful of Lucky Charms midway to his mouth, not sure what to say. Bertie continued, confident of his tacit support.

"It's on the Christmas cards and everything. Every year. *Love, Frank, Karen, Cord, Aria, Sky, the twins, and Quince.* It's how you introduce us when we're out someplace: *'Oh, and you remember the kids, don't you? Cord. Aria and Sky. And the twins. And Quince.'* Sometimes you put Quince's name first, even though he's the youngest."

"Oh, now, sweetheart, I don't think I always do—"

"—Is it really that much more effort to write out *Bertie and Trace?* I know we share a birthday and all, but we are two separate people."

"Of course you are. I certainly never meant anything by it."

"Dad does it, too. All of you, sometimes. I just… I'm my own person, you know? I'm not half of some sideshow act or something."

"Nobody thinks that, I promise," their mother was saying, but Bertie was flouncing out of the room, so she turned to Trace.

"I had no idea," she said, chagrined. "If anything, I suppose, I was bragging a little. Not every family has twins, after all. I'm sorry if it's bothered you all this time."

Trace, his mouth full of cereal, merely shrugged. He'd never really paid much attention. But thereafter, he was keenly aware of how careful his mother was to insert both of their names into any discussion that involved the whole family, whether Bertie was within earshot or not. It was painful, almost, and he nearly cringed at the precise way she pronounced them. It made them both stand out in an entirely different way, though he doubted anybody besides himself noticed.

Now, of course, it would never be an issue again. There weren't any twins to introduce. He lifted his oar from the water and rested it across the bow of the canoe. From behind him, Kaye said, "Everything okay up there?"

He nodded, flexing his hands several times.

"Just giving my fingers a break," he told her.

Chapter Five

Their flight home was delayed, and they boarded the plane more than two hours late, making a long day of travel just that much longer. Trace dozed in the middle seat, lulled by the engine noise and the faint sounds of activity and conversation around them. The seat didn't recline enough to accommodate his height, so his head slumped against Marla's shoulder as she listened to music through a headset and turned the pages of the book she held in her lap. After some time, he became aware that her hand was sliding up and down the inside of his thigh. She had set her book aside. He blinked awake and cast a glance to his left.

"Relax," Marla said. "He got up and went to the restroom, I think." She was referring to the stocky white-haired man who had been occupying the seat on Trace's other side.

"He'll be back," he reminded her.

"And when he is, I'll stop." She increased the speed of her strokes and also expanded their target area. They both gazed at the seat backs in front of them as if nothing else was going on. "Or you could reach up and get our coats out of the overhead bin."

"I'm not going to do that."

"Yeah. You probably shouldn't," she said, amused, giving him a squeeze. She stopped moving her hand and rested it on his knee. She allowed a few more seconds to pass before she added, still facing forward, "I've been thinking about going off the pill. We talked about it late last year, remember."

His breath caught, mid-inhale. "Oh," he managed finally.

"I know, with everything going on—with what happened with Bertie—this really hasn't been the best time. And I'm not talking about right away. But soon."

He resumed breathing, and the air rushing in and out of his nostrils seemed very loud. Now he found himself wishing for his seatmate's return, so that this conversation could be tabled and he could have time to consider it.

"What do you think?"

"I... I don't know."

"If I got pregnant this summer, you'd be twenty-nine, nearly thirty, when the baby was born. I'd be twenty-nine. We wouldn't want to wait much longer than that, would we?"

"No," he agreed. "We wouldn't." His arousal, he realized, was a thing of the past.

Marla nodded, sliding her hand back into her own lap and reaching for her book. The white-haired man returned, caught Trace's bewildered gaze, smiled briefly, and buckled himself back into his seat. The discussion was definitely at an end, and from Marla's perspective, had evidently been settled.

It was true that before Bertie's death they had tentatively chosen this year as their target date for getting pregnant. And really, there was no reason to postpone it much longer. They both wanted children; two, they'd decided. So why was this catching him off guard?

He wondered all of a sudden what it would be like if they had both kids at the same time, something he'd never considered until now. Wasn't it said that multiple births run in families? Though he'd also heard somewhere that the tendency skips a generation or two, so probably he was safe. Although how science determined something like that—or if it were even true—he couldn't say. Now, from some dim recess of his brain, he had a murky recollection of Bertie at ten or twelve or some other confrontational age bemoaning a perceived injustice by yelling, *"Well, if I ever have twins, I'm going to treat them different than this, you can bet on that!"*

The memory made him smile. The next time he saw her, he would have to ask her if she remembered that. For now, he closed his eyes and settled his head against Marla's shoulder. Engrossed in her book, she gave his leg another pat—a chaste one this time.

THE NIGHT AFTER THEIR RETURN from South Carolina, his niece Lisa was performing in a ballet recital. Trace groaned when Marla reminded him.

"Well, we don't *have* to go," she said. But they both knew they did.

It was a slippery slope, of course, setting a precedent for attending any event involving nieces or nephews. So far, it had been relatively easy to maintain. Only Cord's kids were old enough to have established a roster of extracurricular activities, and lately Zeke, in his moody teen phase, had withdrawn from most of his. But the others were coming along: Aria's boys—Richie at eight and Lawrence, six—and Emily, Sky's little girl, at five, would soon be participating in things that demanded an audience. Richie was in soccer already, and how do you not huddle on uncomfortable bleacher seats in blustery weather, cheering him on, when you've done likewise for his older cousins?

So Trace and Marla made their way down the aisle of the rec center's small auditorium where Mademoiselle Pineret's Dance Academy held their performances. They'd arrived in plenty of time, yet most of the seats were already filled. Fathers held camcorders or cell phone cameras at the ready; mothers tended to restless younger siblings while the rest of the audience—tangential relations like himself, Trace supposed—gamely waited in a room already too warm and heavy with perfume and sweat.

He spotted Leslie and Cord in the second row, and Quince sitting with them. But there were no empty seats around them. Trace had stopped in his tracks, trying to decide their next move, when Marla touched his arm.

"Over there!" she said. "Sky's waving to us. Looks like she's saved us places."

They retraced their path a few steps and entered a crowded row, apologizing as they negotiated their way around knees and legs until they had reached Sky, Emily, and two seats draped with coats as placeholders.

"Thank God," Sky greeted them. "I'm not sure how much longer I could have held onto these. Ugly glares are one thing, but the mumbled threats and clenched fists are something else."

"I hope that's an exaggeration," Marla said, settling into her seat and handing Sky's coat back to her.

"Just barely."

"Aria and Pete aren't coming, I take it?" Trace asked, glancing around. "Or Mom and Pop?"

He received a snort in response. "You know the folks. And Aria said it would be next to impossible to keep the boys in their seats and quiet for an hour of ballet."

I know how they feel, Trace felt himself about to say, but thought better of it. And, of course, his parents had made their position on these sorts of things clear a long time ago.

"Don't you think we've already done our time?" his mother had said once in a let's-be-reasonable tone of voice. "I mean, six kids of our own... We've already sat through more than our share of pageants, plays, Little League games, and Cub Scout awards presentations. It's really more of a parent's job to go to these things, don't you think?"

Their father had been even more to the point. "Not going to happen," he announced. "Send the grandkids over for a visit now and then, that's one thing. But I'm not going anyplace where I have to put on shoes and clap for a bunch of other kids I don't even know."

Trace had found this attitude somewhat humorous in the past. But now, as he gave a sidewise glance to Marla—specifically her belly—and imagined her carrying a baby, he felt a sudden jolt. If they got pregnant anytime soon, theirs would be the sixth grandchild to come along. Just another in a sea of third-generation faces, nothing particularly special to his folks. Another name and birthdate they would grudgingly have to make a note to remember. For Kaye and Meacham, however, this would be a momentous occasion, their firstborn's firstborn, a child to be celebrated with all kinds of excess and devotion. Maybe that was a good thing; each set of grandparents counterbalancing the other. The kid could feel kind of special, but also humbled.

He listened to Marla converse with Emily.

"So, Emily, are you excited to see Lisa dance tonight?"

His niece's tiny hands gripped her chair's armrests as she frowned slightly, considering the question. "I haven't decided yet," was her eventual answer. Emily was a solemn child composed largely of enormous brown eyes, who gave the impression of someone constantly inventorying everything around her for verdict at a later date. She could not have been more different than exuberant, outgoing Lisa, who wore every emotion on her sleeve.

Marla tried again. "Would you like to try ballet, do you think?"

This question seemed to require less contemplation. "No. I don't like wearing all white, and I don't like having my hair pulled back too tight."

"She's more of a fashionista than a dance enthusiast," Sky explained, rolling her eyes. At this, Emily gave her mother a dubious, searching look. It wasn't an expression suggesting she didn't understand the term, but rather that she was unclear why her perfectly valid opinion was being treated in such a dismissive way.

Trace was intrigued by Emily. More than her cousins, more than anyone else in the family, she was a cypher. Self-possessed without being smug, cautious yet not exactly timid. He didn't have the same easy rapport with her as he did with the other kids, but he was confident she liked him, trusted him in her own quiet way. She was clearly a product of both her parents, yet there was something else in there, too, something miles beyond either of them.

The lights were lowered, finally, and Mademoiselle Pineret entered from the wings, stepping into a spotlight to a round of applause. Her hair, Trace couldn't help noticing, was in fact pulled back the way Emily had described. It gave her forehead a taut appearance and her eyes a faint look of perpetual surprise. She greeted and thanked her audience for being here, gave a brief description of the order of the program, and then things got underway.

The first number featured girls as small or smaller than Emily. The troupe faced their audience with expressions of misgiving, and they seemed only further disconcerted at the chorus of coos and *awwws* their appearance solicited. It was amusing to watch them move awkwardly around the stage, barely in time to the music and glancing nervously into the wings from where they were being encouraged by a chorus of loudly whispered directions, probably from Mademoiselle Pineret herself.

Things grew progressively less entertaining with the subsequent groups, who were older, more skilled, and clearly more comfortable onstage. This was simply ballet, performed pretty much as it was intended to be performed, so far as Trace could tell. It got boring very quickly. After several minutes of this, he released a sigh just a little more loudly than he'd realized. Marla nudged him in the ribs and Sky gave him a quick, disapproving glance, although she wasn't quite able to conceal the smile that came with it. He suspected her sentiments weren't much different than his.

Lisa performed twice, once with the other nine- and ten-year-olds, and again in the final number, which brought together dancers from most of the age groups. She had a brief, featured bit as one of a trio of girls who executed a series of swoops and twirls before retreating to the rear of the stage. Her skills seemed perfectly in line with everyone else's, but it was the beaming expression that really made her stand out. The other girls were much more sober, wearing looks either of absolute concentration or no emotion whatsoever. Probably that was the preferred, traditional method. Lisa's barely concealed giddiness lent the number a much more informal air.

"We should have brought her a rose or something," Marla murmured to Trace as the audience gave the performers a standing ovation at the end. Indeed, it appeared that nearly everyone around them was now producing a flower or an entire bouquet from under their seats or out of their coats, or somewhere.

"I wouldn't worry about it," Sky told them. She pointed to Cord, who was wielding one of the more impressive floral arrangements to be seen anywhere in the room.

They made their way back across the row and down the aisle, jostling through the crowds and flowers to join the others.

"Thank you so much for coming," Leslie greeted them. In a lowered tone, she added, "I know it's a lot to sit through."

"Not at all; we loved it!" Marla enthused, perhaps being at least half honest.

"Where's Zeke?" Trace asked his brother.

"At a buddy's house," Cord told him. "He said he'd watched his sister do the routines around the house often enough, he didn't need to see them again tonight." He set his mouth in a grim line. "We caved. Sometimes, it's just easier to go along with his bullshit than to take a stand on every little issue. There are only so many hours in the day, after all."

Trace slapped his arm sympathetically, but at that moment, Cord's face broke into a wide smile. Lisa, his ray of sunshine, had reappeared from around the curtain, looking over the crowd anxiously until she spotted her family. A look of delight mirroring her dad's spread across her features, and she flew down the steps and into their midst to receive a collection of hugs and lavish compliments. Even Quince, Trace noticed with a twinge, had remembered to bring a flower to the young star. Well, there was nothing left to do but to offer to take everyone out for ice cream to make up for his oversight, he decided.

Trace and Quince were standing on either side of Lisa, their arms on her shoulders, smiling for Cord's camera, when she began to wave frantically and broke away from them. "There's Mademoiselle!" she said. "I want her to meet all of you! Stay right here!" She was back a second later, her instructor in tow. "Mademoiselle, this is my family! You know my mom and dad, but here's my cousin Emily, my aunts Sky and Marla, and my uncles, Quince and Trace. It's okay; it's a lot of names. You don't have to remember all of them."

The ballet teacher shook hands with each of them in turn, laughing. Up close, she looked younger and less formidable, Trace decided. Her offstage voice was more informal, as well.

"Well, I'll try, anyway," she said. "I certainly could have picked most of you out of the crowd. You have a very nice-looking bunch of relatives. They all look like you!" she informed Lisa.

"Oh, there's even more of them," Lisa explained. "Maybe you can meet them another time."

"Well, I certainly hope so," her instructor said in a tone that didn't seem at all insincere. Her wide green eyes swept the circle of Bannerlys one last time, lingering on each of them for just a second. "It was a real pleasure; thank you for coming to see our performances this evening." She turned away then, to a circle of other young tutu-clad girls eager to introduce her to their families.

"She didn't have an accent," Quince pointed out to Trace under his breath.

"Did you expect her to?"

"Yeah. I thought she'd be French or something."

Shaking his head, Trace turned to the others.

"Anybody up for ice cream? It's on me!"

Everyone was.

"THIS IS TO MAKE UP for not bringing flowers, isn't it?" Marla surmised as they all filed into the pink-and-white-striped confectionery parlor thirty minutes later, pulling together a collection of rounded tables and generally disrupting the room's quietude as they settled in to await ice cream.

"Let's see Quince's flower stand up to *this*," Trace joked. "Or even that monster bouquet of Cord's." He pulled out a chair for his wife.

She grinned and rolled her eyes. "That brotherly one-upmanship. Will you guys ever outgrow it?"

"Look who's talking," he jeered. "I just spent a whole week watching you compete with your sister in every conceivable way. Badminton. Swimming laps. Shoes, even."

"Dana has horrible taste in shoes!" was all Marla could offer in defense.

"So, what's the deal with that Pineret woman?" Quince was asking Leslie across the table in a slightly lowered tone.

Leslie, studying the menu, smiled without looking up.

"What do you mean, Quince?"

He idly tapped the bobbing straw in his glass of ice water. "I was just curious, you know. Does... Does she have kids of her own?"

Sky and Trace, seated opposite one another, exchanged an amused glance, but said nothing.

"Oh, Quince." Leslie folded her menu closed and propped her chin in her palm, studying him with just a trace of a smile. "She's twenty-three or four. She's not even married."

"Well, the one does not preclude the other." The color was rising on his neck and cheeks.

"You interested?"

"I'm just curious, that's all."

But now they had the attention of everyone at the table.

"Do you like Mademoiselle?" Lisa demanded. Her look of astonishment was quickly replaced by one of delight, nearly the same expression she'd worn when she'd first spotted all of them after the performance. She turned to Leslie. "Mom, give him her number!"

"You stay out of this, squirt!" Quince instructed, jabbing a finger toward his niece. "I did not say that, and don't you go telling her I did, you got it?" He took a deep pull of water through his straw and slammed his glass on the table. "Jeez, I was just asking a question, is all."

Lisa nodded and fell silent for a moment. But then, when she felt confident that nobody was listening, she turned to her small cousin.

"I bet Quince asks her out," she told Emily. "And I bet she'll say yes!"

Emily, regarding Lisa through wide brown eyes, said nothing, but appeared to give the idea serious consideration.

"LISA'S RIGHT, I THINK," Marla said shortly after they'd walked back into their apartment an hour later. "Quince likes her ballet teacher. And I think the feeling may be mutual."

Trace was pulling his shirttails out of his pants and unbuttoning his cuffs. "What makes you say that?"

She turned off the living room light and followed him into the bedroom. "Her comment about us being a nice-looking family."

"So?"

"She was looking at you and Quince when she said it. And *you're* already taken." Marla unzipped the back of her dress and let it fall to the floor. She stepped out of it and flopped back onto the bed.

Trace glanced at her and then at the clock on the nightstand. "Are we going to bed already? It's just past nine-thirty."

She wriggled her body up the bedspread so that her head was resting on a pillow. "Maybe not to sleep."

"Oh." He speeded up the unbuttoning of his shirt. "Are we trying to make a baby already?"

Grinning, she moved her head from side to side, watching while he shucked his pants. "No. Tonight's just for practice."

THIRTY MINUTES LATER they were stretched out alongside one another in a tangle of sheets. Marla's chin was nestled against his collar bone, and she watched the steady rise and fall of his chest.

"You asleep?" she asked finally. He shook his head.

"Thinking."

"'Bout what?"

"Oh, stuff."

She waited for clarification.

"Cord, for instance," he said after a moment. "I hope I can be as good a dad as he is."

"Of course you will be."

She snuggled in closer, closing her eyes. As far as she was concerned, the subject was settled.

Trace went on staring into the darkness, less convinced. There was a seven-year age gap between Cord and himself, and his brother had never seemed as much like an older sibling as he had an unchallengeable, slightly younger parental figure than their dad. He didn't pick fights or tease, the way Aria or Sky had done. He settled squabbles, soothed bad dreams, demonstrated how to toss a football. There was a sort of unflappable authenticity to him that nobody seemed to challenge very much.

On one occasion, he'd shown up at school when Trace had been hauled in for fighting. Cord was eighteen, barely out of school himself, standing with quiet authority next to Trace's chair, listening as the principal spelled out the details of the situation. He hadn't nodded, spoken, or reacted in any way, a tactic that unnerved Mr. Peekskill, the administrator, who seemed to pile words upon unnecessary words as if he didn't want to stop talking until he'd gotten some sort of response.

But it hadn't worked, so finally he rambled to an uncertain stop, intimidated by this tall, thin young man less than half his own age, who had only recently begun shaving every single day.

Trace remembered this far more clearly than the fight itself or what it had been about—being called *Tracey* by someone again, maybe. He recalled the way Cord had finally drawn in a breath through his nose, bunched his lips and said, "Thank you for bringing this to our attention. Trace and I will discuss what happened with our parents. And I'll have our sister Bertie collect his homework assignments over his suspension the next three days."

Without waiting to see if there was anything further to be communicated, he had nudged Trace to his feet and, with a hand on his shoulder, guided him to the door. Before reaching it, though, he'd turned back to Mr. Peekskill and said evenly, "I assume you've brought the other boy's parents in for a similar consultation? Maybe we should all sit down together, just to be sure there's a balanced investigation into what happened."

"I…" the principal had faltered for a mere second while he regained his composure. Standing, he smoothed the front of his tie. "…I don't think that will be necessary. I met with the other parents this afternoon. And, yes, the same suspension has been given to their son."

Cord nodded, finally. "I apologize for the disruption and the inconvenience." Looking down at Trace, he said, "You won't do anything like this again, right?"

"Well, but…" Trace had started to protest, until he felt his brother's fingers digging into his back. "No," he sighed, looking back at Mr. Peekskill. "No, I guess I won't."

Satisfied and feeling in control once again, the principal dismissed them with a curt nod.

Outside in the corridor, Trace was prepared to vent his indignation at what he perceived to be an unfair judgment when Cord bounced his fist gently off the top of his brother's head.

"I thought you knew better than to get caught," he said, keeping his gaze straight ahead even when Trace looked up at him. They continued to walk toward the double glass doors at the end of the hallway.

"Well, I won't next time," Trace promised him. Cord merely nodded.

By mutual unspoken agreement, the matter was never discussed at home. If his mother and father were at all surprised that Trace was at the house and underfoot for the next three days, they gave no indication. It was possible they hadn't really noticed.

Was it his brother's mantle of quiet capability that kept Mr. Peekskill from questioning why he showed up in answer to the summons instead of Mom and Pop that day? Or was his parents' cheerful indifference so widely recognized that the administrator was just relieved that anybody responded at all? These were questions that would forever remain unanswered. Others, as well. Trace sighed, and shifted his arm out from under Marla's neck, lowering her head onto the pillow as gently as he could manage. She murmured without waking entirely and rolled away from him. He moved toward her, molding his body to hers, and pressed his face into the back of her neck, taking in her sweet and familiar scent.

What kind of childhood had his brother had? he wondered drowsily.

The first born, the initial recipient of their parents' sporadic caregiving skills… How much had he been self-taught, even in those first two years before the arrival of Aria? After that, things could only have gotten more complicated. Three years later, Sky was born, and then children even began arriving in pairs. Mom and Pop were well-meaning, of course, but so easily distracted.

As he drifted toward slumber, another image took focus in his head, this one of Cord at eleven or perhaps twelve, carrying a naked, squirming Quince in from the front yard, holding him aloft for their mother to see. "Oh, that's right," she'd said, cupping her hand over the mouthpiece of the telephone she was holding to her ear. "I was getting him ready for his bath when Ruth called." And with that, she'd turned back to the phone, confident that the situation was well in hand. Trace didn't remember what had happened next, but it seemed likely that Cord had taken their three-year-old brother on into the bathroom and finished bathing him.

There'd hardly been any time at all between when Cord was keeping siblings from running naked into the streets and when he was a father himself. It was a role he was eminently qualified to play, but there must have been regrets, disappointments. Did he harbor resentment toward the folks, and toward the rest of them as well? Had anybody ever asked him if he minded being the beleaguered big brother to five whiny, sticky, grasping kids, all wanting something of him nearly every single minute? Of course not. Like Pop and Mom, they'd all just assumed he was fine with it, and went on asking for more of his time, his attention, his help.

It had come at a cost, Trace realized now. Maybe greater to them than to him, in fact. They were grown now, at a point in their lives where they could all be contemporaries. At a time when they could value Cord as a friend as well as a brother, none of them knew how. He stood apart, a sibling in name only, and no longer a surrogate third parent, either. It was especially apparent at times like tonight, when he watched them with the same sort of bemusement he displayed toward his own children. He smiled benevolently at the way they joked among themselves, and couldn't keep from lecturing when he felt it was warranted. He hadn't even let Trace pay for the ice cream.

"Don't be silly," he said dismissively, placing his hand atop the check when Trace had reached for it. "We just appreciate all of you turning out for Lisa's big night. Save your hard-earned bucks for something else."

Had he intended to sound so condescending? The remark stirred up a faint resentment. Through most of Trace's life, Cord had been his protector, his confidant; now he seemed like more of a nag, a killjoy. Even letting those disloyal words drift through his brain made him feel guilty, but there it was. Was this fixable? Could they say to him, "*Relax, Cord. Your job is done. We'll take it from here,*" he wondered. He closed his eyes and tried to will away these thoughts altogether.

IF HE WERE GOING to be twins with anyone, it should have been with Quince. Just fourteen months behind him, his youngest sibling had begun toddling after Trace as soon as he could walk. His crib was in the room Bertie and Trace shared, and in a year or so, when Bertie moved in with Sky, Quince took ownership of the bed that had been hers. In fact, Trace actually had no memories of a life without Quince in it. They were explorers together, fast friends, and occasional combatants, a situation that continued through high school—and in some aspects, even to this day. As if determined to be as much like his brother as possible, Quince, by age six, was the same height as Trace, and kept pace with him going forward. They were similar enough in appearance that casual acquaintances and even teachers, sometimes, mistook one for the other. Where Bertie was often a cypher, Trace understood Quince through and through. He could gauge his reaction to almost anything.

But he had no clear idea of how his brother was going to respond to the information he planned to put before him this evening.

"I've been having conversations with Bertie," Trace said.

They'd met for drinks after work and were sitting in a booth at a quiet end of the pub.

Quince looked startled for only a second or so, then nodded. He drummed his fingers on the side of his vodka and grapefruit juice and glanced around the room. When his gaze returned to Trace, he said:

"Understandable. There's a lot of unresolved crap there. Are you angry at her? I sure as hell am."

"I... Well, yeah. But what I mean—"

"—But you just have to let it go now. I know it's only been a few months, and I know you and she were pretty tight, tighter than she was with any of the rest of us. Maybe talk to somebody, if you need to. Don't let it eat you up, especially since there's nothing you can do about it."

Trace squeezed the base of his beer glass and took a deep breath.

"She... She talks back."

Now his brother was studying him with absolutely no expression on his face. He wasn't even blinking.

"Twice, so far. Once at my place, and once in South Carolina when Marla and I were visiting her family."

Still nothing from Quince. Trace forged ahead.

"I haven't said anything. Not even to Marla. But... But she's *there.* Bertie, I mean. I see her. As close to me as you and I are right now. Always when I least expect it. I'm not thinking about her, or anything, but then *boom!* There she is. We have these conversations for a few minutes, not about anything in particular or anything all that important. She's her usual flip self. We talk until somebody interrupts us. The first time, it was Marla, and the next time Kaye, Marla's mom."

"And then she vanishes."

"Yes. Well, no. I don't know. The last time, I didn't look back. I just got up and walked away. Maybe she was still there."

Quince bunched his lips in the standard expression that all the Bannerlys employed when they were considering new information. He looked down at his drink and then up again.

"And both of these times have been since you got the concussion?"

"That's definitely gone through my mind, yes. I even asked Bertie if that's why I was seeing her." Trace paused, considering just how unbalanced that made him sound. "I mean… Well, she said maybe that was it, but I don't know if I believe that or not."

"Bud… you definitely need to talk to somebody."

"That's why I'm talking to *you!* Yeah, yeah, I know what you mean." Trace added, waving away the remark he knew was coming next. "You think I should tell a doctor about all of this."

"Well, shouldn't you?"

"Not now. Not right away. This is just so specific, you see? I'm not having headaches. I'm not hearing voices. Well, not any other voices. It's only happened twice, weeks apart from each other. If this were serious, if it was getting worse, don't you suppose things would have intensified?"

Then, as if reading his brother's mind, and not waiting for what was coming next, Trace added. "Yeah, yeah, I know. Who's to say it isn't going to intensify? I don't know, Quince, I don't. But I don't want to see a doctor. Not not yet."

"Does… Does she realize she's dead? In these visions?"

He didn't particularly like his brother's use of the word *vision,* but he let it slide. He nodded.

"She seems almost as perplexed as me about why she's there. I get the feeling she thinks I'm doing it. I'm making her show up, or something."

He watched Quince chew his upper lip, and knew exactly what was going through his mind. *"Well, aren't you?"* was the question he was debating whether to ask.

Quince must have sensed this, too. He glanced up at Trace and then away again.

"There's got to be a reason this is happening," he said instead. He lifted his glass and took a drink. "Can you think of what it might be?"

Trace shook his head slowly. He understood that his brother wasn't asking why Bertie was appearing, but rather why he *thought* she was appearing. And that was all right. Because the answer, if he could fig-ure it out, would be the same, regardless.

Quince set his glass back on the table. "Why did you decide to tell me about this?"

"I thought it was important. In case, you know, I *am* going crazy. Somebody needs to know that there were some preliminary signs. And nobody besides you would even give me the benefit of the doubt."

They both laughed a little at this.

"Okay," Quince said, growing solemn again. "I want you to prom-ise me something, though. Will you tell me if she... if it... happens again?"

"I promise." Trace hoisted his mug and drained the last of his beer. "So, answer me this," he said adopting a different tone. "Have you called the ballet teacher yet?"

Quince fished the swizzle stick from his glass and pitched it at him. "Oh, like I'm going to give my crazy brother that piece of information."

"I'll take that as a yes."

"You promise to keep this to yourself?"

"After what I just told *you,* do you think I'm going to spill any se-crets?"

Glancing around first, as if he thought some other member of the Bannerly clan might be lurking within earshot, Quince nodded.

"And?"

"And we're meeting for a drink Sunday night."

"Ah." Trace elevated his eyebrows.

"*Sunday,*" Quince emphasized. "Her choice."

They both understood that this indicated caution on the part of Lisa's teacher. Sunday was a safe night, a night that would need to end early.

"Still," Trace said. "It shows potential. Marla was right."

"Marla? About what?"

"She said Mademoiselle-person was definitely showing interest."

"In me?" Quince's face took on a hopeful look.

"Well, in one of us. Me or you. Probably me, but when she found out I was already taken, then you would have to do."

"You are such an asshole," Quince grinned.

After they'd paid their tab and were standing next to the booth sliding into their jackets, he placed a hand on Trace's arm.

"You meant what you said earlier, right? You'll tell me if... if you see Bertie again?"

"Absolutely."

Quince's hand lingered on his brother's shoulder a second longer.

"And... And how about this... Tell her to come see me, too. If she can. There's a thing or two I'd like to tell her."

His face bore a sheepish grin, but behind it, he was serious. Trace could see it in his eyes. "I will," he said.

Somehow, it didn't entirely surprise him that Quince would say something like that.

Chapter Six

"Why aren't you like other moms?" Sky had demanded one time. "Why can't you and Pop be, you know... normal?" There was such energy, such frustration in her voice that the younger three looked up from whatever they were doing, startled, but also interested to hear the response. At thirteen, Sky was finding their mother's quirks more and more irritating, and increasingly difficult to explain to her friends. Aria had passed through this same phase three years earlier.

"Oh, pooh," Karen Bannerly pronounced languidly, her attention barely diverted from the crossword puzzle she was working. "What's normal, anyway?"

It was true her children had nothing more than a passing familiarity with the concept, recognizing it chiefly through glimpses into the lives of their friends and classmates. They were much more versed in the unconventional: sack lunches containing ham slices wedged between two toaster waffles; going dressed as Christmas trees on Halloween, decked out in garland and ornaments from boxes of decorations hastily pulled down from the attic; the sight of their mother careening last-minute into a classroom wearing mismatched sneakers and bearing a sheet cake that read *Happy Birthday* on the day she'd just remembered it was her turn to bring snacks. "They were out of cupcakes," she'd panted. Then, beaming around the rows of desks, she'd added, "But I bet it's *somebody's* birthday today, or just about!"

Loving but distracted child-rearing had been their parents' style. Curfews and bedtimes were languidly enforced. There were days when the entire family overslept, having pursued their individual interests until midnight or later. After too many mad dashes out the door on the following morning, their mother had come up with what she considered a time-saving solution: she prepared a stack of pre-signed notes explaining that something had come up, and to please excuse *whom-ever* for being tardy. These sat in a kitchen drawer, ready for *whomever* needed to grab one on their way out the door. When those were exhausted, their dad taught Cord and Aria how to forge his signature and gave them permission to write the notes for themselves and the younger kids. The gesture seemed both thoughtful and slightly alarming.

Responsibility wasn't so much earned, as self-taught. Most of them had learned to conduct sibling-inventories on outings, having experienced the unpleasant sensation of walking out of a building to find the family car gone from its parking space. Their parents had a way of getting wrapped up in a conversation with one another that made them less cognizant of everything else around them. They touched hands, exchanged glances, and spoke in unfinished sentences that caused them to smile slyly at one another. Mutual adoration made them dreamy and sometimes absent-minded.

As an adult, falling in love with Marla, Trace gained some insight into how this could happen, how watching one other person walk into a room could cause everything else in the world to fade into sepia tones, all sounds besides her voice to be background noise. But it was just the two of them; he couldn't imagine being quite that lackadaisical with a child running around.

That was the thought in the back of his brain as he stood next to his buddy Gil, both of them still catching their breath after a pick-up basketball game at the rec center. Without realizing he was doing it, he sighed heavily.

Gilbert gave him a sideways glance. "Too much, huh? Sorry, I get a little carried away."

"No, not at all." Trace pointed to the picture on the cell phone the other man was holding up. "Keep going."

His buddy studied him a second longer before using his forefinger to slide the next photo into view. "Okay… Here he is with my mom…"

They were standing between two rows of benches in the rec center's locker room, perspiration streaming on their necks and foreheads. It was the first time Trace had seen Gil in a couple of months, and the new dad was proudly displaying a seemingly endless line of pictures.

"That's great, man," Trace told him. "He looks just like you. For now, anyway. Until he starts to grow hair."

Gilbert grinned ruefully, running his fingers across his shining, threadbare scalp. He dropped his phone into his bag. "Yeah, you'll be there one of these days, just watch."

"Never," Trace retorted. "Good game. And good to see you."

He turned away, lifting one foot onto the bench to untie his sneaker. With the back of one hand, he swiped his nose. "*Having a baby changes everything,*" is what everybody said. Trace thought about the wild and careless Gilbert he'd known when they were teenagers and tried to reconcile him with the man he knew now, the Gil with the greasy thumb print, sliding photo after photo across his cell phone's screen. The same guy who, in high school, couldn't be serious about anything except girls and weed was now an excited new dad, responsible for the upbringing of an infant and enthralled at the prospect. One of the overlooked miracles of new life.

When it was his and Marla's turn, how would it change him, and how *much* would it change him? Would he be like Gilbert, embracing a new challenge, or was he cut from the same cloth as his folks, reluctant to make *too* many sacrifices to an established, comfortable way of life?

He thought about this as he showered and dressed, considering Cord, Aria, and Sky. Each had a distinct parenting style of their own, and all reflected a kind of overcompensation for their own chaotic upbringing. Cord was authoritarian, Aria micromanaged, and Sky was cautious—too cautious, in Trace's private opinion—with Emily. Though, in his uninformed opinion, while none seemed precisely right, at least they were all invested in the process. He recalled the jocular way Meacham, Marla's dad, interacted with his girls, and that seemed closer to the mark, creating camaraderie without surrendering leadership. That's what he wanted to aim for, but was it in him to get there?

He'd missed a call from Marla while he was showering.

"*Running late,*" her message said. "*I won't be home before seven. Don't wanna cook. Could you stop and pick up a pizza or something on your way?*"

There was a pizzeria half a block from the shipping store, and he had to stop by there to pick up a bank deposit anyway, so that would work out well. Trace called her back to let her know he'd gotten the message. Then, deciding to place the order first, he pulled his car into the parking lot in front of Stefano's and walked inside.

"Hey, Trace, how's it going?" Cathy, the woman behind the counter, greeted him. "What's up?"

"Oh, you know. I just have a taste for the best pizza in the city is all."

"Then what are you doing in here?" Leo, Cathy's husband, demanded from over the low wall that divided the kitchen from the front of the restaurant. He was spreading tomato sauce across a freshly rolled circle of dough and gave Trace an indifferent sidelong glance before returning the ladle to a silver pot and reaching for a handful of grated cheese.

"It's too late, and I'm too hungry to drive halfway across town, so I decided to settle for what was close," Trace informed him solemnly. Cathy didn't crack a smile, either. She'd heard this routine too many times before. She merely waited, pencil poised above her tablet, for him to get down to business.

"I'm gonna run up the street to the shop," he told her once he'd placed his order and handed her his credit card. "I'll be back in ten." She nodded and gave him back his card and receipt.

Daylight hadn't entirely faded, and the air, though chilly, held the tantalizingly moist smell of thawing earth as he stepped back outside. He decided he'd savor the sensation while walking to the shop, so he zipped his windbreaker and locked the car.

The evening traffic had subsided, and he was able to cross the street without waiting for passing cars and continue up the far sidewalk. It was past six forty-five, so he bypassed the front door and darkened windows to turn into the alley. Mikayla would have set the alarm when she and Zeke left at around six-thirty, so the only way to enter the store was from the rear entrance, where he could step inside and punch in the code to disable the siren that would otherwise start shrieking in less than sixty seconds.

"I don't know why we need it," she'd complained once or twice. "There's nothing in this place except boxes and rolls of tape and stuff. How many times have you heard of an office supply store getting burglarized?"

"That's not the point," he'd tried to tell her once, though privately he saw her point. "It keeps our insurance premiums down. And it gives you peace of mind. Doesn't it give you peace of mind?" he'd added falteringly under her steadfast, unblinking gaze. She did not answer him.

He slipped in through the door, closing it behind him, and flicked on an overhead light to fully illuminate the keypad on the wall to his left. He punched in the code, and when the tiny green bulb came on signaling the all-clear, he moved across the room and into the small office that, officially, was his, but in which he spent almost no time. He was generally far too busy helping customers, receiving and unpacking orders, and engaged in other tasks to be sitting down for more than a minute here or there. But he pulled out the chair now and settled into it, leaning forward to spin the tumblers on the small floor safe located beneath the center of the desk. It contained two canvas bags, both secured with tiny padlocks. One held the basic cash drawer till; the other would be the day's receipts. He opened the latter and pulled out the deposit form, already filled out in Mikayla's neat printing and rubberbanded to a stack of currency. She and Zeke had had an impressive afternoon, it seemed; it hadn't been that busy up until the time Trace had left to go work out at the rec center, but the tally was the largest they'd had in several days. Maybe he needed to start leaving early more often.

He returned the first bag to the safe, lowering the lid and twisting the dial to secure it. He tucked the second bag into the waistband of his pants, behind his windbreaker, and got to his feet. He paused in the archway leading to the front of the store, gazing thoughtfully across the room and out at the darkening street beyond the windows. His brain seemed to be trying to pull back some stray memory or fact, but he couldn't quite bring it into focus. He might have stood like that a moment longer except for the figure he saw passing on the sidewalk on the other side of the glass. It didn't register for half a second, but when it did, he turned on his heels and rushed to the back door. He held it slightly ajar while he fumbled to re-set the alarm. In his haste it took two tries to enter the code correctly. Then the little red light bulb began to flicker, signaling that he had sixty seconds to step outside and pull the door closed behind him before the security system would be fully engaged. It took him less than ten of those, and then, pushing the bank deposit bag further down into his pants, he began running around the side of the building into the alley. Not even half a minute could have passed before he burst back out onto the street, but the person he'd seen walking in front of the store was already out of sight.

Trace sprinted half a block looking in all directions. All of the shops to his right were closed for the night. The opposite sidewalk was deserted. A little further down the street, a bus was just pulling away from the curb, and his spirits sank. Too late now, he supposed. Dammit. Sighing, he pulled the sides of his jacket together, but did not zip them. He was too warm, following that burst of activity. He walked to the corner, tossing a resentful glance at the bus bench as he passed it, then crossed and continued down the far side of the street. He held the door for a cluster of people filing out of the pizzeria and then for two women who had come up behind him. They nodded their thanks and he smiled back, entering after them.

"Here you go," Cathy said, thrusting a warm pizza box into his hands. "Don't tip it. We put some garlic bread and dipping sauce in there, too. On the house."

Trace thanked her and turned, promptly colliding with a tall and bulky man who had just stepped out of the hallway from one of the bathrooms. The pizza box ricocheted off of the other guy's chest, one corner of it clipping Trace painfully in the center of his own.

"I'm sorry," Trace said at once. "I didn't see you..." And then he stopped, looking up at the imposing figure. "Oh…"

It was the same fellow he'd been trying to chase down the street just a few minutes earlier. The other man stared down at him impassively.

"It's all right, man. No harm," he said.

Still Trace continued to gaze up at him, entranced by the close-up view of the tattoo that snaked from the back of his neck, up and over his ear, ending in a dragon's gaping jaws breathing fire onto the man's right cheekbone.

"I think," he began, and then cleared his throat. "I think… you knew my sister."

"WERE YOU IN THE shop last night? After I left?" Mikayla demanded.

"Uh-huh," Trace said vaguely. His attention was focused on threading a new roll of tape into the cash register. He pressed the advance button, feeding an inch or so of white paper through the slot. Satisfied, he tore off the protruding piece, closed the door of the register, and locked it. "Just for a couple of minutes. I picked up the deposit."

"I thought so. My folders were moved to the other side of the desk." She turned and walked into the back room.

He crumpled the paper, shaking his head with amusement at her retreating figure. He didn't remember having touched anything during his short time in the office the previous night, but trust Mikayla's eagle eye to notice anything even slightly out of place. It was daunting, sometimes, being her supervisor. She was capable and efficient, and though she never questioned his procedures or failed to carry out any instruction he might give her, she had a contemplative way of looking at him sometimes that left him feeling inadequate in some undefinable way. He felt guilty taking the occasional five minutes to sip a Coke and check his personal email and texts on his phone because she never did. If she took a personal call from her daughter or the grandchildren she was helping to raise, it always began with her saying, "This better be good; you *know* I'm at work right now."

He'd tried—tentatively—to tell her that he didn't care if she wanted to take a break and do nothing productive now and then, but she looked at him until he was done speaking and then said, "Mm-hm," in a way that implied it might be fine for him, but it wasn't a philosophy to which she subscribed. The only outcome of that exchange was that now he felt guilty when he took his own breaks. He had no doubt that when she was assigned her own store, hers would begin outperforming his from the first day going forward.

Trace followed her into the back room.

"I'm sorry," he said. "I was in and out pretty quickly. I may have bumped something or moved it without thinking."

"Mm-hm," she responded without looking up from the spreadsheet she was consulting. He rested his shoulder against the doorframe and watched her for a few seconds before adding:

"A strange thing happened, actually. I saw a guy pass by the front of the store, someone I thought I recognized from Bertie's funeral service."

She leaned back in her chair, giving him her undivided attention.

"I was right, it turns out. No one in the family had ever met him, had ever even seen him until he got up to speak at the church. And then he left right afterward, before I had a chance to talk to him, or thank him."

Mikayla folded her arms on the edge of the desk and leaned forward. "And what did you find out?"

"His name's Patrick. He knew her for about the last six months. The last six months of her life, that is. We're going to meet for coffee in a couple of days."

"Why?"

"Well…" Trace shifted his weight away from the doorsill. "So I can find out more."

"More of what?"

"About Bertie. How she was feeling. How she was, you know… doing. I'd hardly had any contact with her in over a year. I'd left her a voice message at Christmas, but I never heard back. Never heard anything until we got the news she'd died."

Mikayla studied him impassively for several seconds, an expression not so different than the one he'd seen on Marla's face when he'd explained this same thing. Except that his wife had followed it with a carefully worded, "Oh, honey... Is that really a good idea, do you think? You don't know anything about this man."

"I know he cared enough to come to the funeral; what more do I need to know than that?"

Marla had watched him for another long moment, weighing a rebuttal. Finally, she'd just shrugged. "Be careful. Please."

Mikayla's concerns may have run along similar lines, but what she said was:

"*I'd* let it go. It's been a few months. Focus on the living, not those that are beyond our help any longer," she advised. She turned her gaze back to the folder on the desk and flicked one hand his direction. "But you do what you think is best."

He stood a moment longer, trying to decide if there was any point in attempting to explain the guilt he still carried for not having made more of an effort to check on his sister the last year or so of her life. He doubted it would carry any weight with this present audience. And it would be even more difficult to suggest that Bertie wasn't quite as dead to him as she was to everybody else. So finally he just pitched the crumpled bit of paper in his fingers into the wastebasket next to the desk and turned to go back into the front of the store. Before he'd taken more than a step, Mikayla called after him.

"Speaking of a few months, isn't it about time you changed the alarm code? It's been the same since last fall."

He nodded without turning around. "I'll do it today."

"And don't forget to give me the new combination when you do."

It wasn't always entirely clear who was actually running things around here.

THERE WERE MORE TATTOOS than just the impressive dragon that slithered its way around the back of Patrick's scalp onto his temple.

The knuckle of every finger bore curious symbols in red and blue inks. Dark stubble formed a shadow across the top of his shaved head. Despite all of these things, he didn't seem as intimidating as he had in the church or the other night in the pizza restaurant. His soft voice, the baby blue eyes, and the fact that he was drinking cocoa all served to undermine the rest of his appearance.

Trace sipped black coffee from his own cup and tried to decide what he wanted to ask. He thought he'd had the questions all worked out, but now, sitting across from this tattooed man, the obvious ones seemed invasive and rude: *Were you and my sister lovers? Did you get high together? Were you there the night she died?*

"Thanks for agreeing to this," he'd said already. "I looked for you right after the funeral service. I wanted to tell you I appreciated what you got up and said."

The other man had shrugged. "Oh… sure. It wasn't anything."

Which wasn't exactly the heartfelt response Trace realized he'd expected. They sat, pondering their beverages, or pretending to, for another minute or so.

"How did you know her?" he asked finally. "How did you meet, I mean? "

"I don't really remember, you know? She was just… around. We were hanging with the same people a lot of the time. So then we started hanging out together sometimes."

"Were you in touch with her toward… toward the end? I'm not *accusing* you of anything," Trace added hastily when the other man raised his head, looking wary. He sighed. "I'm embarrassed that I didn't know anything about her life the last… well, the last few years, I guess I'd have to say. I didn't know she was homeless, crashing with some girls she barely knew. I don't know if she had a job. I don't know anything."

Patrick shifted his gaze, staring out the window next to their table. He was silent so long that Trace wondered if his attention had wandered to parts unknown. But finally, still looking through the glass, he said:

"You wonder if the O.D. was on purpose."

Which was true enough. Though Trace wasn't prepared for that frankness. "Uh…"

"Maybe, I guess," Patrick continued. "She was angry enough, sometimes. But she wasn't the type, you know? She didn't have that kind of spite."

"Spite?"

"Some people think the world's just against them. They look for excuses to get pissed; they're happy, actually, when they find them. Then they feel like they have a reason for doing whatever they were planning to do all along. Albie had her moments, but I think she planned to go on living."

"Well, that's a relief, I guess," Trace said. He thought about this for a few seconds, then added, "You always call her Albie." Patrick looked at him curiously. "We—the family, I mean— called her Bertie. It just reminds me, I guess, how much she seemed to want to distance herself. To be a whole other person than the one we knew."

Patrick chewed his lip, nodding. "I didn't even know she had family until I saw the whole slew of you in the church. Well, I mean, everybody *does,* but it didn't ever come up. And isn't that better, don't you think, than if she'd spent her time telling people how much she hated you?"

"Right," Trace said, without conviction. "But you said she was angry sometimes. What about?"

"Oh, you know: just shit. When things weren't going her way. Sometimes she'd start swearing about some guy she was going to track down because he'd taken something of hers. Money, or a stash, I figured."

"Did she mention his name?" Trace was recalling something Katie, the girl with whom Bertie had been staying, had said. "Was it Beau, by chance?"

The other man lowered his hot chocolate and shrugged. "Might've been. I don't really remember."

Trace said, "The last time I talked to her, which would have been sometime in late November, she sounded good. She was clean; she said she was, anyway."

Patrick released his lip from between his teeth to smile. "Yeah. Except for when she wasn't." He leaned back and folded his arms in front of him. "Look, man, I'm not sure what you want. I'm like you, I guess. I want to think she was getting better, and that what happened was an accident. Ask me anything you want, but I don't think I have enough answers to suit you. Probably you could ask everybody who knew her and it still wouldn't be enough to find out what you want to know."

"That's true. I feel like there are pieces of her scattered all over the place. I just want to fit a few of them together, I guess. Enough of them to… to make some sense."

"Well, good luck with *that*." Patrick lifted his mug and took a gulp. Then, apparently recognizing the unintentional heartlessness of his remark, he added, "I mean… well, you know. Isn't everybody like that? Scattered?"

The vinyl cracked as Patrick leaned back against the seat and fixed his gaze on Trace.

"Like, at the day spa where I work, clients know me as the guy who gives great deep-tissue massages. At school, instructors see me as the scary-looking dude in the back of the classroom who squeaks by with C-minuses on written exams, but who rocks the hands-on training and will be the best physical therapist that school ever turns out. My ex thinks I'm a self-absorbed douchebag. My dog thinks I walk on water. Friends know I'll come get them when they post bail, but never to call me before nine in the morning unless they want an earful. My folks see me as a fuck-up who has disappointed them at every turn. And you know what? Everybody's right. Every one of them, for what little they see. But none of them will ever have the whole picture, because even I don't have that. Nobody will ever see all the colors. It isn't possible."

"So, you're saying I shouldn't even try?"

He shook his head. "I'm just saying be careful whatever conclusions you come to, because you won't be doing her justice. That's all."

Both men sat staring into their mugs, letting the next couple of minutes slip past in silence.

Chapter Seven

Trace and Marla had dinner with Quince and Mademoiselle Pineret two weeks later. Mademoiselle's first name was Jodi, they learned. Such an affable, informal name for someone usually seen with her hair pulled back into a severe bun, Trace thought. Tonight it was down, loose and bobbing with every turn of her head, and she looked much younger than she had at the recital. Her fingers mostly stayed wrapped around Quince's upper arm, and she frequently pressed her forehead to his shoulder in a gesture of practiced intimacy. Marla shot Trace a glance beneath raised eyebrows, and he knew she was thinking the same thing he was: These two had been seeing a *lot* of each other in a short period of time.

Quince's face was flushed and his eyes shone. He wore a ridiculous grin and mostly kept his eyes lowered, a telling gesture left over from his high-school dating days, indicating he was trying to feign indifference. Marla and Jodi did most of the talking.

"I was a little surprised when he called, since he hadn't said ten words to me the night of the performance," Jodi said, nudging Quince. "And I hadn't given him my number. I figured he wasn't interested."

"I was just giving it some time, first," Quince said airily. As if to underscore his indifferent tone, he lifted his glass for a gulp of beer.

"I was curious to meet the famous uncles that Lisa is always talking about," she continued as if he hadn't said anything. "Not that I had any romantic inclinations at the time, but to hear her tell it, they both walk on water."

"That's the impression they like to give," Marla retorted dryly. She squeezed Trace's thigh under the table. "Actually, they're both ridiculously shy. Quince was probably trying to work up his nerve. God knows, if I'd waited for Trace to make a move on *me* back in college, I'd still be twiddling my thumbs."

"I'd've gotten around to you eventually," Trace said. "I was mulling all the offers." This resulted in hoots of laughter from both his wife and his brother.

"So, anyway," Jodi continued, "I actually asked Leslie for his phone number when she came to pick up Lisa the following week. She said she'd be happy to give it to me, but advised me to hold off a couple more days, since Quince had already asked her for mine. And sure enough, two days later, the phone finally rang."

"What is it with sisters-in-law? Both of you, plotting against me," Quince complained, raising an eyebrow at Marla. "Leave a guy with *some* mystery, won't you?"

"Sorry." Marla turned to Jodi and dutifully reported, "He's very brooding. You never know what's going on beneath that smoldering exterior."

"I've noticed that." Jodi's matched Marla's facetious tone, but when she turned to look at Quince, there was no misreading her adoring gaze.

"Wow, THEY'VE MOVED QUICKLY in just a few weeks," Marla mused later, as they drove home from the restaurant. "She's in deep, did you notice?"

Trace nodded. "Quince has always had that ability to hook them fast. I think it has something to do with being the baby in a large family. You called it shyness, but it's the opposite, actually. He's so accustomed to having all those big sisters looking out for him, catering to him, that he's never felt the need to make too much of a show if there was a girl he liked. He's used to them coming to him."

She gave him a sidelong glance. "That sounds a little like jealousy. But you sort of had that, too: the older sisters, I mean."

He considered this for a few seconds. "True enough. And it's not jealousy. Maybe, for the both of us, it was that girls didn't seem like that big a mystery. We've been around them all our lives."

"So, in other words, you're telling me that they flocked to you the same way they flock to your brother."

Trace laughed. "I'm not idiot enough to admit to anything like that. Maybe Quince projects a kind of I-expect-girls-to-take-care-of-me quality that draws them in. Bertie and I traded too many blows growing up for me to have that kind of entitlement."

Marla was quiet. When he finally glanced over at her, she said:

"So, do you think it's serious this time? She's sweet. I don't want her to get hurt."

"I can't tell for sure," he admitted. "Like you said, they're moving awfully fast." It was clear to both of them from the behavior they'd witnessed at dinner that the pair were already sleeping together, and were already quite practiced at it. This, in Trace's estimation, followed his brother's well-worn pattern with prior relationships. He shifted uncomfortably. "I'd hate to think that Lisa is going to have to find a new ballet teacher in another month or so."

For this, he received a sharp smack across his leg. Marla was looking at him reproachfully.

"*That's* what you're worried about? Bastard."

"Well, but... I mean, you see what I'm saying... right?"

Marla folded her arms and averted her gaze, looking out the side window.

"When we get home, I'm going to call Quince and tell him I'll have his balls if he hurts that girl."

Trace was picturing the way his brother and Jodi had walked out of the restaurant ahead of them, arms encircling each other's waists, Quince's head tilted against hers.

"I'm betting he's too busy to answer his phone right now," he said.

WAS HE SHY?, TRACE WONDERED LATER. He was lying in bed, arms propped beneath his head and pillow as he faced the ceiling, eyes closed. It was early still, but he was fending off a nagging headache that had been poking around his brain most of the evening. Sounds from the television program Marla was watching in the living room drifted through the open doorway. Lines of dialogue were occasionally followed by her laughter, which made him smile.

Who *had* pursued whom back in their college days? He'd always assumed it had been him targeting Marla at some point during their junior year. He'd noticed her first in a statistics class they were both taking, then began to spot her at various other places around campus once she was on his radar. He went out of his way—sometimes way out of his way—to say hi, and finally, spotting her in a pub one evening, he'd sent a round of drinks to the table she was sharing with some girlfriends. Emboldened by the amount of alcohol he himself had consumed, he'd made his way over to them a few moments later to strike up a conversation, and they'd begun dating shortly thereafter. But it had taken him several weeks to get to that point, something she'd pointed out more than once, which indicated she'd been paying attention to him, as well.

Shy, maybe; but clueless, more likely.

Wait… what?

That thought had come from outside his head and voiced from somewhere in the darkened corners of the room.

"No, don't get up," Bertie murmured as Trace lifted his head and blinked. "There's nothing to see, anyway. We can talk just as well with your eyes closed."

"Where are you?"

"I'm here," she answered vaguely. "How's your head?"

"You know?"

"That it hurts? Yeah. How bad is it?"

"Not bad. It's one of those headaches you barely even notice if you're doing something else. It'll go away pretty quickly. By morning, anyway."

"I used to get migraines, remember?" she reminded him.

He nodded, causing a channel to form beneath his head in the pillow. "Oh, yeah. You'd have to lie with a cold cloth over your eyes. With the curtains drawn. For days, sometimes."

"It got so bad that Sky would sleep on the fold-out couch in the den sometimes. She couldn't stand to be in a dark bedroom all the time. And even a little bit of noise would cause so much pain I'd start crying."

"I guess I don't have anything to complain about," Trace said.

They were both silent for a moment.

"So, you haven't been around in awhile," he said finally. "I really sort of expected to see you the afternoon I met your friend Patrick in the coffee shop."

"Why did you think that?"

"I don't know... Because we were there to talk about you. Because... well, I thought maybe you'd want to monitor the conversation or something. Put your own two cents in."

Trace waited a second, but there was no response.

"Bertie?"

"Yeah?"

"I wasn't sure you were still there. You know, it's kind of creepy, just talking to a disembodied voice."

She laughed. "More creepy than talking to your dead sister in the first place?"

"No, but it seems less ridiculous, I guess, to be conversing with a full-bodied hallucination than talking to voices in my head."

"You need to keep your eyes closed," she said. "The headache will go away faster. I'll do something, if you promise to just lie still. All right?"

He didn't answer, but she must have taken his silence as a tacit promise. There was no sound, no stirring of the air, but abruptly he felt a gentle, cool pressure on his forehead and eyelids.

"Oh," he exclaimed, drawing in a breath. "That... that helps." He did not try to open his eyes.

"So, how was talking to Patrick?" she asked. "Did you find out what you wanted to know?"

"I'm glad I did it. He couldn't really tell me much, but... but, I liked him."

"Did that surprise you?"

"He's a masseur, for Pete's sake. And he's going to school. I've always had this image of the kind of people you were hanging out with, getting high with. A bunch of people in some crappy room somewhere, with nothing but a stained mattress on the floor, passing around a glass pipe and lighter. Or shooting each other up. I didn't really stop to think that you wouldn't be the only one there who had a life apart from all that. A job, maybe. Or at least things that fill the other hours of the day."

"And now?"

"Now?" Trace considered a moment. "Now it's not as easily defined. Patrick pointed out that it wouldn't really matter if I could talk to everybody who knew you. It wouldn't give me the complete picture of what happened, or even who you are."

"Oh, don't let Patrick romanticize me." Bertie's voice was coming from somewhere above his head. "It's true of everybody, don't you see? Those of us who stay put and mow the grass and make shopping lists are just as screwed up as those who go out and never call home and eventually overdose in motel rooms. Don't go to any extra effort on my account."

"I do feel a little hypocritical," Trace confessed.

"Oh, really? Why is that?"

"I should have put this kind of effort into finding out things about you before it was too late."

Now it felt as if someone were lifting the hair gently from his forehead.

"Maybe this is a stress headache," Bertie declared. "Maybe that's what this is."

"Oh, I just remembered something," Trace said. A moment or so had passed, and he might have fallen asleep; he wasn't sure. "I have a message for you from Quince. I told him you and I have been talking, and he said I should tell you to go see him, too. He says he has a few things he'd like to say to you."

He waited a few seconds, but there was no response.

"Bert? …Bertie?"

He realized then that the cool sensation was gone from his eyes and forehead.

"Who are you talking to?" Marla asked from the doorway. She did not turn on the light.

Trace pulled his hands free from beneath the pillow and raised his arms in a stretch. "Dreaming, I guess. I must have fallen asleep for a minute or two," he said, avoiding her question. It seemed to work. She asked another one, instead.

"Is your headache gone?"

"I think so," he said. "Just about, anyway."

That, however, was a direct lie. He could still detect the faint throbbing behind his eyes.

"YOU STILL HAVEN'T CHANGED the security code on the door," was Mikayla's terse greeting as he walked into the store the following morning. She turned back from dropping a paper plate into the wastebasket, dusted her hands, and fixed him with an expectant look. One corner of her mouth was drawn up into a clench. He imagined this was the same expression she used often on her children and possibly grandchildren if they'd disappointed her in some way. He'd seen it directed at himself often enough.

"I forgot," he said lightly. "I'll do it today."

"Do it early," she instructed. When he turned back, annoyed, her face softened. "I just mean, before you get busy and forget again."

"Fine," he sighed. "Though I don't know why you care so much."

She did not offer an explanation, but went to hold the door for an approaching customer whose arms were laden with packages.

In truth, Trace had been more or less deliberately avoiding the issue. He hadn't changed the code in more than a year, knowing he would have to unearth the manual and refresh his memory in order to do it. Plus, a change meant his brain would have to discard the old code and learn a new one. No doubt there would be times ahead when he'd be rushed, either arriving or leaving, and try to use the old one again, setting off all the bells and whistles in the process. But it was store policy to change it annually, and he'd already let it slide for a few additional months. Plus, it was clear that, for whatever reason, Mikayla was not going to stop bugging him until he did it.

In retaliation, he took his sweet time, sitting at the desk and thumbing through the instructions, ignoring the sounds of customers in the front of the shop, leaving Mikayla to deal with all of them. She could darn well holler for his assistance if she got overwhelmed, he decided.

The faint smell of something Italian kept drawing his attention as he turned the pages of the manual, and finally he glanced into the wastebasket next to his desk. It emanated from the paper plate Mikayla had pitched there, apparently. He turned back to his book, and after a few more seconds of searching found the information he needed. He stood, carrying the book to the security panel on the wall by the rear door.

"Four-one to disable," he muttered, pressing the keys, then looked at the page once more. "Enter new code…" For the first time, it occurred to him he hadn't considered what new sequence to use. He stood a moment in debate while the panel waited, its lights extinguished. A birthday? An anniversary date? What hadn't he used already?

The store's zip code, he decided finally. In reverse. He punched each number slowly, then the *Enter/OK* button, before referring to the folded-back page in his hand.

"If new sequence has been successfully entered, the red *Engage* light will begin blinking at three-second intervals," Trace read aloud. It was doing exactly that, he noticed, and he closed the booklet with satisfaction. He re-entered the code to disable the alarm for the rest of the work day. Maybe, just maybe, he would be able to remember this process all on his own next time it needed changing.

He was about to turn away from the panel when something clicked in his brain. He scowled at the now-flashing green light for a second. Then he moved slowly back to the desk, where he tossed the manual into the desk drawer atop the stack of papers from which he'd unearthed it. He nudged the drawer closed with his hip, leaned over the wastebasket for a moment, and then headed to the front of the store.

Mikayla was handing a receipt to a customer when he joined her behind the counter. The smile she'd been offering faded as she turned his direction. Her eyes dropped to the object in his hand, and lifted to his face again almost immediately.

"This isn't yours, is it?" he asked quietly, holding out the crumpled, stained paper plate he'd retrieved from the wastebasket.

"What?" she said, although he knew she'd heard him clearly.

"You found this somewhere when you walked in this morning, didn't you?"

She regarded him with a defiant gaze a second longer, then lowered her eyes and turned away. "Finding everything all right?" she called to a woman studying cards on a spinning rack halfway across the room. The woman looked up, surprised, not entirely sure whether she was the one being addressed.

"Somebody forgot it, anyway," Trace said softly, but now Mikayla was on the move, crossing from behind the counter to the package prep table at the front of the store where she busied herself by neatening the rows of tape dispensers, pens, and markers, and the stacks of labels. He suspected that this was perhaps the closest she had ever come in her life to telling a lie, and she wanted to distance herself to avoid further cross-examination.

He remembered now what had momentarily caught his attention a few weeks earlier, the night he'd stopped in just long enough to retrieve the bank deposit. If he hadn't become distracted by the sight of Patrick passing in front of the store windows, it probably would have occurred to him what he'd missed as he was trying to re-set the alarm.

The alarm hadn't been set in the first place. No lights had been blinking when he'd first come in and punched in the code for the all-clear. The green one had come on, acknowledging that he was pressing the right buttons, but the red one hadn't been flashing at all.

That could have meant that Mikayla had simply forgotten to engage the alarm when she'd left earlier that evening. That would have been careless and a slight cause for concern, but nothing more. Except that Mikayla wasn't careless. She just wasn't.

And he'd remembered something else. The following morning, she'd accused him of moving some of her files from one side of the desk to the other that night. He didn't think he had, and now he was sure of it.

An uncomfortable theory was beginning to take form in his brain. Logically, the only two people who would know how to either set or disable the alarm system were the manager and assistant manager: himself and Mikayla. Nobody else was ever even around first thing in the morning or last thing at night when the codes were being entered. Except, once or twice…

Trace dropped the paper plate into the wastebasket under the cash register and crossed to the front of the store. He joined Mikayla at the prep table. They stood shoulder to shoulder, neither looking at the other.

"I understand now why you've been nagging me to change the code," he informed her under his breath.

"Do you, now?" she said carelessly, bending to straighten the stack of flattened, unfolded boxes beneath the counter.

"Uh-huh. I do."

"It couldn't just be because it was past time? And because it's policy?" she flung at him.

He chose to ignore this. "I assume you've found other evidence, other times?"

"Don't know what you're talking about."

"You don't have to cover for him."

She rose from her squatting position, grunting slightly, and smoothed the front of her dress. "I'm not covering for anybody. And what kind of evidence do you think you've got, anyhow? A nasty old paper plate? What's that prove about anything?" As she turned and stalked away, she flung one last comment over her shoulder. "And you be sure and tell me what the new code is before I have to open or close on my own next time."

He did not follow, but turned to gaze at the street on the other side of the plate glass window in front of him. He had a strong suspicion that if he were to step out into the alley and look in the dumpster, he would find a pizza box or two atop the rest of the trash. Maybe some beer cans or liquor bottles, too. But then again, Mikayla was right. What would that prove, exactly?

She was giving him an easy out by playing dumb, instead of coming right out and saying, "Your stupid-ass nephew apparently watched his stupid-ass uncle punch in the security code one night, so now he's coming and going in the off-hours, eating fast food and drinking booze with buddies." Mikayla was going to look the other way on this, allowing Trace to decide what steps, if any, he wanted to take next.

Idiot teenaged boys. Zeke, smart enough to stand by unobtrusively and memorize a code, yet stupid—or lazy—enough to leave behind incriminating and obvious evidence. Trace squirmed uncomfortably, wondering what other items Mikayla might have been finding lately.

Now that he thought about it, he realized he'd probably burst in on Zeke and pals that night, since the alarm was already off. Had they been huddled somewhere in the shop, behind a counter or crouched in the bathroom, while he sat at the desk and opened the safe to retrieve the bank deposit? He drew in a deep breath and let it out slowly, drumming his fingers on the edge of the table and watching the world pass by in front of him.

Chapter Eight

Marla was barely three months along by mid-August. Her belly had only just begun to swell, but oddly, it was her face that had rounded more noticeably than her stomach, giving her a pink and cherubic appearance. She both glowed and glistened, aided today by the sun's relentless glare, permeating even the drooping thick strands of the willow tree under which she and the other women were encamped. Trace's sisters and Jodi all clustered around her, cooing and exploding in fits of giggles every few minutes. Trace himself sat a safe distance away, flopped in a lawn chair, bare legs splayed in front of him, a bottle of beer lodged in the crotch of his Bermuda shorts as he lifted the front of his shirt away from his chest, fanning it to create some small breeze between the fabric and his sweaty skin.

It was as if all the women had nudged their way in, taking possession of his wife, guarding her, exchanging secrets, accompanying her on a journey that somehow no longer included Trace. Even Marla barely seemed to give him a second thought or glance during these gatherings. He considered this for a second, releasing his shirt and allowing it to adhere itself to his flesh once more, then lifted the beer to his lips for more immediate relief from the heat. He wasn't jealous, and that worried him slightly. He felt oddly uninvolved in the whole pregnancy process. Maybe because it had been planned so precisely, and all he'd done was to successfully hold up his end of the bargain. The rest seemed sort of abstract.

At first, the idea of creating a baby, bringing a new life into the world, had been exciting. Then daunting. Recently it had occurred to him that their lives were changing forever. It would never be just the two of them again. Now a stranger was on the way, someone who would arrive with an immediate sense of entitlement. Noisy, demanding constant attention, and, if the nieces and nephews were an indication, it would only become more so with the passage of time. Already he was developing an appreciation for his folks' lackadaisical style of parenting. A child could absolutely consume you, if you gave it half a chance.

He had not shared these sentiments with Marla, nor would he. She already got irked any time he referred to their unborn child as *it*.

"It's not an *it!*"she insisted, violating her own credo. "This is a baby. Our baby. A person."

"I understand that. But we don't know yet if it—if this baby—is a girl or a boy. I'm not demeaning the child. It's just easier right now to say *it* instead of *the baby* all the time."

They had argued more in the last ten weeks than in all their previous years together. Well, maybe *argued* was too strong a word. They were more like nattering little disagreements, here and gone in a flash. Trace had always prided himself on the fact that he and Marla presented a united front, never bickering around others, always supportive, unlike the couples they knew who insisted on trotting out old grudges for feedback from a new audience, demeaning themselves in the process.

Yet now, as he nursed his beer and glanced at the women encamped beneath the willow tree, he could imagine at least some of those laughs were at his expense. *"I never noticed until now how much he tosses and turns in his sleep." "I can't decide if I'm more sensitive because of the pregnancy, or if his feet really do stink that bad." "He was complaining about an upset stomach the other night, and I said, 'Do you really want to whine about a bellyache to a woman who has been puking her guts out every morning for two months?'"* Now, every one of his shortcomings appeared to be fair game for discussion whenever the mood struck her.

The rest of the barbecue guests, the ones with less interest in Marla and her expanding belly, were splashing and shouting in the aboveground pool to Trace's right. His niece Lisa was perched atop Quince's shoulders and they faced her cousin Emily and Emily's dad Matt, similarly stacked, in some sort of face-off that mostly seemed to involve each girl scooping up handfuls of water and hurling them at the other. Now and again some of the spray made it all the way to where Trace was sitting, showering him in droplets. He did not complain, because to do so would invite a full-on liquid assault from all the parties involved, as well as his nephews Richie and Lawrence, currently occupied with masks and snorkels on the other side of the pool. And in the heavy, unmoving air, the droplets felt kind of good across his neck and arms.

He raised his arms over his head in a stretch. Lifting the nearly empty beer to his lips to drain it, he stood and made his way across the lawn to the patio where his brother Cord was intently guarding a grill laden with sizzling burgers and pieces of chicken. He wielded his spatula with the finesse of a conductor leading an orchestra.

Trace clasped Cord's shoulder as he passed behind him. He dropped his bottle into the wastebasket and leaned to open the cooler set to one side of the picnic table. "Anything I can do to help?" he said, already confident of the answer.

"Nah. Except, hand me one of those, too." Cord gestured with the spatula to the fresh bottle Trace was lifting out of the ice. He took his job as host seriously, never leaving the grill or delegating anything associated with the preparation to anyone else. Trace unscrewed the cap, passed the beer to his brother, and reached for another for himself. They clinked bottles in a companionable gesture before taking gulps.

"Zeke's staying out of the pool, I see," Trace said.

Focused on flipping the burgers, Cord did not glance up, but the corner of his mouth curled in amusement.

"Too cool for that," he said. "At least when the rest of the family's using it. He's almost sixteen, you know. In case he hasn't reminded you of that as regularly as he does Leslie and me. Plus..." This time, Cord had to gesture by tilting his head, since the spatula was currently in use, "He's entertaining a guest, I guess you noticed."

They both studied the backs of Zeke and the girl sitting next to him in the grass that bordered the yard. It was clear they had positioned themselves to achieve the maximum amount of privacy available. Whether it was because he knew someone might be watching or perhaps because he was still unsure of himself around the opposite sex, Zeke's posture was rigid, and he sat a good six inches away from the girl, making no move to touch her. Even their shoulders didn't brush casually against one another.

"How's he liking his new job?" Trace asked.

"Fine, I guess. He comes home tired and grumpy, but he takes an extra shift now and then when they ask him to, so there must be some pleasure in it."

"Well, he's got to be making more bagging groceries than I was able to pay him at the shipping store, anyway. That's some incentive. He's saving up to buy a car in a year or so, isn't he?"

Cord nodded, taking another pull from his beer. "Les and I try not to think about that too much; it keeps us awake nights. And we make him put ten percent of every paycheck into a college fund. Not that that's going to keep us out of the poorhouse when it comes time to pay his tuition, but it's the principle of the thing. I want him to understand there are no free rides. Hand me that plate, would you?"

As he began transferring burgers from the grill to the platter that Trace held out for him, he glanced up. "So, how's the dad-to-be feeling?"

Trace watched a slice of cheese bubbling atop one of the patties as Cord slid it off the spatula. "Okay, I guess. A little overwhelmed sometimes." When his brother snorted in amusement, he added, "You know, I sort of envy you."

"How's that?"

"You'd had so much practice with us by the time Zeke came along. You already kind of had a handle on things."

"You think that, do you?"

"Well, didn't you? You were the one we waked up in the middle of the night if we had a bad dream. The one who wouldn't let me go to the movies until I'd raked the whole back yard. You went with Quince and me on that scouting trip when I know you had better things to do. And remember when you wouldn't let Bertie leave the house to go to some party until she went back upstairs and changed into something you said didn't make her look like a slut?"

Cord laughed ruefully. "For all the good that did."

"I know it wasn't easy. Or fair, exactly. I know you gave up a lot, being the oldest and having to... well, you know, fill in the gaps for Mom and Pop. But it also sort of prepared you, didn't it?"

His brother set the spatula to one side, picked up a long-tined fork, and began spearing pieces of chicken. "Another plate, please," he directed. "I guess it did, a little. But the thing you learn about five minutes after the doctor places that squirming new life in your arms for the very first time is that no amount of experience is enough. Whatever you think you know, your kid knows better. Beginning that very first day, he—or she—is going to do things that no baby book will have answers for. By the end of the first week, you're just winging it, and if you're lucky, the kid won't catch on until he's twelve or thirteen. How's that for advice?"

Trace stared at his brother for a second and then took a long gulp from his bottle.

"Terrible."

"It is, isn't it?"

At that moment, he felt a deep rush of love for Cord that he hadn't remembered was there, not for a long time. He might have found a way to say something to that effect, but just then Quince came sloshing across the grass, water streaming from his hair and shoulders.

"So, bro, isn't it about time you got in the pool?" he asked Trace.

"The food's just now ready," Cord began, but Quince had already gripped Trace around his midsection and was lifting him over his shoulder.

"It's all right," Quince called back, heading for the pool. "It tastes the same whether you're wet or dry."

Trace dropped his beer bottle in the grass as he struggled to free himself, but to no avail. His younger brother had been on the wrestling team in high school, and retained both his old moves and superior strength.

"At least let me take my shirt off first," he pleaded before Quince had hoisted him over the side of the pool and dropped him into the chilly water, to the accompaniment of cheers from the kids and his brothers-in-law.

Later, sitting next to Marla as water dripped from his hair and shirt onto the paper plate in his soggy lap, he bit into his hamburger and thought about that earlier conversation. The lawn chairs had been pulled into a large circle so that everyone ate facing one another. Even Zeke and the girlfriend were there, albeit reluctantly. His father had made it clear that it was time they joined the rest of the family. Trace wondered if Cord had any idea that some of his son's aversion to join-ing the group was due to an awkwardness that had begun the after-noon back in late May when Trace had pulled Zeke into the back room at the shipping store. It had been the day after he'd changed the code on the security system. His stomach had been twisted into knots all day in preparation for the conversation they would need to have. As if the persistent headache plaguing him hadn't been enough.

"I'm thinking…" he began hesitantly, though he'd rehearsed the words multiple times, "…that now might be a good time for you to start looking for another job."

"What?" Zeke stared at him. "…But, why?"

"School won't be out for another couple of weeks," Trace contin-ued, ignoring the question. "If you put in your application now, maybe at a movie theatre or one of the fast-food places, you'll beat the rush of kids who won't start looking for summer employment until after the last day of classes."

His nephew was silent, still wearing a faint look of surprise. Only when Trace held up the tomato sauce-stained plate as well as a pint bottle of Jack Daniels he'd retrieved from the dumpster in the alley, did Zeke's expression alter. His eyes widened for a fraction of a second, and his Adam's apple bobbed in his throat as he swallowed.

"Or maybe these aren't yours," Trace said. "Or the pizza crusts that were in the bottom of the wastebasket under the sink in the bathroom, either."

Zeke said nothing.

"I put the temptation out there, I realize that. I was careless, punching in the alarm code with you standing right there some evenings. I don't know how many times you've been back here after the store is closed at night, or who you brought with you. At this point, I don't even want to know. I'm just relieved that nothing more serious happened than a little underage drinking."

"We never did anything!" Zeke blurted. "I promise! I mean, except for what you said. I never let the guys touch anything, honest! We just… we wanted a place to hang out, is all."

Trace dropped the paper plate and the liquor bottle into a desk drawer and closed it. "I'm not going to say anything to your folks," he said. "If they ask, I'll tell them that it's because I couldn't promise you more hours once school is out. So you notified me that you were going to start looking for a full-time summer job. How does that sound?"

Zeke's chin was quivering and he blinked rapidly. After a moment, he nodded.

Trace's own heart was thudding painfully against the wall of his chest, and he resisted the impulse to add any sort of lecture to what he'd already said.

"I've got your final check," he concluded, holding it out.

"Keep it," Zeke mumbled. He stood and lurched away from Trace.

"I'm not going to do that. It's yours; you earned it. You can take it now, or I'll hand it to your mom or your dad later. This is probably easier, don't you think?"

Zeke had snatched it from Trace's extended hand, crumpling it into his jeans pocket. And he had not responded to Trace's offer of a ride home, but moved swiftly through the front of the store, dodging customers and ignoring Mikayla's stare, shoving open the glass door and dashing from view down the sidewalk.

That had been the last real conversation they'd had in two months.

On those unavoidable occasions when they were thrown together—like today—they exchanged terse hellos and made minimal eye contact. Even now, Zeke was pointedly looking anywhere but in Trace's direction. It seemed painfully obvious to anyone paying attention that something had happened between the two of them, but in this large, bustling, noisy family, the awkwardness appeared to have gone unnoticed so far.

"You're awfully quiet," Marla observed. "You feeling okay?"

But when Trace turned to answer her, she squinched her face in distaste. "Honestly, honey, be careful. You're spritzing water all over me. Do you really have to horse around with your brother every time you get together? Move your chair back a little."

He replayed the events of the afternoon in his head as he faced the ceiling in bed that night. The skin felt taut, stretched across his face, and he wondered if he'd gotten sunburned. He pressed one hand to his cheek and temple, but they didn't sting or carry any of the residual oily heat that usually accompanies a burn.

Alongside him, Marla stirred and murmured something unintelligible. He lowered his arm carefully to his side so as not to wake her. In the darkness overhead, Cord's and Leslie's back yard took shape once more: the lush, manicured grass, the layered awnings of leaves produced by thick-trunked elms and willows, and the cheesy, above-ground pool, a concession to perpetual middle-class status. Finally, the circle of familiar bodies hunched over disposable plates heaped high with food and balanced perilously on knees drawn together to accommodate them.

There was Quince, complaining good-naturedly because Jodi had been devoting all her attention to Marla's stomach and none to him. And Jodi, rolling her eyes in response and then reaching to swipe a glob of mustard from his upper lip with the side of her thumb. The gesture was both casual and intimate, and it produced a curious reaction in the pit of Trace's stomach. Annoyance, maybe, at their oh-so-cutesy infatuation with one another, but something else, too. Not... not jealousy, exactly, but a sense of something he himself had forfeited. Not that Marla would ever have done something like that—she'd have handed him a napkin and told him to wipe his mouth—but the giddiness that came with early courtship, a sense of existing on a plane slightly removed from everyone and everything else.

On the other side of Jodi sat Pete, using a plastic knife to saw a hamburger in half for his youngest, Lawrence, squirming in his seat, still wearing swimming trunks, goggles, and one flipper, and displaying no interest in eating. Quiet, good-natured Pete had come lumbering into the family to marry Aria and produce two sons who displayed a nonstop exuberance difficult to imagine had come from him, or from Aria either, for that matter. Calm, collected Aria expressed every opinion and desire in a manner suggesting that there could be no reasonable dissension from her viewpoint on any subject. Even their parents had always seemed intimidated by her unswerving observations, which only fueled her dictatorial way of getting what she wanted. When Aria had brought Pete home to meet everybody during her junior year of college, it was clear to her family that he didn't stand a chance of escaping her clutches. Though from all outward appearances, he seemed happily resigned to his fate, so apparently it was true: Aria really did know best.

Nearly as mismatched, or so it had seemed at first, were Leslie and Cord. Leslie was as giddy and humorous as Cord was grounded and serious. The family had been equally parts enchanted and mystified at the attraction, particularly on Leslie's part. *"She could do so much better than him, don't you think?"* Bertie had confided to Trace and Quince, and they'd nodded in agreement. But nobody wanted her to go away. In fact, they were a little concerned that if Cord didn't loosen up a bit, that was exactly what would happen. But she stayed, drawn in some indefinable way to their eldest brother's grim, unswerving demeanor. To which Bertie added, *"He must be really good in the sack, is all I can think,"* a startling image Trace could have done without.

But on days like today, reflecting back on the barbecue, he could see the things that hadn't been apparent in his callow youth. If Leslie laughed more frequently and moved among her guests with the impetuousness of a hummingbird, and if Cord stationed himself at the grill and didn't go in the pool or join in swatting a plastic birdie back and forth over a badminton net, there was nevertheless a reliable kind of harmony in their separate actions. Out of earshot from one another, they ventured similar opinions, admonished their kids for the same infractions, shared a set of values. Both had a way of knowing, somehow, just before their eyes were about to meet across the field of a family gathering, that each would find the other looking. In observing this, Trace realized how unfounded his earlier fears had been. Once they'd met, there was no possible way Leslie would ever have let his brother go.

Sky was the sister he'd always been closest to, far more accessible than Aria, and less prickly than Bertie who, from an early age, seemed to heed a siren call from some distant shore. He and Sky shared a similar sense of humor and were the two who could look at the rest of the family and question the quirkiness in their parents that everybody else seemed to take for granted. Also, the biggest age gap within the siblings—three and a half years—came between Sky and Aria. It was a division that distanced the elder two from the younger four, physically and emotionally.

If Aria was unflappable in her own confidence, Sky was a mass of insecurities, and she regularly confided these to Trace. He had no answers to give, but he was a sympathetic listener. She worried about failing algebra and then talked herself into doing just that. Fearful that her face would break out right before the day of class photos, that was exactly what happened. She just knew she wouldn't make the cheerleading squad, and so she didn't, managing to somehow forget a part of the audition routine Trace and Quince had watched her rehearse so many times they themselves could have performed it flawlessly. She was the prettiest of his sisters, yet the most unsure of her appearance.

But as it turned out, all she needed was Matt.

He was the innocuous-looking boy who'd been plodding through school alongside Sky from kindergarten upward, resolutely average in just about every way. She knew him, but didn't really know him until they found themselves working together at Burger King the summer between their junior and senior years of high school. There were no romantic inclinations—at least, not on her part—and so no pressure to be funny or engaging or charming in front of him. Eventually, Matt usurped Trace's role as confidant, and that was fine, since he'd never had any substantive answers for Sky, anyway. Matt, on the other hand, did. And his all basically boiled down to a single one: *Who gives a damn?*

Would she really look back years from now and care whether she'd been a cheerleader? Matt wanted to know. *Was that how she planned to define her life? And how many employers were going to care whether she remembered any algebraic equations? And, finally: Of course she was pretty; what was she, blind?*

They went to the senior homecoming dance together, just as friends, just to say they'd been. And maybe because there was nothing at stake and they weren't really thinking about it, their feelings for each other started to change. By Christmas they were in love, and by graduation they were engaged.

Trace's mother was delighted. "Don't they make the cutest little couple?" she said. Trace's dad shook Matt's hand and said he'd figured it was coming, all the signs were there. Aria, on the other hand, was apoplectic.

"Are you out of your little freaking high school minds?" she demanded. "You're eighteen years old! You're a couple of babies, and you don't know what the hell you're doing!" She appealed to her parents, "You're not going to let them go through with this, are you? They have to go to college! They have to go out and live life, first!" And then, two days before the small backyard wedding later that summer, she declared: "I give them a year, tops. Living in that squalid little apartment, trying to work and go to college all at the same time? Yeah, good luck!"

Yet in spite of Aria's dire prognostications—or perhaps partly because of them—the union had succeeded and appeared to be going strong all these years later. Trace had no doubt that Sky loved her husband deeply, but there was also the slightest suspicion that she loved proving her sister wrong almost as much.

And now there was Emily, their thin, wide-eyed daughter, face framed with long, straight hair, standard Bannerly-issue brown. She was a Wednesday Addams child, less macabre, more rosy-cheeked, but just as solemn. This afternoon, she'd sat on a folding chair between her parents, legs dangling a good eighteen inches off the ground, pushing mounds of baked beans and potato salad—she didn't eat meat—around her plate.

And taking it all in.

Whatever *it* was. She had a sort of unquenchable interest in anything this sprawling, ungainly family happened to be doing or discussing at any given time. Somehow, just the right combination of traits had been measured out from each of her parents to create an unobtrusive, observant individual. Trace had concluded some time ago that she was going to grow up to be an interesting person, but the fact was, she was that already.

The topic of Bertie—well, the *topics,* actually: theories about her self-imposed estrangement, her death, and what might have happened toward the end—still came up occasionally when the family gathered, though less often than before. Still, when they did, they were conducted in lowered tones, in quiet corners away from the kids. But now Trace was reminded of one of the last times when the adults evidently hadn't been as discreet.

He had stepped away from the group to refill a drink or something. As he passed the open doorway to the den, he caught sight of Emily, buried in the middle of a large, overstuffed chair, legs extended, with his parents' ancient cat Morty sprawled across her lap.

"Well, hey," he'd greeted her, stepping into the room. "What are you doing in here all by yourself?"

"I'm not by myself," she'd declared without raising her eyes. Both of her hands were occupied with stroking the cat's head.

"No, I guess you aren't," he conceded, moving across the room to crouch in front of the chair. Morty regarded him with a haughty sort of reserve as Trace lifted and stroked his tail. After a few seconds, Morty shifted his weight in order to snatch it free and tuck it around his feet, safe from the unwelcome attention.

Trace shook his head and smirked. "Fine," he said, resigned. "Like her better; see if I care."

When he glanced up, Emily was studying him closely.

"I heard you talking," she said. "In the other room."

"Yeah? About what?" he asked carelessly.

Her fingers continued to trace the stripes in Morty's fur as she looked at him. "'Bout Bertie."

"…Oh." Trace shifted his weight and had to press one hand against the floor to steady himself. "Oh, well, honey, you see…"

But she saved him from having to fumble for any sort of explanation.

"You shouldn't feel bad," she continued. "Because, do you know what I think? I think she's gone to find her real family."

"She's… what? …Her real…?"

Emily lowered her face, then, returning her attention to Morty. Trace stared at her a moment longer, leaving his faltering question unfinished.

"I want to get a kitty," she sighed. "But Daddy's allergic. That's what he says, anyhow. I think he just doesn't like cats."

"Well, uh, maybe he'll outgrow it. People do, you know. I used to be allergic to cheese, but not anymore. Until then, you can always come over to visit this old guy."

Struggling to his feet, he stroked Morty behind one ear with his forefinger, but the cat went on resolutely ignoring him.

"And anyway, Morty might get jealous if you showed up with a strange cat's smell on your hands. You wouldn't want that, would you?"

No response. He had the feeling that neither his niece nor the cat were paying him any further attention.

Now Trace shifted under the covers. Such a bewildering and absurd declaration about Bertie; he hadn't given it much more thought at the time. It seemed pulled from that same peculiar reservoir that children dip into for their theories about Santa Claus and the tooth fairy and where babies come from. If it had been one of the other nieces or nephews who'd said it, or if the statement hadn't been delivered so offhandedly, then it wouldn't still be lurking in some dark recess of his brain. But it was, flitting about his half-consciousness like some annoying moth battering itself against a light.

Her real family? Gone to find them?

Now, as the sides of his pillow closed around him and the waking world began to recede, he found himself questioning not the ridiculousness of the theory, but rather the reasons why it might be true.

"Do you remember the Lawrences? The family that lived in the next block from us when we were ten, or so?"

Trace had fallen into the habit of talking to Bertie whether she was there or not. Today she was not, but he had developed the idea that if he said out loud the things he wanted to run by her, they'd be bookmarked or something, and available for discussion the next time she popped in.

"And do you… do you remember that thing you said when their son Freddie drowned at the swimming pool?"

He was alone in the car, of course, headed to a doctor's appointment. These days it seemed as if his life consisted of large blocks of time spent in medical offices, whether in waiting rooms, exam rooms, or driving to and from them: pre-natal check-ups, ultrasounds, visits to the maternity ward at the hospital where Marla was scheduled to give birth. But today's visit was to a different location, for a different reason.

As he waited at a red light, Trace recalled so clearly that summer afternoon nearly twenty years earlier, when he'd stood on the sidewalk in front of his house with some of his siblings, peering down the tree-lined street past the intersection to where a cluster of cars, including two police vehicles, were parked. There hadn't been any sirens, but somehow word had spread that something awful had happened. People had drifted out of every home along the street, arrayed in silent clusters at the edge of their yards, faces turned to the spectacle one block over. He remembered Mrs. Lawrence, a woman he barely knew, being escorted out the front door by a policeman and accompanied by some other women—her neighbors, probably. Even that far away, he could hear a frantic babble that transformed itself into a throaty wail that floated their way and seemed to go on without ending, not even briefly enough for its issuer to draw breath. Even in the hot, unmoving air, the sound raised goosebumps on his arms and legs.

"No! No!" she'd shrieked as they helped her into the back seat of a police car. Other words, too, although too far away to be distinguishable. The vehicle had pulled away from the curb, red light flashing, moving slowly. No siren. Only then had word begun to travel up the street, passed from one group of people to the next, and moving their way with what had seemed at the time to be unbearable slowness. First they could see only that people receiving the news reeled, or buried their faces in their hands. Then, drawing closer, the gasps and sobs grew audible, along with stray words: "Accident," "Horrible," and so on.

Abruptly, Trace had gone from eagerly awaiting the news—whatever it might be—to dreading it. He had an impulse to turn and bolt into the house, but his legs would not carry him. So instead, he stood, vaguely aware he'd dropped his baseball in the grass, and that Quince had seized the sleeve of his t-shirt and was leaning against him.

"Floating... not breathing... don't know what happened..." He understood the words as they passed by him and continued up the street from neighbor to neighbor, but they held no personal context. Death was something on television and in books, not something that happened to people he knew. He stared into the faces of his family, each of them blanched of color, and they all stared back at him and at each other, penetrating glances seeking meaning and finding none. His mother had herded them into the house then—Sky, Bertie, Quince, and Trace. In the cool, dark foyer, Sky finally dissolved into tears, which made Quince begin to cry, as well. Trace and Bertie had not wept; he could not guess at her reasons, but for him it was the strange hunch that only if he succumbed to tears would the whole thing be real.

"Do you remember that?" he inquired again, pulling into the intersection and turning left when the oncoming lane of traffic was clear. "That day, that afternoon? Mom took us into the kitchen, settled us around the table, and then she got out a can of frozen concentrate and made us lemonade. One of those times when her maternal side really did come through. Sky wanted to go to her room and lie down, and Mom wouldn't let her. She said she needed all of us to just be there with her for a little while. Then Quince threw up, and that sort of spoiled the moment. But it was kind of nice while it lasted. Even though it was all for a horrible reason.

"We didn't talk about what had happened," he continued after a moment's reflection. "We just... sat. I've never asked her, but I think maybe Mom just wanted us to have a few minutes of appreciating one another, and of understanding how easily it could all be taken away. ... Or maybe I'm just giving her way more credit than she deserves."

He was in the parking lot of the medical complex now, guiding the car to a space some distance from the entrance, but in the shade of the overhanging branches of a tree. He shifted into *park* but didn't immediately kill the engine.

"And I remember the thing you said after Sky was finally allowed to go to her room and Quince was off brushing his teeth. How it didn't seem fair, that Freddie Lawrence was an only child, and now he was gone, and here we were, six kids in one family, so it probably should have been one of us, instead. Mom stopped mopping where Quince had barfed. She turned and looked down at you with such a strange look on her face. I half-expected her to slap you, or hug you, or maybe say that it would hurt just as much to lose a child no matter how many were left, but she just looked at you for awhile and then went back to cleaning the floor. I think I held my breath the entire time. I had been thinking the exact same thing myself, except I would never have said it out loud the way you did. I thought you were awful and wonderful, all at the same time."

There was no response, just unmoving warm air pressing against his skin. He was alone in the car, after all.

This was his third visit, each to a different doctor, a different building, and each one slightly more intimidating than the previous one. This latest facility was actually an adjunct to a hospital, which did nothing to help his unease. The reception desk and area were like the others, however, and so was the paperwork he was required to fill out yet again as a first-time visitor. When that was completed and he'd turned it back in, he tried to focus on his annoyance at having to wait, instead of the fluttering feeling in his stomach. When he was finally ushered down the corridor, it was not to an exam room, but to an upholstered chair in front of a desk in an expensively appointed office. The doctor rose to shake his hand and they both settled into their seats.

"Headaches," she prompted, glancing briefly at the folder lying open on the desk before her. She leaned back in her chair, waiting for him to elaborate.

Funny that she pluralized it, Trace thought in the instant before he began to explain. Though it had come and gone over the course of the past few months, he'd begun to regard it as just one. The same headache, popping in and out again, as though it occasionally had someplace else to be when it wasn't bothering him. *There it is again,* he'd think, as the familiar throbbing sensation would kick in, a prologue to the dull, persistent pain that would follow minutes later.

"Yes," he said. The series of questions that followed were as familiar to him now as the waits in all the previous reception areas and the paperwork he'd waded through again and again: *It'd started in late spring, as best he could remember. No, painkillers didn't seem to help. No, he didn't have a history of migraines or even headaches before now. Yes, there'd been that concussion back in March, but these attacks hadn't really gotten going until April. Yes, he'd mentioned them to the doctor who'd been treating him for the head injury, and was told this was typical, and they'd go away after awhile. Except they hadn't. It* hadn't. *It would show up, barely noticeable at first, for a day or two, then three. Then it would be gone for a week or more. Lately, it was there more frequently, and for longer periods of time. No, no particular activity or stress seemed to bring it on or exacerbate it, it was just there when it felt like it.*

Yeah, he admitted reluctantly, *the pain was worse now, and accompanied by a sense of vertigo sometimes. Yes, he had it right now. It focused itself between his eyes, or sometimes behind them.*

The doctor closed the folder and leaned forward, resting her arms atop it.

"All right," she said. "There are some preliminary things we'll want to do before the procedure. But the whole thing shouldn't take more than thirty minutes. I'll have the nurse take you back to check your blood pressure, take your temperature, all of that." She scrutinized him for a moment. "How do you do in confined spaces? Are you claustrophobic?"

IT WAS LIKE A LONELY amusement park ride, he reflected later. Lying flat on his back, gazing upward, senses distorted by incessant pounding noises, he wasn't altogether certain if he was moving or whether it was the tunnel around him that was in motion. "Lie completely still," the technician had instructed him.

"Keep your arms and head inside the vehicle until it comes to a complete stop, right?" he offered with a nervous grin, and had received a grimace in response. Probably they'd heard that line so many times by now it was difficult to even fake amusement.

She was more conciliatory afterwards. "You can rest here for a few minutes, if you'd like. It can be disorienting, I know. Is there anybody waiting for you? I can let them know." Her brow creased slightly when he told her there was no one, and she hovered outside the door as he changed from the gown back into his street clothes, adding to his self-consciousness. It hadn't occurred to him that coming here alone would seem odd, though he did recall now that he'd been the only person sitting by himself in the waiting room. It made him something of a pitiable figure, he decided, especially when the technician thrust a bottle of water into his hand as he stepped back into the corridor, still tucking his shirt into his pants.

"Drink this," she said. She squeezed the back of his upper arm as he accepted it. "You'll feel better the quicker you're rehydrated."

No doubt they offered a water to everyone afterward, but did everybody get a reassuring arm-squeeze, as well?

"Thanks," he told her. "Am I supposed to see the doctor again now?"

She shook her head. "No. We won't have the results of the scan for a few days yet. Someone from her office will call you. Be sure and drink that water, now. I can get you another, if you want."

"No, thanks. This will be plenty," he assured her.

Even though Trace had parked in the shade and left the windows cracked, the interior had still baked in the mid-morning August heat. He stood with the car door open, leaning over the roof and gulping from the bottle as he gazed across the parking lot.

No one had accompanied him today because no one knew what he was doing. It wasn't exactly stoicism that had kept him from telling anybody; if anything, it was the opposite. It was cowardice, or something like it. Marla and his family had stopped asking him about the headaches because he'd led them to believe he wasn't having them any longer. It was easier to pretend that everything was fine when nobody brought it up, and sometimes if there were enough people around, he forgot about it himself for a little while. Even now, even after multiple consultations and today subjecting himself to an MRI scan, whatever was happening to him still didn't seem real, and wouldn't, unless he had to say it out loud to the people he loved. For now, it was something he was observing as nothing more than an interested bystander.

He lifted the bottle to his lips before realizing he'd already drained its contents. Damn. Now he wished he had accepted the offer of a second one.

Chapter Nine

His head was pain-free for the next few days, and Trace allowed himself the faint hope that the MRI process itself had somehow corrected the situation. In any event, there was nothing left to do right now but wait. In the meantime, he was unaccountably cheerful—giddy, even. Mikayla looked at him askance as he moved around the store making little popping noises with his mouth and drumming his fingers on the sides of his legs as he worked. Her granddaughter Jasmine, who had been hired to replace Zeke, watched with undisguised wariness.

"Stop wasting time staring at the crazy man, and get back to wiping down those counters," her grandmother instructed. Jasmine turned away reluctantly, spritzing a generous amount of cleanser and mopping it up in slow, wide circles. She didn't move with any more urgency than Zeke had ever managed, and seemed just as intimidated and uncommunicative around customers as he had been—but fair is fair, after all. They'd tried one of Trace's relatives, and now it was Mikayla's turn. And she clearly offered no favoritism. If anything, she was bossier now than she had ever been before.

"Hey, who wants ice cream? My treat!" Trace announced, turning to face the others after he'd assisted a departing customer through the door.

Jasmine stole what looked like a hopeful glance at Mikayla, who scrunched her lips onto one side of her face.

"Aw, come on!" Trace pleaded. "It's a hundred degrees out there today. Who couldn't use a little break?" In a whisper directed to Jasmine but designed to be heard by her grandmother as well, he added, "She can't say no, because I'm the boss. So, what do you want?" He was rewarded with just the smallest clandestine giggle.

"You're giving her the wrong idea," Mikayla scolded him later, though it was over a heaping spoonful of her own butterscotch sundae. "Work is supposed to be work, not treats and bosses who try to be buddies."

"Oh, come on. She's been here more than a month. You think one ice cream cone's going to give her a distorted view of the business world?"

Mikayla's lips were doing that disapproving twitching thing again.

"It's not the ice cream I'm concerned about."

He shrugged. "It's hot. I had a craving. I couldn't very well get something for myself and eat it in front of the rest of you, could I?"

She let the subject drop there, but continued to watch him stonily between bites of her sundae. He met her gaze evenly, beaming back across licks of his swirl cone, refusing for once to be intimidated.

Trace's twenty-ninth birthday had passed quietly in late June. It had conjured strange feelings in him, even though it had been years since he and Bertie had celebrated the day together. Still, making a big deal of it this time felt disloyal in some way. As if sensing his feelings, Marla had roused herself from the early throes of morning sickness to be especially supportive.

"How about dinner at LaFontainne's?" she'd suggested. "Or maybe just a couple of people over for a quiet get-together?"

"How about just you and me, and we order something in?" he'd countered, and a nearly palpable sense of relief passed between them. Neither was really up to putting forth much effort.

But now it was September, and Quince was turning twenty-eight. It was gearing up to be a big deal, orchestrated by Jodi, who was now widely acknowledged to be The One. The event was going to be held at her parents' back yard in one of the tonier suburbs.

"Seems strange, don't you think?" Trace observed, wending his way through the leisurely Saturday-afternoon traffic. "None of us have met her family yet. She and Quince have only been going out since last spring. You'd expect her to pick more... I don't know... neutral ground for this."

"Well, her own apartment's too small to host very many people, she says. She felt like a restaurant or a bar would be too regimented. And I guess her parents have all this extra space. Their yard backs up to a lake. So why not?" Marla was entering her second trimester and was feeling and acting more like her old self again. She was dabbing lotion onto her hands and rubbing them vigorously. "I'm excited to see this place; aren't you? A *lake!*" she repeated for emphasis.

"You've seen lakes before. Hell, your parents' house sits right on the channel in South Carolina. How is this going to be more impressive than that?"

Marla stopped rubbing her hands and looked at him. "It's not a contest, for Pete's sake. One doesn't have to be better than the other. I just think it's nice, is all. And it's fun to see someplace new. Aren't you interested in seeing where Jodi's folks live? Where she comes from?"

He wanted to answer honestly and say *No, not especially,* but decided that would only lead to allegations of either being a party pooper or perhaps feeling jealous, neither of which was the case, but he wasn't up to defending himself. Instead, he said:

"Have you considered the impact on these nice, unsuspecting people of meeting this many Bannerlys all at the same time? Do you remember what it was like when I first brought you home to meet everybody?"

She considered this for a moment, and went back to massaging lotion into her knuckles. "Well… but that was at your folks' place. Where everybody naturally congregates, anyway. Everybody was… well, they were being… comfortable."

"Aha!" Trace cried. "You started to say *being themselves,* didn't you? Everybody was being themselves. And that was a lot to take, wasn't it? Don't tell me you didn't have a few second thoughts about continuing to date me, after spending an evening with my whole family!"

It was Marla's turn to dodge an accusation. "Everyone is going to be on their best behavior tonight," she predicted. "It's unfamiliar turf.

So as long as I can count on *you* not to do anything obnoxious, we should be fine. Okay?"

She squirted a little more lotion into her hand and then dabbed some on the tip of his nose.

"Okay," he said obediently. But he nonetheless refused to do anything about the lotion, forcing her to finally swipe it away with her finger as they were walking up to the front door of the Pineret's elegant-looking home.

It was the perfect evening for a backyard party on the shore of a lake, Trace had to concede. The heat of the September afternoon had faded to a comfortable level, and layers of pink and orange clouds rested on the western horizon as blue ebbed from the sky. Jodi's parents greeted them with ebullience. Her father was stout, balding, and far less formal than his elegant home would have suggested. Her mother shared Jodi's dark, snapping eyes and wide smile, but neither seemed like the sort of people who might give birth to a long-limbed dancer. She squeezed their hands warmly and escorted them out to the patio, which was festooned with more Japanese lanterns than Trace had ever seen in one place.

"Overkill," Mrs. Pineret confided, reading his mind. "But when Jodi gets an idea in her head, there's no room for compromise. I wonder if your brother knows what he's in for."

"It's like a fairyland!" Marla said breathlessly, and Trace couldn't disagree. In addition to the paper lanterns dangling overhead, strings of tiny white lights were threaded through shrubbery and ran along either side of a path that descended across a wide expanse of lawn, presumably leading to the lakeshore, although he couldn't see that far. The view was partially obscured by the several dozen guests milling about the yard. None of them were people he recognized.

"Who are all of these people?" he spoke under his breath to Marla after their hostess had left them to greet still more arrivals.

"Friends of Jodi's, I guess. Or relatives? Maybe her family's as big as yours."

"No family is as big as mine," he retorted. "Where the hell's Quince, do you suppose?"

She clutched his arm. "Look there," she said in a strange tone of voice.

He followed her gaze. At first he thought she was looking at the enormous cake, set at the near end of a buffet table and tilted slightly to display, embedded in its surface, side-by-side glossy images of a little boy and a recent one of Quince. It took him a puzzling moment to connect the two. "Oh, I guess the first one is from when he was a kid," he was in the process of saying, but then realized that Marla was actually looking past the cake to the genuine article. Both resplendent and uncomfortable-looking, Quince had emerged from between clusters of guests. He was attired in full tuxedo-regalia. Trace grinned broadly. "I don't believe it."

"Quinnie, you look wonderful! So handsome!" Marla gushed, kissing him on the cheek.

"Hey, guys. Thanks," he added in a sheepish aside to Marla. Facing Trace, he lifted his chin defiantly. "Go ahead. Say whatever you like. Though I should warn you, Sky and Matt got here before you guys did, and she's already used up most of the best lines."

"He's not going to say *anything*," Marla hastened to interject, patting the silky lapels of Quince's jacket. "And if he does, just put it down to jealousy."

"The only things I can think of to say are *Why?* And *How?* They couldn't even get you to wear pants to your high school graduation!" Trace pointed out.

"I had a cap and gown on! What did I need with pants? Anyway," his brother continued grimly, "Jodi thought it would be a nice touch if she and I got all dressed up for this."

"I wish I'd known." Marla glanced down at her maternity blouse and black slacks and then at Trace's khakis and polo shirt. "When we heard *garden party*..."

"No, you're dressed fine." Quince gestured around the yard with a sweep of his arm. "Nobody knew. See? The idea was for just us to stand out. Everybody else gets to be comfortable," he finished in a lamentable tone.

"The *idea*," Jodi amended, linking her arm through his as she stepped up to join them, "Was so the birthday boy would stand out. We'll be able to spot him, wherever he is in the crowd. I'm just *slightly* dressed up, and that's only to send the subtle message to any single women on the prowl that the hot guy in the tux belongs to me." Disentangling herself from Quince, she hugged Trace and Marla in turn. "You guys look great! And no matter what I wear, I can't hold a candle to the beautiful pregnant lady, so I'm not even going to try."

Despite such assertions to the contrary, Jodi had clearly gone to some effort. Her hair was swept up, though not as severely as she'd had it at the ballet recital, and a strapless evening gown hugged her slender form, held in place, as far as Trace could tell, by nothing except her breasts. The one concession to informality was that she was barefooted.

"We struck a deal," Quince explained. "I get to shed the monkey suit at the stroke of nine. And after tonight, I don't ever have to wear one of these ever again."

"That wasn't exactly the agreement." Jodi adjusted his bow tie. "I promised I would never ask you to wear one on your birthday again. I never implied that all other events were off the bargaining table."

"Weddings!" Quince challenged. "You said I'd never have to wear one to a wedding, any wedding! We were very clear on that point!"

"Oh, look! There's my friend Celeste, from college. You haven't met her yet." She beamed at Trace and Marla. "Will you excuse us for a minute?"

They watched as she led Quince across the lawn, waving to someone in the distance.

"Huh," Marla said after a moment. "Weddings. *A* wedding. Are they engaged, do you suppose?"

He shrugged. "I don't know. He hasn't told me, if they are."

They stood looking after the departing pair a few seconds longer.

"That doesn't mean anything," she pointed out. "Your family doesn't tell each other a lot of things."

Trace shifted uncomfortably and looked around. He drew his arm around his wife's waist. "You want me to get you something to drink?"

SOMETIME LATER, HE FOUND his sister and his mother in a secluded corner of the yard, seated in a patio swing, gliding back and forth gently. Each was holding a glass. He kissed his mother on the forehead and threw himself into a wicker chair opposite them, sloshing a little of his own drink on his pants.

"So, how about our baby bro, all decked out like that?" Sky greeted him.

"I know!"

"Don't make a big deal of it, you two," their mother admonished. "You poke fun at him now, and he'll never want to get dressed up again."

"When has he ever gotten dressed up before now?" Sky challenged. "He refused to be one of the groomsmen at my wedding because it meant wearing a tux. So, I made him an usher, and even at that, I found out he'd taken off his tie before any of the guests arrived, and by the time the ceremony actually started, he was seating people in his shirtsleeves. When I saw him, I thought about halting the organist just long enough to murder him on my way down the aisle."

"You're probably lucky he stopped at shucking his coat and tie," Trace suggested.

"It's true he was never overly fond of clothes when he was little," their mother said thoughtfully. "Every time we turned around, it seemed he was playing in the front yard or paying a visit to one of the neighbors, stark naked. On laundry days, I'd have to send one of you out to look for stray socks and underpants in the rose bushes."

"That reminds me; did you see the cake?" Sky asked Trace. "Those photos of Quince in the fondant icing? Amazing what they can do these days."

He nodded. "Jodi went all out, for sure. Did she get that old picture of when he was four or five from you, Mom?"

Their mother got a funny look on her face and swirled the ice cubes in her glass, prompting her children to glance at each other.

"She wanted one from when he was a newborn or just a few months old, but I couldn't find any." She didn't lift her face to meet their questioning gazes. "It's the last-baby syndrome, I suppose. The firstborn gets the hundreds of pictures, the next gets a few less, and it goes down from there. I'm sure we must have taken one or two of him during those first few weeks, but when I went looking, I couldn't find a single one."

"Well…" Sky hesitated, seeking a consoling response. "The one you gave her was probably a better choice. Kids only really begin to have distinctive features when they're two or three, anyway. Early on, all babies pretty much look the same."

Trace chimed in. "Heck, yeah, Mom. As far as that goes, you probably could have given her a baby picture of any one of us, and she would never have known the difference."

"Well, that's the thing." His mother took a final gulp from her nearly empty glass and crunched an ice cube in her teeth. Courage bolstered, she said:

"I'm not entirely sure the picture I did give her is one of Quince. I hadn't labeled the back." She looked at Trace. "It might just as easily have been of you. Maybe even Cord." When nobody said anything, she eased herself out of the swing. "I think maybe I want another drink."

They watched her walk across the grass. Sky turned back to Trace.

"You just gotta laugh," she said philosophically.

"Do you? Do you really?" he challenged. His own good mood had faded. He slammed back the rest of his drink and dropped the empty cup on the grass.

She glanced at the discarded glass and then up at him. "What else do we do, at this stage of the game? Make a big deal out of it?"

"Why not? Maybe things like this keep happening because we never *do* make a big deal. We never call her on it, Sky. Neither of them. I wish… I just wish they could be a little apologetic about it once in awhile. But you heard her. It's no big deal. Just another little *oops!* moment that's here and gone."

His sister leaned forward in the swing and rested her elbows on her knees. "I don't think tonight is the time to start holding them accountable, Trace. Think about it: Who's the one who'll wind up most embarrassed? That would be Jodi, who went to all this effort and will look like a fool if you get up there and say, 'Oh, by the way, that's not Quince on his birthday cake, that's an old picture of me!'"

"I'm not going to do that."

"You bet your ass you're not."

They were both quiet for a moment, listening to the sounds of conversation and laughter drift across the yard toward them. Sky rubbed her face in her hands and then leaned back once more.

"Their youngest is twenty-eight now. Do you really still hold out some belief that Mom and Pop are going to change at this stage of the game? They are who they are, babe. They weren't perfect parents, but who is? They didn't do so bad, all things considered. We're here, aren't we? We turned out reasonably okay."

"Not…" he hesitated a brief second, but the built-up indignation was too great, and the amount of alcohol he'd consumed was just right, and the rest spilled out. "Not *all* of us. In case you forgot."

The stinging slap came out of nowhere, or so it appeared. Sky seemed as surprised as he did, and she stared at her hand as though it had moved with a will of its own. She looked up at her brother, his head still turned slightly aside from the force of the blow. She reached again, this time to touch his face with both hands, but he flinched, and she dropped them into her lap.

"I had no right to do that." She spoke in a soft, even tone. "No matter what, and I apologize. For *that*. But don't you ever imply that I've forgotten, or that I don't care. I love her, maybe not as much as you do, but I still grieve every single day. And they do too, Trace, even if they can't show it to your satisfaction. And you know as well as I do that what happened wasn't their fault. I don't know where her demons came from, but not from them."

She stood, setting the swing to jiggling in her wake. She took a few steps away from him and then stopped. When she looked back, his face was still averted.

"You're about to be a father yourself. It will change how you feel about everything, wait and see. It changes everything."

Sky waited a moment longer, but when Trace did not move or speak, she walked away, swallowed into the party noise and the glare from all the Japanese lanterns.

"Where are you?" he said thickly several minutes later. He raised his face to the open sky above him. "Where are you, when I really need to talk?"

"WHERE YOU BEEN, BRO?" Quince hollered at Trace's approach. "You're missing everything!" You missed singing me a happy birthday, and you missed the cake cutting." He had discarded his tuxedo jacket and his bow tie now dangled in two black strings on either side of his unbuttoned collar.

"I'm here now," Trace declared, stepping beneath the canopy that housed the bar and a half-dozen or so of the more exuberant guests, his brother included. He swept up a fresh gin and tonic and clinked against the glass in Quince's outstretched hand. "Cheers, baby bro. Welcome to middle age." He looked around them. "Where's everybody else?"

"Screw you," Quince retorted amiably. "I'm in the flower of my youth." He enunciated each word with slurred precision and followed them with a beaming smile. "I don't know where the rest are. It's not my birthday to keep track of them." This produced laughs from the cronies standing behind him, buddies and co-workers Trace recalled having met once or twice.

He rubbed his temple with the heel of his hand, sloshing a bit of his drink onto his shoulder. "Well, here's to your flower, then." More hoots and guffaws.

Quince downed his own beverage in one gulp. The act of tossing back his head caused him to stagger a little.

"Careful," Alan, one of his buddies, cautioned. "You don't want to get too messed up in front of your girlfriend's folks. Not if you're planning to marry into the family."

"You're right." Quince nodded vigorously. "Fort... Fort-you-nut-lee," he pronounced with some difficulty, "I'm still a ways away from that."

"Which?" someone else asked. "Getting married or getting messed up? You may be closer than you think."

Quince tapped the edge of the counter as a means of indicating to the bartender that he wanted another. While he waited, he faced the others.

"I love her, it's true. I love my little Jodi. But we just met...what?... six months ago. *Waaay* too soon to be thinking about more than... well, you know." He might have been attempting to wink, but all he succeeded in doing was squinting with both eyes. "My flower isn't ready for more than that, not yet. Anyway, we gotta take these things one event at a time."

He looped his arm around Trace's neck and pulled him close.

"Next up is a baby—this one's. My brother's having a baby, can you believe it? Aren't you? Aren't you, Trace? You're having a baby!"

"Well, I started it," Trace said, blinking from Quince's warm scotch breath so near his face. "But Marla's doing all the heavy lifting."

Quince laughed heartily. He reached for his fresh drink without removing his arm from around Trace, causing them both to stagger.

"It was a secret for awhile," he told the assembled group. "Only the family was supposed to know." He pressed his nose into Trace's cheekbone. "But I told Jodi. I hope that's okay, bro. I hope it's okay that I told Jodi."

"It's fine." Trace was trying to disentangle himself from his brother's grasp. "We didn't think you'd keep it from her."

"Hey! Hey!" Quince repeated emphatically. "Did you tell you-know-who? Did you tell her, speaking of secrets?"

He'd renewed his grip on Trace's neck. Trace stopped struggling momentarily, confused.

"What do you mean? Who are you talking…?" The question died away unfinished as a suspicion rose in his somewhat inebriated brain. "No. No, Quince. Don't—"

"—I hope you didn't," his brother interrupted. "Because that would mean either you didn't ask her about me, or you did, and she doesn't want to come see me."

"Shut up, Quince."

"Not even on my birthday." Quince was grinning broadly at the assembled group who stared back at them with expectant smiles, awaiting a punchline of some kind. And the more Trace attempted to free himself from the crook of his brother's elbow, the more determinedly he held on.

"Just be quiet," Trace ordered through clenched teeth. But Quince had already traveled far enough down the road, spurred on by scotch.

"Our sister," he explained to the others. "He talks to our sister. I don't mean the *live* ones. I mean the other one. Bertie. You remember her?"

"Stop it, Quince. This isn't funny! Shut up and let me go!"

Quince leaned forward, causing them both to stagger a few steps. He finished his story in an exaggerated whisper, spewing flecks of spittle toward his audience.

"And the thing is… the thing is… She *talks back!* Tell them, Trace! Tell them how you have these conversations with Bertie!"

With a final tug born of fury, Trace wrenched himself free and fell backward onto the ground. One arm made stinging contact with the edge of a brick planter, but he barely noticed. He was on his feet again in a flash, pile-driving himself into Quince's chest with his shoulder. Quince fell against the portable bar, which in turn toppled, taking the bartender and all the bottles of alcohol and mix with it.

"Shut up, you little asshole! You drunken son of a bitch!" He reached for his brother's lapels, but Quince twisted aside, then ducked and rose to deliver a glancing blow to Trace's jaw. Through streaks of sharp white light in his periphery, Trace returned the favor with a more substantial blow to the side of Quince's face. Quince staggered backward again. He was raising his hand, preparing for another swing, but he became tangled in a folding chair and fell over it into the grass. Trace advanced, kicking the chair out of the way and would have thrown himself atop the other man, but he suddenly found his arms pinned efficiently behind his back. He struggled to free himself, only to be brought up short by a kneecap nudged in his ribcage and a commanding voice in his ear.

"Knock it off! Knock it off right now, or I'm hauling your ass onto the dock and pitching you in the lake, you got me? ...I *said,* Do you *understand* me?"

And for a minute, Trace was ten years old again, held in the same vise-like grip Cord always used when breaking up another of the countless squabbles between his little brothers. Panting, he nodded, the heat of battle slowly ebbing from his brain. Still Cord did not release him. They stood like that, both watching as their father and Jodi lifted Quince to his feet. Quince's expression was still one of glowering madness, and once on solid ground, he lunged for Trace, pulling free of Jodi's grasp, but not from his dad's, who reigned him in as efficiently as Cord continued to hold Trace.

"Easy, son. We're done here. You got that? All done."

At last the onlookers seemed to shake off the spell that had held them motionless throughout the fight. A few moved to lift the bar upright once more. Someone was escorting the bartender to a chair. Still others were collecting bottles, glasses, and stray oranges and maraschino cherries from the grass. Everyone else who was still at the party had grouped some distance away, watching in silence. Jodi scurried to Quince's side again, resting a hand on his shoulder. She and their father led Quince away, taking care to keep a wide berth between them and Trace and Cord. Jodi threw Trace a bewildered but nonjudgmental glance as they passed. Quince, blood streaming from one nostril, did not look at him at all. Only when the others had crossed the yard and entered the house through the patio doors did Cord relinquish his grip on Trace with a small shove.

"Happy?" he asked, as Trace stumbled a couple of steps away from him. "Maybe it's time you grew up some." And then he crossed to where Leslie stood among the crowd, linking his arm through hers and steering her into the night somewhere beyond the glow of the Japanese lanterns that continued to bob merrily overhead.

No one else came near him, not at first. Some stared his way from a safe distance; most acted as if they couldn't see him at all. He ran his tongue over his teeth and tasted blood. He gripped the elbow that had made contact with the planter, realizing now that it hurt mightily. When he looked up, Marla was standing a short distance away.

"I think we should go," she said. He nodded and moved toward her, but she did not wait, turning instead and walking several steps ahead of him. They walked around the side of the Pineret house rather than going through it. On the street, Marla stood by the driver's-side door with her hand extended.

"I'm going to drive," she announced. "Hand me your keys." He dug in his pocket and handed them to her without comment.

Neither of them spoke again until they'd entered the apartment. Standing in the hallway after she'd flicked on the overhead foyer light, she appraised him from head to foot.

"You're a mess," she said. "You're covered with grass stains. There's a big welt on your chin, some dried blood in the corner of your mouth, and the back of your shirt is ripped." That summation complete, she turned on her heel and went into their bedroom. It was clear she had no intention of administering any first aid. She didn't even know, he thought as he rubbed it, how much his arm was hurting.

"I'VE BEEN SEEING AN awful lot of you lately, it seems," Dr. Gorham said. He was supporting Trace's elbow in one hand while moving his arm back and forth with the other. "Does that hurt?"

"A little. Well, a lot, actually. I kept hoping it would get better on its own, but that doesn't seem to be happening. Did I break something?"

The physician continued to work the arm back and forth, then turned it over and pressed his thumb into the soft underside of his arm, probing up and down.

"If something were broken, you'd be going through the roof right now. But we'll take an x-ray, to be sure. I'm guessing it's just a real serious bruise, but better to be safe than sorry."

Dr. Gorham glanced up. His gaze lingered on Trace's jaw and the finely-etched purple bruise there. "Hate to see the other guy," he quipped.

"I haven't seen him, either," Trace confessed. "Not since it happened, more than a week ago. It was Quince," he added sheepishly.

His doctor's eyes widened. "Well," he said noncommittally, "They do say that nobody can push our buttons like family. Was alcohol involved?"

"A lot."

"Uh-huh." The doctor lowered Trace's arm and reached up to run a gloved finger across his discolored jaw. "All your teeth still in there?"

"I think so."

"Good. Keep it that way. Okay, in a minute, I'm going to send you across the hall for that x-ray. Anything else that needs looking at?"

"I hope not."

His physician nodded, peeling off the rubber gloves and tossing them into a wastebasket. He rested his hands on his knees.

"I saw the results of the MRI, and read the neurosurgeon's report. I'm sorry, son."

"Yeah. Me too."

"I really did think the headaches were just an aftereffect of the concussion, and they'd go away with time."

"The way I hoped my arm would stop hurting?"

"Something like that. The good news is, they've caught it early.

Well," he amended, "Early enough that there's something that can be done. In another six or nine months…" He let the sentence go unfinished. "How did the family take it?" Gorham looked closely when Trace didn't answer. "Ah," he said after a moment.

"I'm going to tell them. I just… I haven't found the right time yet."

"And Marla?"

"I… I can't right now. Not with the baby on the way. I can't put her through that."

Chewing his lower lip reflectively, the doctor got to his feet. He continued to look down at Trace. "I hate giving advice when none has been asked for. I picked the wrong field to go into, maybe. Maybe the rest of the family doesn't need to know just yet, but you can't keep it from her, boy. She'll never understand. She'll never be grateful and say, 'Oh, thank you for sparing me that news as long as you did.' It's like your arm here. And like that tumor up there. Those aren't situations that improve the longer you put them off." He was not mollified by Trace's nodding. "Your wife is stronger than you give her credit for. And you need her support, just as much as she needs yours.

"You think I don't understand," he continued. "You think that anyone who hasn't faced what you're looking at couldn't really know how it feels. Well, that's probably true. But try this on for size: You haven't said anything to anyone so far, because it isn't really true until you say it out loud. It's just a word, just an academic concept until the first time you tell somebody you have cancer. You have a tumor. Once you've said it, you can't take it back. It changes who you are, and it changes how other people view you." He resumed a businesslike tone. "Anyhow. I'll go get that x-ray lined up." And then he was gone, closing the door behind him.

Trace hadn't been looking at the other man for several minutes. He'd been staring across the small exam room at the row of jars on the counter holding tongue depressors and rubber gloves and cotton swabs, willing back the tears that were blurring his vision. Now they began to spill down his face, dripping steadily off his chin and soaking into his pant legs. They seemed scalding, almost, as they rolled across his flesh, and he wondered if this was somehow a side effect of that malevolent mass growing behind his eye, working its evil magic in ways they hadn't told him about yet.

HE WAS A BIT OF a pariah within his own family, it appeared. No one had called or come by since the night of the birthday party. He mentioned this to Marla, who had adopted a peculiar distance of her own.

"Is that so?" was her response. "And why would you think that?"

"There have been squabbles before," he rationalized. "Maybe… Maybe not on this level, but still. You'd think somebody would call just to tell me how pissed-off they are. That's what usually happens."

"I'm guessing it's implied. Maybe they're waiting for you to make the first move." When he didn't answer, she sighed and lowered the magazine she was holding. "I'm trying to understand, Trace. What happened? What went on that night?"

"Why don't you ask Quince?" he countered, then regretted it. If Quince hadn't said anything already—at least not since blurting his secret at the party—he didn't want it coming out now.

"Oh, for God's sake, stop acting like a four-year-old! I'm asking you!"

"Too much alcohol, the both of us, that's all. He was being a prick, and I got pissed. He said something-or-other, I told him to knock it off, he kept it coming, and then… well, you know."

He was aware she was still watching him closely even after he'd turned away.

"Sky said you'd been spoiling for a fight even earlier," she told him. "That she may have set you off with something she said."

"Sky gives herself too much credit."

Marla set her magazine on the coffee table, aligning it carefully with the others already stacked there before she spoke again.

"Your sisters think it might be nerves, about the baby coming. All the added responsibility."

Trace whirled on her. "My sisters are full of crap! How dare they?

That's the last thing you need to hear these days, in your condition!"

"My condition is fine," she told him evenly. "It's yours we're worried about."

He got up from the couch. "Nobody needs to be worrying about it! Nobody needs to be discussing it behind my back!"

"Then let's talk about it now!" With difficulty, she got to her feet and followed him across the living room, putting her hand on his arm. "This isn't just about you picking a fight with Quince the other night. You've been different for a while, now. Not... not present, exactly. I didn't need your sisters to point that out to me, or for me to wonder if you're having second thoughts about us becoming parents. I know I kind of pushed the issue..."

He turned and pulled her to him, pressing her face into his chest.

"Don't think for one second I don't want this baby," he ordered, kissing the top of her head. "That I'm not twice as excited about it as you are, because I am. You're my hero, the one dealing with all of the changes this pregnancy is putting you through. I sit next to you in those birthing classes, watching you accept so calmly the information about what's going to happen in the delivery room, while I'm crapping my pants in terror, and I'm not even the one the baby's going to come out of. If that's what's worrying you, then stop it right now."

"Nice to hear," Marla's muffled voice rose from the front of his shirt. She took a half-step back, wrinkling her nose as she looked up at him. "Now, how about we talk about the real issue, here?"

"There's no issue," he assured her. "No issue. Just an overabundance of booze and testosterone. That's all it was."

As she had been before her death, Bertie was a willful, unreliable presence, darting in and out of Trace's life at random intervals. The more he'd wondered and worried about her, the less frequently she called or showed up to put his mind at ease. And so it was now. When he would have welcomed a visit from her most, she was nowhere to be found. Perhaps she sensed that she blamed her for his estrangement from Quince and was keeping her distance.

"Hey," he would announce, alone in the car on his way to work. "I just want to talk; get your impression of things. Of what's happened."

He'd taken to talking out loud a lot lately, hoping it might encourage her to put in an appearance.

Funny, how he'd stopped questioning his sanity. Whether his sister's return was a side effect of his concussion or perhaps the newly discovered tumor behind his right eye hardly seemed relevant any more.

"I know what you told me," he murmured, sitting in his office with Mikayla safely out of earshot in the front of the store. "That you can't tell me anything I don't already know. But still, it would just be nice to hear your voice again."

Abruptly, he sensed without turning around that he wasn't alone. He knew it wasn't a spectral sibling, but somebody else who had arrived without making a sound. He took a second to steel himself before he looked over his shoulder. Of all the possibilities for who might be standing in the doorway, one that had not entered his mind was that it might be Emily, his six-year-old niece. She was regarding him with her standard impassive gaze.

"Well, hey there! Look who's come to visit!" Trace said in a tone he immediately recognized as patronizing and too high-pitched, besides. He adopted a lower register. "What brings you by?"

"My daddy," she said simply. "He's talking to the lady out front."

Trace pushed his chair away from his desk. "I'm glad you came with him. Should we go see what he needs?" He was in the process of rising when Emily said:

"I do it, too. I talk to my grandma sometimes. Not the one who's your mother, but my other one. My daddy's mother."

"Oh? You mean your Grandmother Peggy?" Meaning Matt's stepmother, since his own mom was deceased and his father had remarried.

But Emily was shaking her head. "Huh-uh. The one who always wears blue. The one who's my daddy's real mama."

"Oh," Trace said again. He realized he had paused midway between standing and sitting, one hand propped on the back of his chair. His niece moved nonchalantly around the room, studying the shelves lined with unpacked supplies along the far wall. Methodically she touched the front of each box with a small, pink forefinger. When she reached the final shelf, she turned and focused her attention on him once more.

"Does it make you feel good to speak to her?" he asked when she was looking at him. "Do you miss her less that way?"

Emily said nothing more until she had come around the desk and climbed into Trace's vacated chair. Her legs dangled several inches above the ground, but by leaning forward and using one of his knees as ballast, she was able to spin the seat in a full circle. As it came to a stop, she confided, "We're pretending to buy paper or something, but it's really just so we can see how you're doing." She pushed off from his knee once more, leaving Trace to consider this as the chair spun around again a few times.

"Well, that's nice of you," he said. "I'm fine, though. Did you think something might be wrong?"

Her shoulders rose and fell in an indifferent shrug. "I wasn't supposed to tell you. It's supposed to be a secret."

He nodded. "Well, I won't say anything, then."

Brow furrowed, Emily scanned the top of his desk. "Do you have any glitter pens?"

Mikayla was sliding something into a bag and Matt was signing a credit card receipt when they emerged from the back room, hand in hand. Matt looked up and smiled apologetically.

"Sorry. She was supposed to stay out here with me." He gestured to the *Employees Only* sign posted above the rear entry. "I'd offer the excuse that she hasn't learned to read yet, but I doubt it would make a difference if she could." He knelt as his daughter approached. "You have a little bit of an entitlement issue, don't you?" he asked her.

Either because she didn't understand the term or she didn't care, Emily held up her free hand, displaying two highlighters.

"Colored pens," she told her father. "Trace gave me them. One pink, and one green."

"Since we don't have glitter pens," Trace explained. He gripped Matt's shoulder in greeting as the other man rose. "Good to see you."

"You too," Matt returned. To Emily he said, "Did you thank your uncle? He's not in this business to be giving things away, you know."

Mikayla made a snorting sound that Trace assumed meant she was seconding that sentiment, but she was moving briskly around the counter and wedged her way past him to the display marked *Back to School Supplies*.

"Who says we don't have glitter pens?" she snapped. "You come on over here, darlin'." Apparently even she wasn't immune to Emily's charms. "What kind you be needing?"

"She doesn't *need* any," Matt started to protest, but Trace silenced him with a wave.

"Don't bother," he said. "There's no point in wasting your breath."

TRACE WALKED THEM TO their car a few minutes later and stood to one side watching as Matt buckled Emily into her child's seat. She was absorbed with holding each pen up to the light and admiring the vibrant color within as her dad fitted the straps around her twisting hands with some difficulty. Finally, he stood back and turned to face Trace, heaving a sigh of mock exhaustion.

"Let me pay you for those."

"Not at all. I didn't even know Mikayla had ordered them, and that's probably the only set we'll move, anyway. Believe it or not, most people don't do their back-to-school shopping at a shipping depot."

"All the more reason..."

"Forget it." Trace leaned around his brother-in-law's shoulder to make sure Emily's attention was still captured by the pens, and then said in a lowered voice, "Look, I want to apologize for my behavior the other night."

Matt folded his arms in front of his chest and tilted his head in the direction of the open car door. "I'm guessing a little someone already blew my cover," he smiled. "If you hadn't figured it out on your own. But look: It's all going to blow over. Most of it already has. Are *you* okay?"

Trace nodded. "As much as I deserve to be, anyhow. Have you seen Quince? How's he?"

"Fingers and toes," Matt cautioned Emily. She nodded absently, and he slid the car door shut before continuing. "He's a little sore and a little pissed, still," he informed Trace. "But he's not giving up any details about what went down, despite all your sisters' cross-examination. It's nobody's business besides yours and his, anyway." His grin faded, and he placed a hand on Trace's shoulder. "I'm here because Sky is not quite ready to let you know she's more concerned than she is mad. Some conversation you and she had, evidently, has got her worried. And she has an idea that you're more likely to spill the goods to a more neutral party like me."

"I get it," Trace nodded. "But there's nothing to spill."

"I didn't figure there was. But you know your sister. Anyhow…" Matt allowed his hand to drop to his side. "…She's mostly done being upset. If you wanted to come over Sunday to watch the game, I don't think she'd object. Especially if you bring Marla."

"I'll think about it; thanks. Um, hey," he continued as his brother-in-law started to cross around to the other side of his car. He waited until Matt had stepped back onto the curb to continue. "I know this kind of comes out of left field, but…" he hazarded a quick glance through the window. His niece looked up at him. A smile crossed her face and she waved his direction. He returned the gesture. "How well did Emily know your mother? Your biological mother, I mean."

"My mom died when Em was about six weeks old, remember, so not at all. Why?"

"I… that's what I thought," Trace fumbled. He waved one hand dismissively. "I was confused, is all. Something she said when we were back in my office. For just a second, I wasn't sure who she was talking about. We were discussing grandmas, and… and what they wear."

Matt regarded him dubiously. "Well, it would have been your mom or Peggy, then. My stepmom. Those are the only ones she knows."

"Yeah. Yeah, of course. Well, anyway, I'll let you know about Sunday. I'll check with Marla to see if she has any other plans."

Matt had crossed around the front of the car and was opening the driver's door when, on impulse, Trace called out: "Hey!"

He leaned over the metal roof.

"I... I lied before," he confessed. "There *is* something to spill. Maybe... Maybe I'll tell you on Sunday, if we come over. But I need to tell Marla first."

A city bus chugged behind Matt, ruffling his hair in its wake. He nodded at Trace. "Yeah... okay..."

"I mean, I know it's kind of unfair to say only that and then leave you hanging. But, since I just said that everything is fine, and... and actually it isn't, I'd feel like a real asshole to show up on Sunday and spring it on you."

"It's all right, bro," Matt assured him. "Whatever it is, Marla should know first. We'll see you on the weekend, then."

Trace nodded. He felt a rush of warmth for a friend who could accept that kind of a dramatic teaser without pressing for more detail. He remained on the sidewalk for several moments after the vehicle bearing his brother-in-law and his niece had pulled away from the curb and had vanished into traffic.

Without turning, he said, "It wasn't me she was waving at a minute ago, was it? I saw your reflection in the car window."

No one answered, and when he turned, he was alone on the sidewalk.

"Bitch," he muttered under his breath.

Chapter Ten

"It's… It's about the headaches," was how he began when he told Marla everything that evening.

She listened without saying anything, without uttering so much as a gasp, merely watching as he paced the length of the kitchen. Midway through the story, her gaze dropped to her hands, fingertips curling, resting in her lap. When he was finished, he leaned against the counter, his own clammy palms thrust into his armpits. Even then, she didn't look up. He wanted to reach out to her, but he wasn't sure his trembling legs would carry him even that short distance.

"I'm so angry," she said finally, though it wasn't reflected in her tone. She leaned back in her chair and released a pent-up breath.

"At… at me?"

"At everything. At that *thing* in your head, at the diagnosis, the uncertainty, the pregnancy…"

"The pregnancy? No, sweetheart…"

"The timing of it, the fact that it kept you from saying anything until now, making me wonder if *that's* why you've been so different, so angry lately, the whole thing that happened with Quince…"

Somehow Trace found the strength to push away from the counter. He knelt by her chair and gathered her hands in his.

"Don't ever think that. If anything, it's the thought of that baby on the way that's kept me from falling apart altogether—"

"—And yes, at you. I'm so angry at you right now."

"I know, I know." He raised her hands to his face. "I should have told you right away. I shouldn't have kept it to myself."

"You shouldn't have gotten sick in the first place!" She shoved him so hard he fell backwards, his shoulders slamming against the cupboard doors below the sink. She struggled to her feet. "*That's* what you shouldn't have done! What am I supposed to do now?" She towered over him, arms flailing, making circles in the air. "Answer me that, why don't you? You can't, can you? No!" she shouted, thrusting a finger at him as he pulled himself into a sitting position. "You stay right there! You stay away from me, you hear?"

And then she was gone. He could hear her footsteps stumbling through the living room, into the hall, and then the slam of their bedroom door.

He leaned back against the counter, one hand pressed to his forehead. A cupboard handle was digging into his back, but he didn't care. He might have remained like that indefinitely, but gradually, over the distant sound of Marla's sobs, there was a closer one, a soft splattering noise, and he lowered his hand from over his eyes to take a look.

In her ungainly rise, Marla had tipped over the glass of milk she'd been drinking, and now a steady white trickle was running off the edge of the table. An ever-expanding puddle had just reached his foot and was soaking one of his pants cuffs. Trace drew his knees to his chest, sighed heavily, and using the cupboard handles, pulled himself to his feet.

He tore off a few sections of paper towel to wipe up the spill, then threw them in the trash. He stood at the sink, washing the glass, along with a couple of stray dishes, so he was unaware of Marla's return until her arms encircled his waist and he felt her cheek resting between his shoulder blades.

"Don't die," she pleaded. "Please, please, don't die. I need you. This baby needs you. We all need you."

Trace shut off the tap and turned. Hands dripping, he gathered her against him, resting his chin atop her head.

"I'll try," he promised. "I'll try my very best."

SHE ACCOMPANIED TRACE TO his next appointment. He put forth his intention to delay surgery until after the baby's arrival, but both the doctor and Marla shot down that idea in no uncertain terms.

"This is an aggressive tumor." The doctor swiveled in her chair and gestured to the pair of x-rays clipped to the screen of an illuminated box on the wall. "You see how much it's expanded in four weeks? Postponing isn't an option."

To Trace, leaning forward and even squinting, the offending cloudy masses to which she was pointing looked nearly identical in size in either picture. But he heard Marla's sharp intake of breath. Her hand, resting on the back of his, clenched abruptly.

"We're not putting this off one day longer than we have to," she declared. "This is not some macho action-movie where the hero's hurt, but he refuses treatment until he's gotten everybody else out of harm's way. This is about getting your sorry ass through this with as little permanent damage as possible. Trust me, doctor," she said, facing the woman watching them from across the desk. "He can't afford to lose however much brain is still up there."

Following the emotional breakdown when he'd first broken the news to her, Marla had rallied, taking on an unflinching resolve to see the both of them though this crisis. She had poured over his test reports more thoroughly than Trace had done himself. She'd gone online to garner more information and had pumped both his physician and the surgeon for every detail she could get out of them.

"I'm getting our team together," the doctor said. "And checking you in a week from Thursday—ten days from now. Someone from the hospital will be in touch with the specifics; in the meantime, I want you to see your own doctor for another round of blood tests as soon as possible."

"Ten days?" Marla protested. "Can't it be sooner than that? You already said the tumor's growing."

"I know it seems like an eternity," the other woman began, even as Trace was thinking with fresh fear rising in his throat that it didn't seem nearly long enough, "But we want to go into this armed with as much information as we can possibly have. Trust me: I'm as committed as you are to getting the best possible outcome."

"*The best possible outcome,*" Trace muttered later as they were driving home. "That phrase doesn't inspire a whole hell of a lot of confidence."

"It does to me," Marla said quietly. "The best possible outcome is that you live."

He snorted more derisively than he'd intended, and she glanced at him.

"They're cutting into my skull," he reminded her. "Poking around with sharp objects in all the stuff that makes me *me*. The last thing you need, when all of this is done, is to be looking after *two* drooling infants. And who knows what I'll look like, by the time they put me back together again."

It was, he knew, an unnecessarily graphic thing to say to a pregnant woman, but he allowed himself this indulgence.

"You think I care about that?" she snapped back. "As long as you're still with us?" But of course, that was the wifely supportive thing to say.

His family instantly forgave his recent transgression once he and Marla broke the news, though Trace himself didn't believe it was the tumor that had prompted his outburst at Quince's birthday party. He felt as though he was trading on his diagnosis, when he ought to be held accountable for what he'd done. Worse, though, was the newly guarded, almost reverential way he was being treated.

"I'm not made of glass," he reminded Aria irritably one afternoon when she'd ordered her boys to stop pestering him. He watched them through the sliding patio door, playing in their back yard. "I can still pitch a ball to them, or play catch."

"And you will," she said lightly. "Later on."

"I dunno. Seems to me they ought to be taking advantage now. While I'm still in my right mind."

It would have been the perfect opportunity for his sister to come back with something like *You were never in your right mind,* but instead she said, "You know, having a positive outlook is the most important thing when you're facing something like this. You read stories about it all the time."

"I wouldn't say it's *the* most important thing," he retorted. "Maybe the second-most."

"You know what I'm saying." She leaned forward, arms folded on the kitchen table, looking at him earnestly. "You have to tell yourself that you're going to get well. *I* know it; the rest of us know it. But you have to know it, too. You have to convince yourself."

"I'm doing what I can." He uttered a short laugh and raised his hands in a helpless gesture. "Trust me, nobody wants it more than I do."

As he stood, Aria drew him to her in a hug. It wasn't the perfunctory, this-is-what-people-do kind of embrace that she tended to dole out on birthdays, Christmas, and other dates of importance. It wasn't the clenching sort, either, where the other person can hardly breathe. It was insistent, though, her hand stroking his hair several times, then coming to rest on the back of his neck.

"That's not true, you know," she murmured. "However much you want it, the rest of us want it more." She stepped back then, studying his features so intently that it made him self-conscious. And she said something odd, something very un-Aria-like.

"You're the heart of this family," she told him. "If you go, the rest of us will never be able to hold it together."

"That's ridiculous," he retorted. "Nobody is that. Least of all me."

She did not contradict him, but instead called through the patio screen, "Richie? Lawrence? Come get your uncle. He's got just ten minutes for a game of catch, or whatever you want to play."

ARIA'S LAST REMARK HOVERED around him the rest of the day, a buzzing, nattering thought. That night, lying awake alongside Marla, he waited until the soft buzz of the snore she'd recently developed had taken hold, then slid away from her, raising the covers by inches until he could lower his legs to the floor, pausing whenever it seemed his movements might wake her.

But she was resolutely out, and he was able to stand and pad across the carpet, closing the bedroom door behind him. He took a wind-breaker from the hall closet and draped it over his shoulders before stepping out onto the balcony.

The night air was weighted and still, and the windbreaker unnec-essary, but he left it where it was and leaned against the brick railing, staring across the rooftops of the buildings opposite his own.

"God…" he began, "…or Bertie. Whoever's listening…"

He paused, half-expecting a response from someone. But there was only the far-off wail of a siren, some city vehicle responding to an emergency somewhere.

"I just want you… her… I want my *sister* to find whatever it was she was looking for. Whatever she needed that she couldn't find here, please let her find it wherever she is now."

Still nothing. There were only the sounds of the city going about its after-hours business. God was being His usual circumspect Self. And Bertie was evidently busy elsewhere. Still Trace remained as he was, the fingers of both hands threaded together, elbows resting over the balcony railing, while he contemplated the past and resolutely ignored the future.

WAS IT HIS IMAGINATION, or had his father aged a lot in just the last little while?

It was a phenomenon Trace had regularly come to associate with the nieces and nephews. He saw them often enough that he didn't no-tice the day-to-day changes until he happened to look a photo of one of them from only a year or so earlier; then he would be brought up short by how much a few months had altered their appearance: taller, slimmer, freckles faded, missing teeth grown in, hair longer, turned darker. But these were young humans cycling through the whirlwind of adolescence. Things slowed down considerably after individuals reached a certain age, or so he'd thought.

Trace tried not to stare too closely at the man by his side as they crouched on the roof of the work shed in his parents' back yard, nailing shingles over freshly laid tarpaper. But in sidelong glances, he took in the paper mache-like texture of the skin that sagged in pockets beneath his father's eyes and draped in folds from his neck and throat. It looked fragile enough to disintegrate under a stiff breeze. The corners of his mouth turned down in a natural sort of grimace that hadn't been there once upon a time. Even focused on a steady, repetitive task like this one, he moved hesitantly, picking up shingles, examining and then discarding them for others that, to Trace, looked identical. The sun beating down on their heads and necks was fierce, yet he apparently wasn't perspiring, while Trace's shirt was already plastered to his back. They'd been working in silence almost since Trace had first climbed up the ladder to join his dad, but now he blurted:

"Should you really be doing this?"

"Should you?" his father responded. "With... you know?" He gestured to his temple with one finger.

"They didn't tell me *not* to. I mean, nobody said anything about avoiding physical labor before the procedure." He leaned over the side of the building, studying the ground below them. "I realize this is just a dinky little shed, but it would still hurt a lot if you fell."

"Then I guess I won't." The older man pounded a nail into place with particular emphasis.

"Okay..." Trace swiped his brow with the back of one hand. "But promise me this is it. That you aren't going to re-roof the house when you're done here. It's one thing to tackle a ten-by-twenty-foot shack fifteen feet off the ground. You don't need to be up on anything bigger than this, especially something with those steep slopes."

"You sound just like your brother," his father retorted noncommittally.

"Ordinarily, I'd be insulted by a nasty crack like that. But, Pop, in this case, I'm squarely in Cord's camp." Trace gestured to the large square of tarp-covered materials sitting on one side of the carport. "You either way over-ordered the amount of shingles you need, or you have some other project in mind after this one."

"Did he send you around to nag? Is that why you're here?" Frank Bannerly's gaze swept over his son's polo shirt and slacks before he fitted another shingle into place. "Because you aren't exactly dressed for the work at hand."

"No. The nagging's a bonus. I came by for a visit, is all. I had some extra time after work and thought maybe you'd offer me a beer or something if I stopped in."

"Could be." His father shoved a stack of shingles toward him. "We'll see how you finish up here, first."

"I'VE HIRED A CREW to do the rest of the job," Frank assured him later as they sat in lawn chairs under the limbs of the elm tree just off of the back porch. "Even though it means cutting into you kids' inheritance."

"Well, it should pay off in the long run," Trace replied solemnly. "With a new roof, we should be able to unload the place for big bucks after you and Mom are gone." He clinked the base of his beer bottle against his dad's.

His father smiled, but otherwise left the remark untouched.

"Speaking of Cord," he said, although they hadn't been, not for several minutes, "I think I'll hire Zeke to help around here while they're putting on the new roof. You know, for things like stacking the old shingles once they come off. Just general toting and carrying. Stuff like that."

"I thought Zeke was bagging groceries this summer."

Frank's eyebrows rose and fell. "Guess you hadn't heard, what with your head thing and the brawl at Quince's party and all." He took a pull from his beer. "He got canned when the manager caught him and a couple of other kids passing around a joint on the loading dock behind the store."

"Oh." Trace ran one hand across the persistent itch on the back of his neck. He was just now realizing that he had sunburned himself while atop the shed. "The little shit."

"That's pretty much what his dad said, except in stronger terms."

Trace shook his head. "There are a lot of scary things about becoming a father. And if Cord is having difficulties with it, what hope is there for the rest of us?"

"Oh, it's not that big a deal. The kid smoked a little weed. It was a stupid move, right there at work. I'm not advocating that fifteen-year-olds ought to be doing it, but it's not the worst crime he might have committed."

Trace shifted uncomfortably in his chair, thinking back to his own discovery of Zeke's after-hours activities at the store.

"You're not excusing him, are you?" he asked. "Because what he did was still wrong."

"I'm just trying to keep it in perspective," his father said. "Especially since your brother is freaking out enough for all of us. He's worried that Zeke is heading down the same path Bertie took."

"But you're not?"

"It's early days yet. He's a good kid."

"Bertie was a good kid, too, Pop. I'm not sure that's enough to make a difference."

"Of course she was. I don't need you reminding me of that," he snapped. "Or reminding me just how scary it is, being a parent. I've been through it six times. I think I know a little something about it. Or at least realize how little any of us knows."

He gazed across the back yard, working his jaw back and forth. Trace gave his father's profile a sidelong glance. He was trying to think of what to say when the older man spoke again.

"But the difference between the two of them," he said, "Between Zeke and your sister, is that Zeke wants to be here; he won't admit it, maybe not even to himself right now, but he likes having a place in this big, crazy family. He recognizes his role here, and once he's done with this rebellious phase, once he's satisfied that he's proven he doesn't need any of us, he'll settle in and things will be fine."

He paused to take a gulp from his bottle and wipe his mouth with the back of his hand.

"Bertie, on the other hand… Bertie never found her place. And, who knows? Maybe we just didn't make one for her. And if that's the case, that's our fault, your mother's and mine. But don't you ever tell her I said that, you hear me?"

"Pop, it wasn't your…" Trace began, but his father cut him off.

"I've thought about it, you know? Going all the way back to when the two of you arrived. You were born early, remember? Way too early."

"No," Trace said, surprised. It was the first he could remember hearing of this.

"You were on ventilators for a while, the both of you. You got to come home after a few days, but they kept Bertie for two weeks. And one night, we got a call. The doctors were afraid they were losing her. By the time we got to the hospital, they'd had to resuscitate her. It was a terrible time, but they pulled her through. Finally we were able to bring her back here. But… I don't know… From the very beginning, it was as if she was trying to leave, trying to correct some mistake that only she recognized had been made. And once she was home, well, it seemed to me that it was too late."

"Too late?"

"Maybe if we'd been able to bring both of you home at the same time, things would have been different. But you were already here, you were… established. From her first day in this house, Bertie was having to catch up, to figure out where she fit in the scheme of things. And maybe she just never did."

"Pop…"

"It's just a theory, nothing more." His father dispensed a resounding belch and patted his stomach. "Something I occasionally find myself wondering about when I lie awake at night."

"We'll never know why she did a lot of the things she did," Trace said, "But I'm certain of one thing: Bertie never blamed you or Mom, not for a second. Her demons, whatever they were, came from somewhere else."

Without turning his head to look at his son, Frank lifted his arm and placed his hand on the back of Trace's neck.

He winced at the touch of his father's hand on his sunburnt skin, but allowed it to remain.

Chapter Eleven

On Friday morning, Mr. Sanders from the corporate office came to the store, bringing with him a young woman in a dark blazer and matching skirt.

"This is Carolee Olsen," he said, and she and Trace shook hands.

"Hello," he greeted her.

"It's so nice to finally meet you," she beamed, sliding the strap of her bag up her shoulder after taking back her hand. "Dalton has certainly been singing your praises. I've heard a lot about this location."

As she looked around, taking in the layout of the room, Trace's eyes moved to Mr. Sanders, whose own smile wavered slightly. The regional supervisor was a tall man with an exceedingly narrow face and shiny hair slicked back from his forehead. He reminded Trace of one of those character actors who frequently turned up in old black-and-white movies, playing a nervous store clerk or a supercilious waiter in a fancy restaurant—the type who might wind up with a pie in his face by the end of the scene.

"I guess that's good. We do what we can, my staff and me," Trace added pointedly, still scrutinizing the other man. He'd known about Sanders's visit this morning, but no mention had been made of anyone accompanying him.

Dalton cleared his throat before speaking.

"Why don't you just look around a little bit, Carolee, while Trace and I talk for a couple of minutes?"

"Oh, sure. Sure." She drifted to the front of the otherwise empty store in an obvious move to give them privacy. Mikayla hadn't arrived yet.

"Got any coffee, by chance?"

"Not yet, but I can make some," Trace said as they moved into the back office.

"No, no, that's all right."

Nevertheless, Trace stood at the counter, measuring grounds into a filter while the other man watched without voicing further objection. It gave both of them something to do as they gathered their thoughts. Trace poured water into the back of the machine, turned the switch to *on,* and then faced Sanders.

"I assumed Mikayla would be running the store while I'm… while I'm out of commission," he said, taking the offensive. "But that's not the case?"

"Oh. Well…" Sanders ran one hand over his shiny hair. "Mikayla is wonderful, of course…"

"Yeah, she is. And she's the assistant manager. Her goal has always been to have her own location. You know that, don't you?"

"Well, I suppose I had an inkling…"

"She's been working toward it for a long time. This would be the ideal way for you to see just what she's capable of, if you were to put her in charge."

Sanders sighed. "I understand that. But that's not how these things work, Trace."

"Don't they? I thought corporate's policy was to promote from within."

"It is, of course."

"But let me guess: You didn't just bring Ms. Carolee-What's-Her-Face along today because—"

"—Olsen. It's Carolee Olsen."

"You didn't bring her along today for a joy ride, did you? You're planning to give her this place."

"Nobody's giving anybody anything, Trace."

Trace took three cups from the overhead shelf and slammed them on the counter. "Do you take cream or sugar?" he snapped.

Sanders ignored the question. He stepped forward, placing a hand on Trace's shoulder.

"It's temporary. Just until you come back. And of course Mikayla will continue to be assistant manager. This could be a really good thing, you know. Each of them can learn things from the other. Ms. Olsen came to us through our recruiting program. She's been learning the ins and outs of the corporate office, and it's time to put her out in the field so she can get a taste of how things are on the front lines. And who better to teach her than someone like your assistant? They'll both come out of this stronger."

Trace clutched the edge of the counter, staring down at the coffee dripping into the pot and resisting an impulse to brush Sanders' hand off his shoulder. He'd engaged in enough physical demonstrations of annoyance lately.

"What I want to know," he said quietly, "Is whether Mikayla will come out of this with a better opportunity of being given her own store. Can you answer me that?"

"I can't, Trace. All I know is that it's not in the cards right now."

Sanders took back his hand and Trace faced him, leaning against the counter. "Then why should she be motivated to teach Ms. Carolee-Whatever how to run this place?" he demanded. "If there's nothing in it for her?"

It was apparent that he was close to exhausting the other man's good will. Sanders did not bother to supply Carolee's last name this time, but drew in a noisy breath through his nose. His pressed his lips together in a thin line in an effort to rein in his irritation.

"I couldn't quite say," he managed finally, in a pleasant-enough tone, but with a steely gaze. "Maybe to remain employed? But I guess that's a question you'll have to ask her."

"Right," Trace muttered. He turned back to the counter and snatched up the pot, even though a stream of brown liquid was still flowing into it. He filled the three mugs as coffee continued to drip onto the bare heating pad, spattering and hissing loudly. This was going to be a very strong brew, he realized with bitter satisfaction.

HE'D EXPECTED MIKAYLA to be furious upon learning the news. She arrived thirty minutes or so later and he introduced her to Ms. Olsen. She knew Sanders already. Trace explained the purpose of their visit, though she must have figured it out at once, just as he had. He watched her closely as explanations were officially given and also in the few minutes as she and Carolee conversed before their guests departed for the day, but she seemed thoroughly unruffled.

"I'm sorry," he told her as soon as they were alone.

"What for?" She seemed genuinely surprised. "This wasn't your idea, was it?"

"Of course not. I'd assumed that corporate would just let you run the place while I was out. Didn't you?"

They were in the back office where Mikayla was preparing her own cup of coffee. "What the hell happened here?" she demanded, staring at the puddle of brown liquid inching its way out from beneath the machine and dripping down the side of the counter. She took a step back, surveying the additional mess on the floor and then checked the bottoms of her shoes.

"I got impatient," Trace told her.

She regarded him through narrowed eyes. "Well, you better get to cleaning it up," she said finally. "Because I'm not going to."

"No, I don't expect you to…"

But she had already snatched a handful of paper towels and was tilting the coffee maker back to dab at the liquid gathered around its base.

"Don't," he said, stepping forward. "I'll do that."

"I never assume nothing." She squeezed the drenched paper towels over the sink and dropped them into the wastebasket before rinsing her hand under the tap. "I know how these things work. You don't need a college degree to do what needs doing around here, you and I both know that. The head honchos must know it, too. But they have a *system,* and if you're going to go to all the time and money to have a *system,* then you might as well follow it."

Trace crouched to wipe the streaks of coffee from the side of the counter. "You could run one of these places with your eyes closed, and do a better job than half the managers they've hired. You deserve to have your own store."

She looked down at him, one hand planted on her hip, the other holding her cup of coffee. "What you deserve and what you *get* are usually miles apart. You ought to know that about as well as anybody these days. How about you just worry about your own stuff right now and let the rest of the world sort out its own problems?"

She did not wait for an answer, but headed out to the front of the shop to greet the first customer of the morning.

This philosophical response was more troubling to him than if she'd gotten angry and stormed out. Mikayla wasn't the sort to internalize her emotions, and he suspected her offhand acceptance of this new development was in deference to his own situation. As the morning wore on, he came to another sobering realization: the corporate office was putting Carolee What's-Her-Face in place because they believed that even if he survived his surgery, there was a significant chance he wasn't going to be coming back.

He'd had those fears as well, but it was the first time he understood that others were actively taking steps to deal with whatever the outcome was going to be.

"I saw the flowers you sent my folks, and read your note," Jodi Piner-et said after settling opposite him and placing her order with the cock-tail waitress. "Both were lovely. Oh, and they asked me to give you this."

She wriggled sideways to dig in the large bag she'd swung across the cushions before climbing into the booth a moment earlier. She'd come from the last class of the day at her studio and wore a loose-fitting sweatshirt, despite the heat of a late August afternoon. Trace watched, fascinated, as she flicked her ponytail off her shoulder and continued to search the depths of the canvas tote.

"Here," she said finally, producing a crumpled slip of paper she slid across the table to him. "They don't want it."

It was the check that Trace had sent her parents to pay for the damage he'd caused at Quince's birthday party.

"No," he said weakly, but she swatted the word aside with a wave of her hand.

"You take it up with them, if you like. I've done my job as courier and you can leave me out of it from now on."

He let it remain on the table, studying it for a few seconds before continuing. "I appreciate you meeting me like this. Just the two of us, I mean."

"Sure. What's up?"

He looked up and was momentarily waylaid by her electric green eyes watching him.

"Well… you know. Just to say I'm sorry, after what happened. After what a douche I was a couple of weeks ago."

"You did that already. Over and done with," she pronounced firmly.

Their server was back with Jodi's beer and a large basket of onion rings.

"Another for you?" The waitress gestured to Trace's nearly empty glass. He started to decline, but Jodi answered for him.

"Yeah, he'll need one to help wash these down." She was swinging an onion ring around her index finger. "Plus, I'd feel conspicuous, drinking by myself."

As their server departed, Jodi bit into the golden coating and immediately began to fan her mouth with her free hand. "Oooh! Hot! Hot!" she declared.

"Well, it's probably directly out of the fryer; what did you expect?"

"I'm hungry," she retorted defensively. "I couldn't wait."

He watched, amused, as she chased the stinging bite with several gulps of beer. A trickle of foam slid from the lip of the glass and down her chin. She wiped it away with the heel of her hand.

"What?" she demanded, seeing his grin.

"I was picturing all those little girls you instruct, them seeing you right now. Mademoiselle Pineret, slugging a brew and chowing down on greasy junk food. Their idol, with ballerina slippers of clay."

"You think they don't show up for lessons all wired on sugar and soft drinks? That I don't have to spend ten minutes peeling them off the walls before I can teach them a thing?"

"I thought ballet dancers were supposed to be super-disciplined. I figured you'd sit here, nursing along a mineral water with lime, or maybe a glass of very dry white wine."

"You thought that, did you?" She nudged the basket of onion rings his direction. "And that all my students are girls, incidentally? You have a lot of faulty perceptions, it seems."

"Oh. I guess I... So you have boys, too?"

"Sometimes," she hedged. "Not right now, but there have been, in the past. So be careful with your blanket pronouncements."

"Sorry. And, speaking of sorry..."

"No, we're done with that. I'm not interested in another apology." She was serious now. As if to underscore her stance, she picked up the check he'd made out to her father and tore it in half. "That's what he would have done if you'd presented it in person, by the way. He'd say that accepting the money would be letting you off the hook way too easily. Better that you have to keep feeling bad about what you did."

"All right." He waited to continue until the waitress had brought his second beer and left again. "In that case, why did you agree to meet me?"

She looked surprised. "Why wouldn't I? You invited me. I like a drink after work now and then. Especially when someone else is paying."

Jodi laughed as she watched him process this.

"And I accepted because you're my boyfriend's brother. I'd like to get to know you better. To see what you're like when you're away from Quince."

"Well, better-behaved, usually. You'd probably already figured that out, though."

She nodded. "The same is true of him. It's easy to tell he's the baby of the family. He takes on a whole other persona when he's around the rest of you than when it's just the two of us, or a group of our friends."

Intrigued, Trace folded his arms and leaned forward, resting them on the table. "Really? Like how?"

Jodi considered this for a minute as she picked apart another onion ring with her fingers. "He's quieter. He becomes more serious away from you guys. And less competitive."

"Competitive? You think he's competitive around us?"

She nodded. "As if he feels he has something to prove. That you don't take him seriously. So he talks louder, faster when he's in a crowd of Bannerlys. And he does goofy things, like at your brother's barbecue earlier this summer, when he ran around squirting people with that water pistol and threw you in the pool. Like it's his way of saying, *I'm here, too. Don't forget about me.*'"

"I can't imagine any of us ever forgetting about him," Trace said dryly, lifting his mug to his lips.

"You disagree with what I said?"

He shook his head, returning his beer to the table. "I guess I just never thought of it from an outsider's point of view before. Someone not in the immediate crazy family, I mean," he added hastily, in case Jodi might take offense at being called an outsider. It intrigued him to consider for the first time how all of them must appear to someone who hadn't grown up in their midst. He made a mental note to ask Marla what her first impression of the Bannerlys, taken as a whole, had been.

"When there's six kids in a family, there's a lot of shouting and jockeying for attention," he added finally. "Nobody ever feels like they get their fair share of anything. And since Quince was the last to come along, I guess maybe he had to shout the loudest and the most often."

"And don't forget, everybody else is married," she reminded him. "That draws another line in the sand between him and the rest of you. I think he sometimes feels like he's still sitting at the kids' table."

Trace leaned back from the table, dropping his hands into his lap. "No, but…" He paused, studying the greasy folds of paper lining the basket of onion rings for a few seconds before lifting his gaze to meet

Jodi's. "Really?"

She shrugged.

"I guess I feel like everybody thinks I still belong at the kids' table, as well," he confessed. "Especially after what happened at the party the other night."

"He felt awful, you know. About the fight. He was so upset."

"I know. Everybody was. And I don't blame them."

"No!" Jodi leaned across the table to tug at his shirt sleeve. "Quince wasn't mad. Well, not after a little while, anyway. He was… he was scared, I think."

"Scared? Why?"

She shook her head. "I don't know, not for sure. He said he'd fucked things up, but he wouldn't say how. At first, I thought he meant he'd never forgive you, but instead… Instead, I think he was worried it was the other way around."

"Well, that's just… that's dumb."

"Is it?"

Trace looked down at the slender fingers still pinching the sleeve of his shirt.

"Wow," he said. "You're in this for the long haul, aren't you?"

"I think maybe I'm in love with him," Jodi confessed. She took back her hand, lifting it to brush a strand of hair from the side of her face. "Crazy, huh?"

"You don't know the half of it. But he's a good guy. A really good guy. Now, if you can just put up with the rest of us…"

"I'll take my chances," she assured Trace solemnly.

HE'D STARTED TO CORRECT Jodi when she'd referred to Quince as the only unmarried one. He'd been about to point out that Bertie had never gotten married, either. But then he changed his mind. Jodi had only recently come into the fold, and for her, for always, there would only be five Bannerly siblings. She knew about Bertie, of course, but only by association. Bertie was a memory, a topic of conversation, not an actual person to anybody that any of them would meet from now on.

"Get used to it," he told himself. His own unborn child wouldn't know her. Even for some of the younger nieces and nephews already here, his sister would fade in their memories, a shadow who populated only a few half-recalled experiences, someone the grown-ups mentioned occasionally, less real than somebody they'd see on television.

And for a second, she was there, sitting in the passenger seat alongside him as he drove home. Her fingers brushed the back of his neck, as tangible as Jodi's had been when they were touching his sleeve in the bar earlier.

"It's all right," Bertie assured him. "It is. It was my choice, after all."

Her smile was unwavering, even as he glared at her.

"What do you mean, *your choice?*" he demanded, his hands squeezing the steering wheel in frustration. "Was it on purpose? Is that what you're telling me?"

But she was gone already, putting in a fleeting appearance and leaving without explanation, as capricious in death as she had been in life.

"WHAT?" QUINCE STARED at him uncomprehendingly. "Now? You mean *right* now?"

"That's what I mean," Trace assured him. "I mean right now, right this minute, as in *get in, we're going.*"

He'd been idling at the curb in a no-parking zone for several minutes, running the risk of being ticketed, just to be sure he wouldn't miss his brother emerging from the bank where Quince was employed. Now a parcel delivery truck had pulled up behind them and its driver was laying on his horn to point out the fact that Trace was blocking access to his drop box. Additionally, rush hour traffic was whizzing past, mere inches from where Trace stood in the street, causing the back of his shirt to flap in its wake.

"Fine." Quince grimaced, but obeyed, yanking open the passenger door and ducking inside. Trace had to wait several more seconds for a gap in the oncoming barrage of cars to get his own door open wide enough to join him, and another full minute before he could pull away from the curb.

"Inconsiderate asshole!" someone yelled from behind them, probably the driver of the parcel truck.

"You're an idiot; you know that," his brother informed him. "You could have called me and saved yourself the near-death experience."

"And given you the chance to turn me down? No, sir."

The silence that followed assured Trace that that's exactly what he would have done.

"Just because I got in the car doesn't mean I'm going."

"Sure you are."

Quince tapped his chest. "I'm wearing a tie, dress shoes, and my best slacks. I'm not dressed for the amusement park. Plus, I have plans with Jodi tonight."

"No, you don't," Trace told him smugly. "Not anymore, you don't. And you can take off the tie. Everything else you have on is fine." Glancing in the rear-view mirror, he swerved across two lanes of traffic in order to make a left-hand turn at the next light and head for the on-ramp to the interstate. "She's the one who suggested this, and made sure you would think you had plans with her, so you'd be free for the evening. Call her, if you don't believe me."

"All right; I will."

Quince dug into his pocket for his phone and held it up to his ear after tapping the number. "Hey, it's me…" he began, and then fell silent, listening.

Trace kept his eyes on the road and his smile in check. Jodi wasn't giving his brother a chance to object to the change in plans.

"Yeah, but I thought… Weren't we… And I'm not dressed for… Well, then how about you…" Exasperated sigh. "Okay, fine. 'Bye, then."

He lowered his phone to his lap and chewed the inside of his mouth for a moment.

"All right," he said finally. "The two of you cooked this up together. But why? Why do you want to go to an amusement park in the middle of the week, and why do I have to come along?"

"Because I want to. And it's no fun to go by myself, and Marla's pregnant, so she can't ride anything."

"We have a bazillion nephews and nieces; isn't that what they're for? Doing stuff like this with?"

"You just answered your own question. There's a bazillion of them. Taking everybody would cost an arm and a leg, and if I just take one or two, I'd never hear the end of it from the rest of them."

Quince tucked his phone back into his pocket. "Does that mean you're paying my way?"

"I guess. If that's what it takes."

"That's what it takes. Plus, corn dogs and soft pretzels and anything else I want to eat."

Quince took Trace's non-response as acceptance of his terms. He was quiet for a moment, unknotting his tie and setting it in the console between the seats.

"Are... Are you sure it's okay?" he asked finally.

"Is what okay?"

"You. You know... Riding stuff. What if it... I dunno... jostles something? Knocks something loose, or makes it bump into something else?"

"Are you talking about the tumor?" Trace asked. When Quince didn't answer right away, Trace grinned. "You can say it, you know. Saying *tumor* doesn't change anything. Doesn't make it get any bigger or do anything it isn't doing already."

"Fine," his brother snapped. "*Tumor.* So, couldn't going on the Tilt-a-Whirl or the roller coaster or some of those upside-down things jolt your *tumor* or bang it against your eye, or your brain, or something? Because I'm not sure your brain was firing on all of its cylinders to begin with."

"Everything is fine, trust me. That sucker is wedged in there so tight that it's going to take scalpels and knives and maybe even a backhoe for the surgeons to dig it out of me next week."

Though, in fact, now that Quince had brought it up, Trace wasn't altogether sure his doctor would approve of what he was about to do. Quince seemed placated, however.

"Just so you know, if either one of us pukes on my shirt or my best pants, you're buying me new ones," he informed Trace.

Quince's initial reluctance vanished within minutes of them setting foot inside the park.

Trace had stopped for a second to look around at the garish neon affixed to every moving surface, casting their skin in shades of yellow, green, and orange. The smell of popcorn, the groan of grinding machinery, and the warm air of an early autumn evening combined to pull him back to when he was eight, ten, twelve, in this same spot. In the distance, the clacking sounds of cars mounting the wooden coaster tracks gave way to the roar of them plummeting down the other side, to the delighted screams of their passengers.

"Come on!" Quince snapped. "If we're going to do this, then let's do this! Let's go get in line for Sidewinder's Revenge!"

They rode the three roller coasters, two of them twice, and one of them three times. They ventured aboard the Octopus and the Scrambler and half a dozen other things that dipped and swirled and hurtled them against the unyielding sides of metallic cars and shoved safety bars painfully into their legs. Afterward, they sat at a table under a canopied awning to eat burgers and drink beer that was nearly as much foam as liquid.

And though they'd been on solid ground for a while, Trace was experiencing phantom motion that seemed to tilt the earth beneath his chair ever so slightly. It made him wonder for a second if perhaps it was possible, after all, to shake a tumor loose from its grip on a brain.

"You okay?" Quince asked, eying the french fry that Trace gripped between two fingers, just inches from his mouth.

"Yeah, fine," Trace assured him. He completed the fry's journey, chewing it and chasing its remnants with a gulp of beer. Wiping his mouth with the heel of his hand, he said:

"I would like it if you'd be the baby's godparent."

He had intended to lead up to this request with more finesse. But bringing it up as they'd jostled their way through crowds and into the queues for rides hadn't seemed right, either.

Quince was staring at him again.

"What baby? Your baby?"

"My kid, yeah. Who else's do you think I'd mean?"

"I don't know." Quince shifted his gaze, staring into the distance. He worked his lower jaw back and forth for a few seconds. "*Your* baby?" he said again, finally. "And me?"

"That's who I mean, yes."

"But why? I… I wouldn't be any good at that. Shouldn't you pick somebody with a track record? Like Aria, or Chase, or Sky?"

"I don't want them. I want you. Unless you'd rather not."

"I'm not saying that. I just… jeez." Quince leaned back, wiping his fingers on a paper napkin. "This is a person we're talking about, Trace. A small, helpless person. What if I do something wrong?"

"Of course you're going to do something wrong. You'll do a lot of things wrong. You think I won't? Or Marla? Or anybody?

"And you understand, don't you," he continued a second later, "that it doesn't exactly mean you have to raise him. Or her. You don't have to pay for the college education or anything. It just makes you the favored uncle, is all."

"Unless something happens to the both of you. Then I'm supposed to step in, right?"

"Well… right. But what are the odds of that? And if it did happen that way, you'd have Jodi to help you out. And Marla's sister Dana and their parents, as well as everyone on our side. You'd be fighting people off, I imagine, who'd insist on helping. But, look: I don't need an answer right now. You can think about it. And it's okay if it's something you don't feel like you can do. I understand."

"Of course it's something I don't think I can do," Quince announced firmly. "Look at me. Up until now, I haven't even been able to keep a houseplant going. But I don't need to think about it, Tracey. Yes, I'll be the godparent. Of course I'll take the kid if it comes to that. With or without help." He dipped one finger in his sudsy beer and flicked it at Trace. "Did you think you had to bribe me with a trip to the amusement park to sweeten the deal?"

"I figured it couldn't hurt."

"And Marla is actually okay with this arrangement?"

"Of course she is," Trace assured him. The truth was, although they had briefly discussed the idea of godparents, they hadn't settled on anyone yet. And though she might be somewhat miffed that he'd extended the offer without including her, she wouldn't fault his choice. It was largely symbolic, after all.

LATER, AFTER HE'D DROPPED Quince off outside his apartment building and was heading home, Bertie again appeared in the passenger seat next to him. Tonight she was wearing the plaid flannel shirt that he recognized as the topmost item from the stack of her belongings he and his sisters had retrieved from the apartment where she'd been crashing during her final days. Her wiry brown hair stuck out in tangled flyaways, and her fingers drummed on the knees of her jeans. This was the washed-out Bertie from their early twenties, the one showing up unexpectedly at the door or at his place of work, trying hard to look pulled-together, engaging in a few moments of polite chitchat before asking to borrow money. Perspiration would dot her forehead and she would flash a series of smiles that were more grimaces than anything else, somehow convinced that she was pulling off an air of normalcy.

"Oh, great," he greeted her. "It's Crazy-Bert."

"Shut up," she retorted. "I'm dead; what do I need with money or a fix? This just happens to be how you were thinking of me right now. If you don't like it, remember me some other way."

They drove in silence for a few seconds. Bertie began to grin, an authentic smile this time.

` "So, the baby bro is going to be your baby's godparent." She nudged Trace's arm. "I know why you picked him."

"Do you, now?"

"And I know why you took him to the amusement park tonight."

"Enlighten me, then."

She slunk down in the seat, planting both her feet against the dashboard. Trace started to order her to sit up once more, before he realized it didn't really matter.

Now Bertie seemed occupied with plucking at the front of her shirt, watching the fabric tent outward and then settle back against her chest, a maddening gesture, as useless as it was familiar.

"Here's why," she managed finally, in a sort of distracted tone. At last she smoothed the front of her shirt and turned to look up at Trace from her crouched-down position. "You're worried you're going to die. That you won't survive the brain surgery. Or that something will get jostled or somebody will slip, and they'll accidentally slice into something vital, and you'll come out a gibbering idiot."

"Fair enough." His hands gripped the steering wheel a little tighter.

"If that happens, then who better than our own Quince to educate the kid on who his dad really was? Who can fill in all the gaps better than he will?"

"So it's an ego thing," Trace conceded.

"Maybe. And why not? If you aren't there, your little snot-nosed brat is going to want some answers. Marla can't provide them all. But Quincey… well, Quince's been there practically from the beginning. He knows you, warts and all. And you know he isn't only going to share the good stuff. He'll spill it all."

"That's true enough."

"You trust him. More than any of the rest of them. Cord helped raise us. Aria made sure we had lunches when we headed out the door to school every day. But Quince is the one who'll make sure the kid knows the real you."

Trace nodded. He drew in a deep breath.

"So… you think I'm not going to make it, then."

"How the hell am I supposed to know that?" she raged. "Jeez, how many times do I have to tell you, asshole? I only know what *you* know! I'm not a fucking psychic, I'm just your dead sister!" She slammed her fist into the upholstery.

She didn't say anything more until Trace had pulled the car into the parking garage beneath his apartment building. He guided the vehicle into its parking space and killed the engine. They sat, listening to the measured tick of the cooling motor. Finally, he turned to her.

"Still here, I see. Was there anything else?"

Bertie lowered her feet from the dashboard to the floor and struggled up in her seat. She tugged down the front of her rumpled shirt and tucked some of her unruly hair behind one ear.

"You were trying to fulfill a promise. You didn't tell him that, but that's what you were doing tonight." She turned to him, her good humor restored. "I told you I knew."

"So, how was your grand adventure this evening?" Marla greeted him as he stepped inside the apartment. Not unlike Bertie had been in the car, she was slumped on the sofa, a bowl of rice pudding balanced on her rounded belly.

He threw himself down alongside her, wrapping an arm behind her head and kissing her sticky lips. "Grand, simply grand," he reported. "Thanks for letting me do it."

"You want some pudding?" Marla held out a spoonful in front of his face.

He waved it away. "I'm full of beer and carnival food crap."

"Delightful," she smirked. "What kept you, by the way? Quince called a few minutes ago to say thank you. He was surprised you weren't home yet."

He shrugged. "Just took my time, I guess. Didn't feel like going too fast, not after being on all those rides."

"Uh-huh." She inserted the spoonful of pudding intended for him into her own mouth. When she'd swallowed, she added, "So, he's pretty flattered about us asking him to be the baby's godparent."

"Oh." Trace's fingers squeezed her shoulder. "He brought that up, did he? I, uh, I'm sorry I didn't check with you first."

But she was smiling as she prodded the contents of the bowl on her stomach with the spoon. "It's fine. I was going to suggest it, anyway."

"You were?"

She laughed at the look of relief on his face. "Well, that we ask your brother and my sister to be co-godparents."

"We can do that. We can totally do that!"

Marla elbowed his ribcage. "Not that either of us is going to go anywhere."

"Of course not."

"So… why the amusement park? Why now? Was this like, your last hurrah or something, before the procedure next week?"

"Sort of." Trace took back his arm from around her neck. He took the bowl of pudding from her and set his hand on her rounded belly in its place.

"When I was eight or so, my folks were going to take the lot of us to Disneyland. We'd been planning it for months, especially Quince and me. We'd gotten a guidebook and maps, and we had a video from the library or someplace that we watched again and again. The whole thing was mapped out, the places we'd stop along the way, and the rides we were going to ride when we got there. And then, just days before departure, both Aria and Sky came down with mononucleosis. So everything got cancelled. I was disappointed, but Quince… he was devastated. I don't think I'd ever seen him cry like that, before or since. So I told him—promised him—I would take him there someday. On my honor, and everything. Except that I've never gotten around to it."

"And that's what tonight was about?"

"Well… kind of."

Marla laughed softly as she leaned her face into his neck.

"Sweetie, I hate to burst your bubble, but the local amusement park is in no way an acceptable substitute for Disneyland. I admire your good intentions, I guess, but they're pretty sucky."

"I know. It's the best I could do on short notice. It's really just a place holder," he acknowledged. "Until we can manage the real deal."

"Well, good. As long as you understand that."

Chapter Twelve

Zeke had been pacing back and forth across the living room. Finally he stopped, plunging his hands into his pockets and facing his uncle. "Life is fucked, you know? Life is just totally fucked."

Trace settled on the arm of the couch, a towel folded over one arm. "Yeah," he said. "A lot of people think that."

"And you don't?" Zeke fired back.

Trace ran his free hand up and down the leg of his jeans as he gazed through the sliding glass door leading out onto his apartment balcony.

"I've mostly been too busy to give it much thought," he said at last. "But, yeah. I guess there are those moments now and then when it seems that way. Why do you think so?"

The hands came out of the jeans pockets, flailing in the air.

"Oh, because of pretty much everything. School… Mom and Dad, mostly Dad. Nothing I do is right, according to him. He hates all my friends. I failed my driver's exam. All because of some dumb flashing light I was supposed to see. This girl, Tress, that I've kind of been seeing this summer, now she wants to go out with another guy who's a total tool. Then there's *you*, with that thing you've got going on now."

"Oh, yeah. This thing of mine."

"So, you see? Fucked. Everything is all screwed up."

"Sucks to be you, I guess."

Zeke grinned. "Shut up."

"Plus, of course, some asshole fired you from the shipping store awhile back."

"Oh, that was two whole jobs ago," Zeke said unselfconsciously. "I'm not even mad about that any more. The grocery store paid way better than you did."

Trace pondered his response. He wasn't in a mood to suggest that most of his nephew's misfortunes were of his own making. No doubt Cord had done this already. And, in truth, the memory of his own adolescence wasn't so far removed that he couldn't recall holding a steadfast belief that the world was deliberately allied against him. It didn't particularly matter how well-ordered or how haphazard the upbringing a person might have; the two of them were proof of that.

But Zeke mistook his silence to mean something else.

"I guess you think I'm a screw-up, too," he sulked. "Fine. That's what I am."

The tone was so self-pitying that Trace had to fight back a laugh. "You've got it about halfway figured out, buddy-boy. We're *all* screw-ups, across the board. You. Me. Your folks. My folks. And not just our family; I'm talking everybody. Your teachers, your bosses. Well, your *ex*-bosses, I guess I mean. That girl Tress. And the tool she wants to go out with now. Screw-ups. Most of us just get better at hiding it, the further along we go. That's where you're falling down. You're still lousy at concealing the evidence. But you'll get better. That's what they call *growing up*."

He stood, unfolding the towel draped across his leg and shook it out with a snap.

"So, are we going to do this thing, or what?"

Zeke followed him out through the sliding door onto the terrace, momentarily at a loss. He stood to one side, the clippers dangling at his side, watching while Trace pulled out a chair from the patio table and sat down, draping the towel around his neck and shoulders.

"You really believe that?" Zeke asked finally. "You think Gram and Gramps are screw-ups? And my dad? You even think your brother is a screw-up?"

"My parents? Oh, yeah, most definitely, dude. Most days, they don't even bother to hide it. Now, Cord, on the other hand... Well, it's harder to point to any concrete evidence, but I have to believe it's there, don't you?"

"I... I don't know."

"Yeah, I know." Trace nodded. "He's really good at concealing it. I've been looking for a lot of years now, and eventually, I'm going to turn up something. It's been my mission for a long time."

"But why?"

"You think you're the first? Your father is seven years older than I am. He raised me as much as anyone did. I had a big dose of the same stuff you're getting. In fact, it's been distilled way down for you. One time, when I was ten or so, I was messing around in the yard or something, and he told me to get inside and do my homework. I told him I didn't have to, because he wasn't the boss of me. So he picked me up, carried me into the house and into the bathroom, turned me upside down, and gave me a swirly. You know what those are?"

"Yeah." Zeke's eyes were wide. "Did he get in trouble?"

"I went running to your grandma, head dripping wet, and told her what he'd done. She looked at me, trailing water all over the floor, and asked if the toilet bowl had been clean when he dunked me. I told her I thought so, and she said, 'Well, consider yourself lucky, then.'"

"Gram said that? And then what?"

"And then nothing."

"I… I don't believe you. That never happened."

"If you say so," Trace said. "So, let's get started. I'd like to have this done before Marla gets home."

THEY WERE DRINKING COKES on the terrace when Marla walked in thirty minutes later. The evidence had been swept up into a neat pile to one side with the broom resting against it. She stopped on the threshold of the sliding glass door and stared. Trace raised his drink in salute. Zeke, looking cowed, shrank back a little in his seat.

"You…" she began softly. "You shaved off all your hair."

"Well, technically, Zeke did it," Trace informed her. "I just sat there." He shot his alarmed nephew a malevolent smirk.

Marla lowered the bag she'd been carrying to the floor.

"I thought Zeke was sitting out here with a stranger, at first. I just saw your back. I didn't even recognize you. Until…"

"It's weird, I know." Now Trace's heart was beginning to thump harder. His wife suddenly looked so vulnerable that he wondered if he should have given her some warning about what he'd been planning. He set his Coke on the table and got to his feet. "But we knew this would have to happen, didn't we? I figured I might as well get it out of the way."

"I… I guess." She took a step forward and then stopped again. He watched her eyes travel from his face to the top of his skull and then back again. "But why now? The surgery isn't for two more days."

"I figured I might as well start getting used to the look. Plus, I thought it might be easier—on you—if we did it when you weren't around. Did… Did you want to watch? Or do it yourself?"

"I don't know." Her voice still had a faraway quality, as though she was commenting on a scenario that hadn't actually happened yet.

Trace reached for her hands. He threaded his fingers through hers on one, and placed the other against his face.

"I'm sorry if I upset you."

"You didn't upset me. Not… not exactly." Her eyes were suddenly brimming, and he awaited with dread the tears he assumed would be spilling down her cheeks at any second.

"I mean, yes, you did. A little," she continued. "Well, no, not *you*. Or you either, Zeke." She looked at Zeke and managed a smile. The teen's shoulders sagged in relief. "What upsets me—what frightens me, actually—is, now the whole thing seems real. Before, it was just a scary idea like the monster you think might be hiding in your closet. But now… now, the door is opening, and…"

"…and the monster is coming out," Trace finished for her. "So it really was in there, after all. It wasn't just your imagination."

She took her hand from his cheek and placed it tentatively on the top of his head, moving it back and forth.

"It feels so strange."

"It feels strange on this end, too."

"Your head is so warm."

"And your hand is cool. It feels kind of good, actually. Sort of like a massage."

Now Marla was plucking at bits of stubble. "There are little tufts here and there. Where the hair is longer than in other places."

"You'll have to talk to my barber about that."

"Hey," Zeke protested. "I did the best I could. I've never given anybody a haircut before. And anyway, you've got bumps on your head. They made the clippers bounce."

"He's right; you do," Marla concurred. "You've got kind of a lumpy head." As if to demonstrate, she pressed her thumb against several places on his skull. The tears that had seemed imminent moments before were gone now.

"Hey!" Trace retorted in mock indignation. "The shears are still sitting right here. Suppose we scalp the both of you as well, and then we can determine just who has the most beautiful bald head. It might turn out that mine is much better looking than either of yours."

"Yours is just fine," she assured him. "Lumps and all."

"And hey, look at it this way," Zeke added, "The next time anybody tries to give you a swirly, they won't have much to work with."

In the middle of the night, Trace woke to the sensation of a hand stroking his head once more.

"What're you doing?" he mumbled, rolling to face his wife.

"Sorry, I woke you," Marla whispered. Her fingers were tracing small circles just above his ear.

"S'aright." He cleared his throat. "Like I said earlier, it feels good. Different. I've never had bare skin there before."

She was frowning slightly, he noticed.

"Something wrong?"

She shook her head. Her fingers remained in that same spot, and he realized abruptly what she was doing.

"Can you feel anything?" he asked. "Like a different kind of bump or something?"

"No. I'm not even sure if I'm feeling in the right spot."

"Me, either. Plus, I don't think you could feel it through my thick head, anyway."

"I guess not." She slid her hand over his crown, index finger probing. She smiled. "You've got a scar right there. A sort of wrinkled valley, from the skiing accident last spring. I noticed it earlier, when you were brushing your teeth."

"And I guess now I'm going to have another. One that will put that one to shame." He considered this for a few seconds. "I hope the hair will grow back. Where they open up my skull. I hope it doesn't, like, kill the follicles or something."

Marla tilted her forehead against his on the pillow.

"I don't care. As long as they fix whatever's wrong in there and you're still with us, I don't care how awful it looks."

Trace pulled her hand from his head and kissed her fingers.

"I sort of wish you hadn't used the word *awful*," he told her.

He had a steady stream of visitors the following day, a few friends and most of the family members, all affecting a casual and lighthearted demeanor, as though they had stopped by to see him off on an ocean cruise. Trace's new look provided an excellent distraction and topic for conversation.

"Remember when you guys were sophomores, and Bertie got that mohawk?" Sky reminded him. She'd been surveying his patchy scalp with a critical eye. "What's weird is, I guess I never actually realized how much the two of you looked alike, until just this minute."

"Oh, my," his mother remarked upon her arrival. "It's *your* head, after all, I realize," she said, as if this had been nothing more than an arbitrary fashion statement on his part. "But don't you think this is a little extreme?" She turned to her husband for validation. "Don't you think it's a little extreme, Frank?"

Trace's dad pursed his lips in the standard Bannerly-contemplative way. Trace found himself shifting uncomfortably under their continued scrutiny.

"I'm remembering now we thought his head was way out of proportion to the rest of him when he was a baby," he declared finally.

"Oh, that's right. Sort of like one of those bobble-head figurines."

ZEKE, VISITING AGAIN, THIS time with his sister Lisa and their parents, exhibited a newfound pride in his work.

"He picked me to do it," he announced. "I thought he was crazy, but he just handed me the clippers and said to go for it, so I did."

"Was it hard?" Lisa asked. Her mouth still hadn't entirely closed since she'd first laid eyes on the new Trace.

"Not really," her brother said. "Those things just plowed right along. It hardly felt like they were cutting anything at all."

"I'm not talking about *you*," she told him. She looked at her uncle. "Was it hard to get it all taken off? To know you were going to be all bald when you were done?"

"I didn't even give it much thought," Trace said honestly. "It was just one more thing to check off the to-do list. And I figured, why do it at a barber's or a salon? It's not like I was going for style."

Lisa was shaking her head. "I couldn't do it. Not in a million years. You're so brave."

"Bravery has nothing to do with it," Trace laughed. He squeezed her shoulder.

"Of course you could do it," Leslie informed her daughter. "If it's what would make you well again." She looked at Trace. "And you *are* brave, by the way."

"I'd shave your head for you, Lisa," Zeke interjected helpfully. "I think I'd be pretty good at it, now that I know what I'm doing. Hey! Maybe that's what I want to be… a barber for cancer patients!"

"You're not getting anywhere near my hair, ever!" To underscore the point, Lisa flipped her hair over her shoulders and took a step away from her brother. "I'd rather die than get it all cut off!" Then, realizing what she'd just said, she looked at Trace and then at each of her parents in horror.

"I… I didn't mean… I was just…"

"How about this, then?" Trace knelt in front of his niece. "If it looks like mine has trouble coming back after the operation, could I just have some of yours? Would you grow it out so there'd be enough to make a wig for me?"

Mouth quivering, she nodded emphatically. He tugged on her bangs.

"We're good, then."

Cord had been quiet through all of this. Trace figured the man was simply being his usual stoic self, but as he got to his feet, he felt a hand grip his shoulder. He turned to find his brother frowning at him.

"There were times, growing up, I wasn't too sure about it," Cord told him, "but you've turned out all right."

Trace grinned. "Don't go getting all sentimental. It sort of scares me," he said, only half joking. He started to turn away, but the hand on his shoulder pulled him back.

"I'm going to be there tomorrow. Right outside in the waiting area, with Marla. As long as it takes."

"That could be awhile," Trace cautioned him. He tilted his head. "Depending on what they find inside here. It could be twelve hours or more."

"As long as it takes," Cord repeated firmly, shaking Trace's shoulder. His voice was low and hoarse. Lowering his hand, he turned away abruptly, leaving Trace staring after him.

Of the entire family, he wouldn't have pegged his steadfast big brother as the one who'd cry first.

"I WASN'T SURE WHETHER I should bring the boys over," Aria said. "But Pete thought it was a good idea. He said we can't be shielding them from *everything*. He says I'm too sheltering sometimes."

"He's right; you are."

The boys in question, Lawrence and Richie, stood on the far side of the room, surveying Trace with identical wary expressions. Neither of them had spoken since setting foot in the apartment. He beckoned to them.

"Come on over. It's still me; just with less hair. Hey, you want to rub my head? It feels sort of gross, but it'll bring you good luck. Come on!"

Aria rolled her eyes, but the invitation, phrased like that, was too tempting to resist. His nephews approached the couch and Trace obligingly lowered his head.

"What kind of good luck?" Lawrence asked. He'd dabbed at Trace's scalp experimentally and was now studying the palm of his hand.

"I don't know. How about chocolate good luck? There are peanut butter cups on the bottom shelf of the refrigerator."

"One apiece; it's nearly dinner time." Aria glared at her brother as the boys made a beeline for the kitchen. "You know we don't let them have candy except on the weekend and special occasions."

"I'd think this qualifies as an occasion, if anything does. Now you." He seized her hand and placed it atop his head. "But only one peanut butter cup for you, too."

"Oh, honestly." But she didn't immediately remove her hand. "It doesn't feel gross," she commented after a minute. "Just strange. And by the way, I wouldn't make a habit of giving little boys candy to get them to feel your head. That's not the kind of story you wanting getting around."

"Listen to you," Trace grinned. "You *do* have a sense of humor, after all."

The kids were back, clutching their peanut butter cups.

"Mom says you have a bad thing in there," Richie commented, gesturing with a chocolate-smeared finger. "And that doctors are going to go up inside your head and get it out. How will they do that? Do they use a laser beam to open up a hole?"

"I'm not sure," Trace admitted. The intriguing notion of lasers had not occurred to him. It sounded a lot less brutal than what he expected they were going to be using. "I guess they'll be doing whatever works best."

"And then will you be okay again?"

Trace glanced at Aria, who was twisting her fingers in her lap and avoiding his gaze. He considered his brother-in-law Pete's comment about shielding the kids.

"Not exactly," he told his nephews. "Whatever happens, whatever they have to do in there, I'll be even better than okay. Because then, we'll know for sure what the bad thing is. Even if it means things are different afterward. Understand?"

They didn't, he knew, but they nodded anyway.

He smiled at his sister, who responded with an unconvincing smile of her own.

"WE'LL GIVE YOU JUST a couple of minutes," a member of the surgical team told Trace and Marla. "And then we need to get you in there."

She stepped out into the corridor. For a few long seconds, they both simply watched the door close behind her, saying nothing. At last Marla faced him.

"Your head is shiny now."

"They shaved it all the way down. So that there's no risk of infection. From, you know, stray hairs."

She nodded. "And they've made marks. Like, with a felt tip pen or something."

"That's the treasure map," he quipped. "Telling them where to dig."

"Don't! Please, just… don't. I can't listen to you be funny right now." She settled with some difficulty into the chair alongside his bed and lifted his hand in hers. "You know what this is, don't you? What they're doing? They're giving us this time to say good-bye. Just in case."

Trace stroked her fingers with his thumb. "And is that what we want to do?"

Marla didn't look at him. "You're going to come through this," she declared, although she sounded anything but certain.

"I think we should," he told her. "We tell each other goodbye when we leave for work in the morning."

"That's different."

"Is it? Isn't there always a chance—a little one, anyway—that any goodbye will be the last one? Isn't that why we all do it, just so that, if anything *does* happen, we don't have to say later, *I just wish I'd told him—or her—goodbye that time?*"

"Well, that's a pretty morbid point of view."

Trace rolled on his side and pressed her hand to his lips. "Just in case, on the very slim chance that I'm unable to convey this personally when the time comes, I want you to tell our kid this: *Be brave, be kind to smaller children and animals, and always do what your mother tells you to, except for finishing your vegetables. When it comes to those, you have my permission to hide them in your napkin when she isn't looking.*"

The corners of her mouth twitched.

"Asshole. You *would* take an emotionally charged moment, and make it even more difficult to let go of you."

He grinned and grasped her hand even harder. "Oh, I'm not letting go, I promise."

But when the nurse and orderlies returned a moment later, he did.

Chapter Thirteen

Oddly, the fear that had been a constant companion for some time deserted him now. As they wheeled his gurney through the corridor, bearing him head-first toward the operating room, his gaze drifted from the ceiling lights flowing by so rapidly to the faces of the people gripping the railings on either side of his bed. Their expressions were impassive until they saw him watching, and then they smiled. The floor was level, he knew, yet it felt as though he was lying atop a Flexible Flyer, careening down a sledding hill with no idea of where he was headed, yet confident that it was safe to relax and just enjoy the ride. He'd surrendered total control, and whatever was going to happen was out of his hands. It seemed like an unbelievable luxury.

"The hard part is over," he told his green-garbed chauffeurs. "For me, anyway."

Chapter Fourteen

Trace's son Jack—they'd picked the name shortly after learning Marla was pregnant, but hadn't told anyone until later—was the first grandchild to break the Bannerly mold... somewhat. His hair was brunette, darker even than his mother's. His eyes—a compromising turquoise color—were inherited, as best anyone could speculate, half from his grandmother Karen, whose were blue, and the other half from Marla, whose were green. But his nose was narrow and pointed and freckled, and his hands large and fingers thick, just like those of all his cousins. And when he smiled, he reminded people so much of his father that, caught off-guard, they would freeze, spellbound for a second or so.

Jack's older sister Sarah had not just the nose and the freckles and thick hands, but the copper-hued Bannerly eyes and hair, besides. Still, she was resolutely her mother, with perhaps a little of her mother's sister Dana tossed into the mix. She was bold and forward-thinking, knew what she wanted, and worked doggedly to achieve it. She was the apple of her grandparents' eye—Marla's parents, that is, not Trace's—and a more-than-willing co-conspirator, colluding with Grandpa Meacham on summer visits to North Carolina. In fact, it was she with whom Meacham was finally able to experience tandem parasailing, when she was fourteen and he seventy-something.

Jack was whom Trace might have been, raised in a household with just one sibling and sterner parental guidance. Quiet and introspective, he said and did everything at his own measured pace, and was pronounced by his sister to be a nerd. She wasn't entirely wrong. He liked superhero movies and science-fiction stories, and seemed at a loss to find common ground with his peers and cousins. No one was particularly impressed by his wealth of knowledge on topics ranging from Tolkien novels to the properties of black holes and how often the latter term was inappropriately used by people who ought to know better.

His parents had long since ceased to be intrigued or puzzled by the disparities in their offspring, or even to take notice. It was a matter of rote to occasionally rein in Sarah or to encourage Jack to pull his nose out of a book or a video game. Neither had presented especially daunting parenting challenges so far, though friends and relatives with older kids sometimes issued the vaguely threatening prognostication, "Just wait."

"We try to learn by example," was Marla's answer to those advice-givers who'd dealt with teenaged pregnancies, runaways, rehab facilities, arrests, or just plain estrangements. Some of these had occurred within the immediate family, making a diplomatic response all the more critical.

As nervous as he'd been about taking responsibility for a new life unleashed upon the world, the uncertainty had fallen away the moment the doctor had lifted his newborn daughter into Trace's arms. Fear was still there, compounded a hundredfold, in fact, since all at once the earth seemed like a barbaric landscape filled with dangers he would have to hold at bay for however many years he would be this child's father. But there was determination, as well, to live up to the task. And by the time Jack arrived, two years later, Trace felt as if he almost had a solid foothold on the parenting-wall.

MONTHS HAD GONE BY following the surgery without an appearance by Bertie, nearly convincing him that her post-funereal visits really had been nothing more than a by-product of the tumor. Until one day she was back again. He was alone in the apartment—well, except for the baby, whom he'd just put down for a nap. Marla was at a yoga class, striving to lose some of the accumulated pregnancy weight, and Trace was standing in the kitchen, drinking orange juice out of the carton, when he turned to find his sister leaning against the counter, hands plunged into the pockets of her jeans, watching and smiling. He choked just a little and a trickle of juice ran from the corner of his mouth and off his chin, dripping onto his t-shirt.

"I don't fucking believe it," he greeted her, wiping his face with the back of his hand. He set the carton on the table.

She scrunched her nose. "It smells like poop in here."

"It smells like poop everywhere. Everywhere I go, even when she isn't with me, I smell it. It's infested my clothes. The walls, the furniture. People in stores or on the streets pass me and they frown and give me a wide berth. I want to tell them it's not me; I didn't crap my pants, I just have a nine-month-old who did. And when it isn't coming out one end, it comes out the other. Used to just be formula or a sour milk kind of smell. Lately, it's other stuff, too. Mashed pears, and strained turkey. Sometimes there's stuff in her upchuck I swear she never ate to begin with."

"And who says parenting isn't a barrel of laughs?" Bertie pushed away from the counter and crossed to stand just in front of him. She extracted one hand from a pocket and raised it as if to touch his face. Her fingers paused just inches away from his ear. "Look at you," she added softly.

"Yeah, look," he grunted.

"You look the same. Almost."

Trace reached around her to pick up the orange juice. He put it back into the refrigerator and closed the door. "That's what everybody tells me. Frankly, I don't see it."

"Oh, very droll. They didn't take out your sense of humor, anyway."

"No, just a big old ugly mass. Well, not that big, actually. Pretty small, in fact. As worked up as everyone had gotten about the whole thing, I figured it was going to be the size of a tennis ball back there. More like a grape, it turns out."

"Did they let you see it?"

Trace shuddered. "God, no!"

"I bet they would have. If you'd asked. It was yours, after all. If it had been me, I would have asked if I could keep it."

He pulled out a chair and sank into it. "Well, you should have dropped by, in that case. I'm sure you could have gotten a peek. Sometimes I forget just how weird you could be. And where the hell have you been, by the way? It's been a year."

"Beats me. Not here, is all I know." She leaned over him, looking down at the side of his head. "I guess I haven't been on your mind much lately. Wow, that's a hell of a gouge."

"Yeah. I try to comb my hair over it, but I don't think I'm fooling anyone except for myself."

"I like the glasses. They make you look..."

"Studious?" he suggested.

"No..."

"Intelligent?"

"No, not that, either. ...Fatherly! Yeah, that's it. They've disguised that baby face of yours. You *look* like someone who would have kids. Or someone who would teach a really boring subject in school."

Trace used the knuckle of his index finger to push the glasses back up the bridge of his nose, a gesture he'd become practiced at performing. "I'm getting better at judging distances, but I'm not perfect. You saw the near miss with the orange juice."

Bertie settled in the chair alongside his and leaned forward, studying him earnestly. "But you see okay out of your left eye, don't you?"

He nodded. "It's a depth perception problem. Half the time when I reach for something, I'm either grasping at empty air, or like a minute ago, bumping into it. The glasses are just helping one eye do the job of two."

She was still peering close. "You can't really tell," she said after a few seconds' inspection. "They both look the way they always have."

"Small victories," he smiled. "I'll take what I can get. On the list of things they said might be an outcome of the surgery, losing sight in the eye was one of the more alarming ones, but when you stack it up against death, it loses some of its intensity."

Now Bertie leaned back in her seat. "It should have been me, don't you suppose? Hell, if I was going to die so young anyway, why didn't whoever's in charge of these things just put the tumor in me? It wasn't like I was going to go out and do great things with my life. It should have been me, instead of you."

Trace drew in a long breath before answering.

"You can't think that way, Bert. You can't. Who's to say what you might have done, if you'd gotten clean and stayed that way? And anyway, the jury's still out on me. It's not like I've done anything so special with mine."

But without being consciously aware of it, he glanced to his right, the direction in which, two rooms over, his infant daughter was sleeping.

His sister smiled. "You can't tell me it hasn't gone through your mind, though. A few times: If Bertie was going to die anyway, why couldn't *she* have had the cancer?" And when he didn't respond right away, or meet her gaze, she laughed. "It's all right. You think I wouldn't have felt that way, if our positions were reversed? It's okay if you thought that, Tracey. I'm dead. It takes a lot to offend me these days."

"Well, good to know. I don't suppose dead people are willing to change diapers, in that case?"

"Some might. I wouldn't have done it when I was alive, so I'm not going to start now."

"WHAT DO YOU SUPPOSE constitutes *doing something with your life?*" he asked Marla later. They'd finished dinner and Trace was wiping down the counter and stove with a dishcloth while Marla sat at the table, cradling the sleeping Sarah in her arms. She looked up at him, amused.

"Where did that come from?"

He shrugged. "It's just been on my mind this afternoon, is all. Are we here to make a difference? Is that what we're supposed to do while we're on this planet?"

She looked at him earnestly for a few seconds before responding. "Is this the start of your midlife crisis? And if so, aren't you a little young to be embracing it?"

He draped the dishcloth along the edge of the sink and rinsed his hands under the tap, then pulled out a chair and sat opposite his wife and baby daughter. He rested his folded arms on the table.

"I think it's more the outcome of a near-death experience. A really delayed reaction to one, I mean. Nothing's happened lately, don't worry."

To this, Marla had no response. She continued to look at Trace expectantly. He took a deep breath and said:

"Bertie dropped by this afternoon. Before you got home from yoga."

"Ah." Marla clasped one of Sarah's tiny hands between her thumb and forefinger, massaging it gently. "I see. It's been quite a while, hasn't it?"

The whole account of Bertie's visits had come to light in the early days of Trace's recuperation. Perhaps it was the combination of the anesthetics leaving his system and the relief he'd felt at waking up at all that had prompted it, but his guard had been lowered enough to disclose details of the experiences to Marla and visiting family members. Reactions, not unexpectedly, had been mixed.

Trace nodded. "It's been a year or more since I've seen her."

"Did she come to meet Sarah? It's about time. Past time, in fact."

"Well, she did comment on how the place stinks of baby poop."

"That sounds about like your sister. And?"

"She… She asked if I'd ever wished that it had been her, instead of me, who…" he gestured to his head. "…You know."

"Oh. And what did you say?"

"I told her of course not." Trace considered this for a moment. "There were times when I thought, *Why me*, but I don't think I ever thought, *Why couldn't it have been somebody else, instead.* Not Bertie, or anybody, for that matter."

"I did." The words were spoken so softly he wasn't entirely sure he hadn't imagined them. He looked across the table. Marla's head was bent over the baby's. She continued to press Sarah's impossibly tiny fingers between her own.

"When… when I was most frightened, in the wee small hours when it's dark and quiet, and everything seems intimidating and insurmountable, I would lie in bed and look over at you. At your silhouette in the darkness. I'd watch your chest rising and falling with every breath, and think, someday, someday *soon*, it could stop, if things went wrong. And how could such a thing happen, just when our lives were underway. It just didn't seem fair. And then, I would think… I'd think about…"

Trace reached across the table and clasped her wrist with his hand. "It's okay."

Marla shook her head. "I hated myself for wishing your illness on somebody else. But I went on wishing it anyway."

He shook her wrist gently. "So what?"

She looked at him then, eyes glistening.

"Bertie said the same thing," he continued. "That it might as well have been her who'd gotten my little *gift*, instead. So, you both wished a dead girl had maybe died for a different reason than the one she did. I don't think that's much of a sin."

"It *feels* like one."

"Well, Bertie absolves you of it, then."

Marla made a noise that sounded like a small laugh, or she might have just been clearing her throat. "I'm going to put the baby to bed," she said, boosting herself up from her chair.

Trace was on the patio when she returned, watching darkness settle over the city. She nudged his leg to one side in order to claim a corner of the chaise lounge where he was lying.

"It's not that I'd given up Bertie as a lost cause," she said. "I kept hoping she'd eventually get her act together." She looked over her shoulder at Trace. "I hope you know that."

"We all did." He stroked her back. "Wasn't the phrase that we kept passing around—something like, *If only she'd get cleaned up, she could do something with her life?*"

Marla nodded, then a thought occurred to her. She swiveled on the chaise so that she was facing her husband. "That's what you said, at the start of all this. You asked me what I thought constituted that exact thing. Doing something with your life. And then we got off-topic."

"Not really. It all ties in. I think the presumption—for some, anyway—is that I'm likely to do more with mine than she ever managed with hers. But I have to wonder… who decides these things? What, exactly, are any of us supposed to accomplish? There are the obvious things, of course: invent something that benefits mankind, or find a cure for something, or commit an act of heroism that saves lives. A few people get to do that stuff. But how about the rest of us? I get the feeling that, for the majority of people, it's mostly just not wreaking too much havoc while we're on this planet." He tapped the center of his chest. "I manage a shipping store. I make sure that people have tape and boxes when they want to send something somewhere. I pay taxes, and I make a real effort not to break any of the major rules while driving a car. Is that really all it takes?"

"You have a wife and a daughter who depend on you," Marla reminded him.

"For which I am more grateful that you can possibly imagine. But let's face facts: anybody with a functioning penis and a heterosexual inclination can manage that. You get my drift, don't you?" he added hastily, feeling the muscles of her back tense beneath his massaging fingers.

"I suppose," she said, shrugging. "When it comes to the concept of doing something with your life, then Sarah and I are a ways down your list."

"You're at the top of my personal list, you know that. I just wonder, sometimes. Was I supposed to wake up after the surgery with a newly defined sense of purpose? Or, no pun intended, a new way of looking at things?"

"Or maybe," Marla said, without turning to look at him, "All you were supposed to do was to wake up. As far as most of us were concerned, that was enough."

Trace returned to the shipping store four weeks after his release from the hospital. He was still on medical leave, with no official time designated to resume work. But the maddening inactivity of staying at home all day, and a curiosity to see just how the business—and Mikayla—were faring, prompted an early visit. He wore a baseball cap pulled low, covering some of the puckered scarring on his scalp, diminishing the severity of his appearance. Still, the skin surrounding the incision had remained white and showed through his returning hair like a ghostly beacon.

"Good Lord," Mikayla had remarked upon his entrance, though she had seen him in the hospital when half his head was still swathed in bandages and his face had a sunken, withered appearance.

Carolee Olsen, who hadn't seen him since before the operation, was nevertheless warmer in her welcome. "Trace—Mister Bannerly. What a nice surprise!" She had blinked away her initial startled expression so swiftly that it might not have been there at all.

"Just *Trace*, please," he'd assured her. "I thought I'd come by for just a few minutes. I don't want to disrupt the work flow."

"Any time. It's good to see you." She was, he realized, using the inflated tone of someone talking to an elderly or infirm person, as if she wasn't entirely certain the message was getting through. "How are you doing? You look great!"

A disparaging sound slipped through Mikayla's closed lips, indicating that this opinion might not be unanimously shared.

"How did you get here?" she demanded. "Did you drive?"

"I did." He refused to relinquish his smile, despite her unwavering scowl. "One-eyed people are allowed to be behind the wheel. I checked."

"Allowed, maybe. Doesn't mean I want to be on the road when you're out there."

"Well, I promise to be back home again before you're done here," Trace assured her. "If you get yourself run over this afternoon, it won't be at my hands."

Carolee shifted her weight from one foot to the other. "I have a couple of errands I need to do," she interjected. "But please, stay and get caught up, why don't you." She glanced at her watch and then at Mikayala. "Maybe I'll grab lunch while I'm out. Can I bring you back anything?"

"I'm fine," Mikayala told her. "Can't stand looking at him another minute, is that it?"

"Oh…No, of course not." She raised one hand in a limp sort of gesture. "You look absolutely fine. I hope you don't think… I mean, I really do have errands."

"Not to worry," Trace assured her. "It was good seeing you again."

After Carolee had made her escape, he turned to Mikayla. "Poor woman, putting up with you every day."

"Oh, shut up," she returned, moving around from behind the counter, pulling him against her in a most uncharacteristic embrace. It was over nearly as quickly as it began, and she'd turned away before either of them could feel self-conscious about it.

"So, how's it going here? Neither of you looks broken or bloodied."

"Why would we?" Mikayala's unflinching gaze caused his grin to falter. "It's no different than when you and I work together."

"No?"

She moved to the display of greeting cards along the far wall, tidying the few that were, to her discerning eye, anyway, out of alignment.

"She has her sights set on something a whole lot bigger than running a place like this, don't you know that? This is her tour of duty, is all. She's corporate material, you can smell it on her. That's why we're getting along just fine. She's not aiming to be my boss. *Yours,* maybe. So her and me, we get along fine. She's easier to deal with than you, most days."

"Yeah, I've missed our tender relationship, too," Trace retorted. "And I'm glad, I guess, that it's working out okay, you two together. I thought maybe you'd… Well, you'd go someplace else."

"Quit, you mean." Mikayla turned away from the cards she'd been neatening and gazed at him. "You thought I might quit."

"Well… yeah. On principle."

Her mouth, bunched into a grimace, relaxed into something very nearly resembling a smile.

"On principle," she repeated.

"Maybe," Trace reiterated. "I'm just saying, I thought, *maybe…*"

"Principles are like a fancy car, Mister Bannerly," she informed him. "Real nice to have, but other things have got to come first. An old clunker or a bus pass will get you where you need to go. You buy yourself a big expensive ride when everything else has been taken care of. That's not me, not yet. If I was twenty and a damn fool who thought she had something to prove, I might've quit. I've moved past that stage, thank goodness."

"Well…" Trace dug his hands into the back pockets of his jeans. "Whatever the reason, I'm glad. I'm happy you're still here."

"Mm," she acknowledged and added something else he couldn't quite catch. It might have been, "And you, too," but he knew better than to ask.

Chapter Fifteen

The person who seemed most receptive to Trace's disclosure that Bertie was continuing to pay him visits was their mother. At first, like everyone else, Karen had reacted with little more than stunned silence; but later, when he was home from the hospital, she'd arrived one afternoon, casserole in hand, thoughtful expression on her face.

"Three hundred fifty degrees for thirty minutes should do it nicely," she instructed, handing off the dish to Marla's mother Kaye, who was visiting them at the time in order to help with the baby. "Or if you want to freeze it to have later, then a little higher temperature and a little longer. It's a sort of enchilada-lasagna thing," she added vaguely. Kaye, familiar with Karen's eclectic cooking style, nodded and bore it off into the kitchen with murmurs of thanks.

"How are you, dear? You look well, all things considered," Karen said to Trace, who was settled in the recliner in the living room. "Still having the bouts of vertigo?"

"Some," he acknowledged. "But it gets a little better each day."

"It's odd, don't you think?" his mother declared, settling herself on the couch opposite him. It seemed natural to assume she was still talking about the vertigo, and he was starting to reply when she cut him off.

"For as much time as your sister spent avoiding all of us *before* she died, I gather she's visited you quite a lot lately." Karen glanced over her shoulder, but it appeared that Kaye had decided to remain in the kitchen for the time being.

"Well, actually, not so much *lately*. Not for a few weeks, anyway. I'm starting to wonder whether—"

"—How does she look when you see her? Does… Does she look happy?"

"I guess. Never unhappy, anyway. Unflappable, mostly. The way she always is. Or was, I guess I mean."

"Oh." His mother received this news with a slight frown. "I was hoping, after everything she struggled with in this life, that she would at least be happy now. Where does she come from? When she pops in to see you, I mean."

"I… I don't know." Now that the question had been put to him, Trace felt a little foolish. It seemed like such a logical thing to have asked, yet he never had. Though, of course, Bertie wouldn't have told him, regardless. "See, Mom, she explained to me once that she can't tell me anything about herself that I don't already know."

"Well, that makes no sense whatsoever," Karen pronounced, as if everything else about his sister's reappearance had been logical up until this. "What do the two of you talk about, in that case? If you don't mind my asking."

He considered for a moment. "It's mostly pretty nondescript, I guess. She reminds me of things that happened in the past. She's told me we shouldn't feel bad about how things ended for her, and that it wasn't our fault."

"Well, naturally," his mother said. "Whatever her challenges, your sister was a kindhearted person. She wouldn't want any of us feeling guilty, after all." She reached over to give his knee a reassuring squeeze. Trace couldn't help but smile.

"So… You're acting as if you believe all this. That this really is happening to me."

She fixed him with a mildly inquiring gaze. "Why shouldn't I? You aren't lying, are you?"

"Well, no… But—"

"—Then of course I believe you."

"But you realize that we could just be talking about some sort of full-blown psychosis on my part, don't you? That it's just all in my head? Nothing more than a way of alleviating any guilt I might be feeling? Or a subconscious need to conclude any unfinished business with my twin sister. That's Aria's theory, by the way."

"Oh, that's such bunk," Karen said calmly. "What do you have to feel guilty about? I love Aria, but she does have that compulsive need to slap a convenient label on everything, doesn't she? *'Subconscious need.' 'Psychosis.'* I get so tired of people using psychobabble to defend every little thing they do. You're far too levelheaded to buy into any of that."

"So, you think that's a more far-fetched theory than the idea that Bertie might actually be haunting me?"

"She is not *haunting* you. Checking up on you is what she's doing. Making sure that everything is all right."

Trace laughed. "That doesn't sound like her. She wasn't ever the caregiver type, particularly."

"Well, maybe that's changed. Who knows what she's picked up on the other side. Wherever that may be."

"I suppose," he ventured dubiously. "Although from our discussions so far, she doesn't seem to have much more of an idea why she keeps showing up than I do. ...Would you like something to drink?" he added belatedly, as his mother sat frowning into space. Eventually, she shook her head.

"I wonder sometimes," she said finally. "There were so many of you children... Did she feel somehow as though she'd slipped through the cracks?"

This was maybe the most self-aware thing Trace had ever heard from his mother. Delivered without fanfare and long since he'd ceased expecting anything of the sort, it felt rather like a gift he'd wanted for a long time, but had now outgrown. He considered his reply carefully.

"We *all* thought that from time to time, Mom. I suppose anyone from a large family experiences those feelings. Once in a while, I mean. We all knew you loved us, even when one of us got left behind at the grocery store."

"One time!" she protested. "*One time* I left one of you, and I never hear the end of it! And it wasn't even Bertie I forgot!"

"See? There you have it. You're in the clear, Mom. I can promise you that none of us—Bertie included—holds that against you. We all made our own choices, and we're all smart enough to own them, good or bad. We learned that from you and Pops."

"Well, we did try to encourage you to think for yourselves," his mother said tentatively.

He'd lied, of course. Trace had certainly held some resentments toward his folks' laissez-faire approach to child rearing, but now that his mother seemed willing to own at least a portion of the blame, he realized with some surprise that this didn't seem to matter very much to him anymore.

Maybe it was having had a tumor yanked from his skull, or perhaps it was becoming a parent himself, but the acts of confronting one's own mortality and cleaning baby vomit off his shirt as often as three or four times a day had provided a new perspective.

Life is unavoidably messy, both in and outside of your head.

Chapter Sixteen

Just days after his surgery, Trace had an unexpected visitor.
He was still in the hospital, half his head swathed in bandages. He'd opened his eyes—the exposed one, at any rate—to see the fuzzy outline of a tall, slender figure standing in the open doorway to his room.

"Um, hello," it had said. "I hope I have the right room. Are you... Are you Albie Bannerly's brother Trace?"

"Uh-huh," he'd managed, his tongue still thick with having just awakened and the lingering effects of the pain medication.

"Is it all right if I come in? I won't stay long."

"Uh-huh," he said again, rousing himself and struggling up onto his pillow.

"I don't know if you remember me, but I'm Katie. You and your sisters came to my place to get Albie's things last spring?"

Trace nodded slightly. He remembered having done that, although he wouldn't have recalled Katie specifically without the prompting, despite the colorful and unusual attire she'd been wearing then. Today's outfit was somewhat more restrained: jeans and an off-one-shoulder blouse revealing a pink bra strap straddling the exposed skin. But as she drew close, and the purple-framed glasses and nearly colorless blonde hair came into focus, the full memory clicked into place.

It was clear that his guest was having more difficulty, however, fitting his current appearance with the way he'd looked at their single previous encounter.

"What... what happened?" she asked. "If you don't mind my asking. Were you in an accident?"

"Sort of. I collided with cancer." He grinned, but she only stared back, solemn-faced.

"I went by your store," she explained. "They said you were on leave, or something. A girl who was cleaning the windows told me you were getting surgery, and where. I don't think she was supposed to say anything, because the older woman behind the counter told her to work more and talk less. I hope I didn't get her in trouble."

Trace uttered up a hoarse laugh. "No more than she's usually in. That was her grandmother who told her to be quiet, I'm sure."

Katie looked uncomfortable. "I should have called first."

"No, it's all right. I like the distraction. It's too hard to watch TV or read with my face covered like this, so company's great. Pull up a chair. On the other side of the bed, so I don't have to turn my head to see you."

She did as instructed, then perched on the very edge of her seat, hands limp in her lap. "Are you going to be okay?"

"Yeah, that's what they tell me. Why? Do I look that bad?"

"No, I guess not," she conceded, though both her tone and expression indicated some dubiousness. "I would have contacted one of your sisters, except I didn't have their numbers. You were the only one I knew how to reach, since you left me your business card the day you came by."

"I remember." Trace had given it to the young woman on the off chance that she or one of the other roommates might find anything else of his sister's around their apartment. "Did something else of Bertie's turn up?"

"Well, sort of." Katie looked at the bandage on the underside of Trace's arm, securing an IV needle to a tube that trailed to a bag some distance away, and sighed heavily. "I really wish I'd known what you're going through right now. I would have waited until later to come see you. This doesn't seem like the greatest time."

"You're here now," he pointed out. "So you might as well tell me. Or show me, if you brought it along." If Katie's reticence was any indication, it wasn't going to be anything particularly good or uplifting.

"I didn't bring it along," she said, although she was digging in her purse. "It isn't an *it,* it's a *who.*" She extracted a folded piece of paper and ran a fingernail along its crease. "You remember that guy Beau I told you your sister had been seeing?"

Trace stared at her. "The guy she'd been fighting with, you mean? The one who kicked her out onto the street?"

"Well, anyway... Last week, he came by the Grease Trap, the place I work, remember? He'd been asking around and heard that she'd been crashing with me those last few weeks."

"Yeah? So what did he want?"

Katie shifted in her seat. "Well, uh, he didn't... He didn't know what had happened. That she had died."

"He didn't know? All this time later, and he's just now finding that out? Where the hell's he been?"

Katie shook her head. "Dunno. Anyway, I don't think he really believed it, not at first. He stood there by my counter, with people lining up behind and jostling around him, because it was our busy time, and he was staring at me and saying, *'Are you sure? Are we talking about the same person? Are you really sure?'* My boss was getting pissed, because this guy is standing there, blocking traffic, making it hard for customers and the wait staff to move around. And all I could do was to keep telling him that yes, I was sure. It really was her who had died." She blinked owlishly at Trace, her eyes huge behind those purple frames.

He was at a loss. "What did he want, especially after all this time? To get back together again, was that it?"

Katie twisted her mouth to one side and glanced away, clearly uncomfortable at what she needed to say next. "No. He felt awful, I could tell, once he really believed me. But he didn't want her back. He... He said he needed her to sign some papers. Some legal documents, I think."

"He... Now, wait... What kind of papers?"

"I'm only telling you what he told me, that's all." She leaned forward in her chair. "I really should have waited to tell you this at a better time, but it seemed kind of important. Oh, I *wish* I'd had one of your sisters' numbers, instead. You aren't going to have a heart attack or anything now, are you?"

"No," Trace assured her grimly. "I'm not going to have a heart attack."

"That's good. Anyway, now it's done, one way or the other." She stood, looking down at the piece of paper she'd been worrying between her fingers for the past several seconds, then thrust it at him. "Here's his name. His full name, I mean. I got that much out of him. I figured you could track him down from that, if you really want to."

He accepted the paper from by rote rather than conscious effort. It remained folded, resting in the palm of his hand as he watched her push her chair back to its original position and move to the doorway.

"I guess we hadn't really ever expected to see each other again, did we?" she said, tugging up the side of her sagging blouse. "Especially for anything as weird as this. So, who knows? Maybe it'll happen again sometime. But goodbye again for now. And I hope you get well real soon."

"Thank you." He continued to look through the open doorway long after his visitor was gone from view. He allowed his thumb and forefinger to rub either side of the folded note, feeling the fibers of the paper until it slipped from his grasp and fluttered down into the folds of the bedclothes.

The slip was nowhere to be found when he awakened later. He asked one of the nurses if someone might have picked it up while he slept, but she just looked at him blankly and shook her head. Not surprising, since the whole experience could only have been a dream.

Chapter Seventeen

L ife picks up speed once children are in it.

Just two days after being born, Sarah was home from the hospital, mostly sleeping and nursing. Then, somehow, she was four months old, shattering the night with her howls, waking her parents regularly to frantically pace the floor with her, jostling her in their arms in an effort to lull her back to sleep. And, in what seemed only a heartbeat later, she was tottering around the house, bottle in one hand, clutching the edges of furniture with the other, her face an etched mask of concentration as she began to negotiate passage in the big world.

In no time at all her brother Jack, usurper of the undivided attention that had previously been hers, arrived. For a while it appeared that she would be unable to forgive that transgression, yet when no one was quite looking, they moved past that hurdle and on to other ones, to all the challenges that advancing through life with a sibling creates.

That was the key, Trace realized belatedly: *when no one was looking*. So much happens when you aren't paying strict attention. He'd been there for all of those moments, from toilet training to bedtime stories, from first day of kindergarten to mastering a two-wheeler, yet it all seemed to have passed in a blur.

"How is it we have two teenaged kids?" he demanded of a startled Marla one evening. "I don't remember getting old."

"*We?*" she snapped, looking at him over the rims of her glasses. She lowered the book she was reading. "*We* aren't doing anything of the kind. If it's happened to you, that's strictly your own affair."

He could have pointed to the reading glasses balanced on the tip of her nose as evidence to the contrary, but decided to keep that observation under wraps. Instead, he looked down at the expanse of belly protruding over the top of his boxers and jiggled it between his thumb and the rest of his fingers and sighed. It wasn't that he'd gained much weight—well, not *that* much. It just seemed that his skin wasn't doing as good a job at holding everything in as it used to. Even his face had relaxed, somehow. He turned back to the mirror to study the places where jowls seemed poised to make an appearance and wrinkles had settled permanently around his mouth and eyes, regardless of the expression he was wearing.

"Anyway," he heard Marla say from over his shoulder, "Isn't that sort of the point?" He looked at her reflection in the glass.

"Isn't what the point?"

"Getting older," she clarified without lifting her eyes from the page. "It means we're doing things right."

"I guess," he said, after considering this for a second. "Although that's not a heck of a lot of consolation."

Chapter Eighteen

"Your family is rather… rambunctious, Alberta, aren't they?"

The question was posed by Mrs. Allison, one of the neighborhood mothers.

Bertie, ten at the time, wasn't sure what the word meant, but the hesitation Mrs. Allison had interjected before using it suggested it wasn't a particularly good quality to possess.

She didn't answer, but merely stared up at her inquisitor. After a few seconds, the woman shook her head and smiled.

"Never mind," she said, and patted her own daughter, Megan, on the back. "Why don't the two of you run along and play. Stay in the back yard. Don't go out in the street."

Later, Bertie sought clarification from her sister.

"Ran… *what?*" Sky asked.

"Ran*bunctious*… I think."

They looked it up online. The word was easy to find, despite Bertie's mispronunciation.

"'Rambunctious,'" Sky read. "*Wild and uncontrollable. Unruly. Noisy.*" She glanced up. "Where did you hear it, anyway?"

"Just somewhere." Bertie sensed it might be best to keep the specifics to herself.

She wasn't particularly offended by Megan's mother's observation, though she understood it had been a veiled criticism. She could see how Mrs. Allison, who kept freshly cut flowers in a vase on the dining room table and who didn't let Megan stay outside after six, even on summer evenings when everybody else was playing tag or having water fights with the garden hoses, might think the Bannerly family seemed… well, rambunctious.

But it was, in some way, revelatory. Until then, if she thought about it at all—and she hadn't—she'd made the assumption that all families were basically the same, that all mothers and fathers went about their parental responsibilities in similar fashion. Now she saw this wasn't so.

If anything, her oldest sister Aria fit the mold of a traditional parent more than their genuine articles did. "You don't need another cookie," she might admonish. "Put them away now."

"You're not the boss of me," Bertie might retort, and then appeal to her mother, who'd been sitting in the room the entire time. "Mom, Aria's trying to tell me what to do!"

"Mm?" her mother might say, as if snapping out of a reverie. "Oh. No, your sister's right. You've had enough." Though a second earlier, it seemed she would have let Bertie go on eating as many more as she liked.

Aria didn't even have the decency to look smug, as if she'd managed some sort of victory. As far as she was concerned, the matter had been decided before their mother had gotten involved.

In time, Bertie and her friend Megan began to drift apart. They'd been near constant companions, being the same age and living on the same block. There hadn't been a falling-out, no shouting match or seemingly unforgiveable act perpetrated by either. They just gradually saw less and less of each other. Megan enrolled in dance classes, which occupied some of her time, and then they entered middle school, where there were new people and new activities to further divide them. Later, Bertie wondered whether Mrs. Allison might have suggested that Megan might find some playmates whose families were less noisy and uncontrollable. Or perhaps Megan herself had arrived at the conclusion that Bertie was too unruly. More likely, things were just following the natural flow of events.

Whatever the reasons, it didn't particularly bother her. As a general rule, not many things bothered her, not the way they did other people. Like when Quince hadn't made the varsity basketball team, or their father had forgotten to pick up Sky and a friend after a movie one time.

"What did you expect?" she'd quizzed her brother. "You're five-five.

Your teammates wouldn't even see you on the court, much less pass you the ball." To Sky, she'd said, "Well, if Pop had forgotten *me*, I would have gone back in and watched another movie for free." But her non-chalance went largely unappreciated.

She tried alcohol at twelve and grass at fourteen, not as an act of re-bellion or dissatisfaction, but out of idle curiosity. She'd sat through the school's anti-drug lectures, but hadn't found their arguments particu-larly convincing. They cautioned against trying controlled substances just to feel popular or to be part of the crowd, things that had never appealed to Bertie anyway.

Only Trace knew for certain what she was doing. He'd heard about it from a classmate who'd seen Bertie and a friend handing off a joint in the bathroom at the mall.

"Are you crazy?" he'd demanded.

"We both know the answer to that," she'd shot back. "So go ahead and tell."

"I'm not gonna do that. But you just better watch it. You could get yourself into real trouble."

"Don't get your good-girl panties in a big wad, Tracey. I was curi-ous, is all. I don't even like it all that much."

Which was true. Weed left her mouth dry and weird-tasting, and was barely worth the effect it provided. In sampling it once or twice, her interest was satisfied. But it rankled that her brother might think his comments had influenced her decision.

As a rule, she had an okay relationship with him. If she had to be a twin with anybody, he wasn't a bad choice. God forbid it should be somebody like Aria, Miss Perfect. Miss Here's-the-rule-book-and-we'll-never-deviate-from-it. Trace was no angel, himself. He got into fights, sneaked friends into movies, and had a stash of dirty magazines under his mattress.

At sixteen, Bertie tried sex, for the very same reason she'd tried those other things. Because it was something new, and because she couldn't think of a compelling reason not to. She picked a boy she had no strong feelings for, and was confident he felt likewise. Turns out, she liked it better than pot, but found it no more addicting. It was an activity to do now and again to break up the monotony and sometimes was useful to clear her head. It was annoying how bodily impulses could slow you down and keep you from focusing on more important things. Trace was evidence of that, chasing after girls or locked in the bathroom masturbating every time she turned around.

Though she told no one, Bertie thought she'd be a writer. Odd, since she wasn't much of a reader and had never done well on school reports or term papers. Maybe it was by default, because everything else seemed either boring or too difficult. It was a long-term goal, though—one she hadn't really explored, because there were more immediate objectives to tend to first. One of those was making it through high school without flunking out. Another was replacing some money she'd stolen.

Some of it had come from her mother's unguarded purse, and some from the kitchen drawer where cash was kept to handle everyday expenses like lunch money or ordering pizza or buying tickets for school raffles. But those were small thefts she didn't worry about too much.

One afternoon when no one was around, she'd been going through the chest of drawers in the bedroom she shared with Sky. What, exactly she was looking for, she couldn't have said. Something worth pawning. Something that wouldn't be missed for a while.

What she found, tucked under several pairs of underwear, was a savings account booklet, and when she looked inside, she saw there was a balance of almost twenty-five hundred dollars. It was Sky's money from babysitting and part-time jobs.

Things had moved quickly at that point. It had been frighteningly easy to copy the account number and take it to the bank, where she filled it in on a withdrawal slip and took it up to a teller window. Beads of sweat dotted her hairline as she stood there, but she affected a bravado and smiled at the clerk.

"No, it's not short for anything. Just *Sky*," she'd said offhandedly when the teller looked at the driver's license she'd managed to borrow from her sister's wallet. "Not *Skyler*, or anything like that. Just *Sky*. And isn't it a terrible picture? I had my hair shorter, then." She understood that the best defense was a strong offense, should the person behind the counter suggest that she didn't look much like her photograph. But in fact, she and her sister shared enough broad features that it hadn't even come up. She was good at copying Sky's signature, and a moment later she was back on the street with two hundred dollars in her pocket.

This was when she was seventeen.

It was a *loan*, she told herself. An unapproved loan that she would pay back in no time at all. She was planning to get an after-school job herself, one of these days. Anyhow, the money was just sitting there in the account, not doing anything. So, really, there was nothing very wrong with borrowing it for a little while.

"This is for textbooks, and other stuff. I'm in college, you see," was what Bertie told the teller—a different one—the next time she presented a withdrawal slip at the bank. It was so stupid, really; she should have withdrawn a larger amount the first time, so she wouldn't have had to risk coming back for more. The beads of sweat were there again, and the smile she wore was a little shakier this time. She willed herself to hold it together as best she could, but she nevertheless knew that she wasn't presenting quite as authentic a picture of nonchalance as before. It didn't help that her friend Derek was pacing back and forth on the street outside, so agitated that he was drawing curious stares from passersby. She never should have let him come along.

This teller stared at her ID far longer than the other teller had, frowning as he glanced from the photo on the card to Bertie herself and back again.

"I... It... my hair, it was shorter..." she'd started to mumble, but then he handed back the license and asked what denominations she wanted her cash in, and her knees nearly buckled in relief. *Never again,* she promised herself as she watched him count out the money. *Next week, I'll find a job and start replacing all this.*

Derek was the one to blame, actually. Through him, she'd become acquainted with something she liked better than alcohol or weed or sex. At a party one night, he'd plopped down on the opposite end of the couch where she was sitting. Pot, hash, coke and other party favors had been making the rounds. The crowd had thinned, and the rumor was that some people had gone off in search of more intense experiences.

"That's nasty stuff," he'd advised her. "Heroin. You aren't into that, are you?"

She studied him, amused but not impressed by his solicitous, easy-going manner. He hadn't introduced himself or even bothered to say hello. "Heroin?" she inquired. "Why? You against it or something?"

"Or something."

"Then why are you here?" She shifted her position to look at something across the room.

"You didn't answer my question," he reminded her.

She continued to avoid his gaze. "So, what's your beef with it? Not that I really care, but since you brought it up."

"It's ragged, man. Not that it doesn't have its good points, but you got to be careful. It's better as a cocktail."

"What do you mean?"

Derek pointed to the glass-topped coffee table in front of them where, earlier there had been small piles of white powder. They were gone now, but he nevertheless licked one finger and ran it across the empty surface. Baring his teeth, he applied the finger to his upper gums. "You mix it with a little blow. Each counterbalances the other, and you come in for a clean landing. It's called a speedball."

Bertie stared at him, her own mouth twisted in revulsion.

"Yeah. Well, you have fun with that."

That should have been the end of it. Except that it wasn't.

She tried it. Not right away, and not with him. But because of him, because he'd been so smooth and so disaffected when he'd talked about its alluring effects.

And he was right; it was great. She'd puffed, rather than injected. It seemed cleaner, less "druggy" that way. Derek's analogy of coming in for a clean landing was perfect, because within seconds of breathing it in, it seemed to Bertie that the world just sort of fell away beneath her feet. She wasn't flying, exactly, but moving at a speed faster than the earth itself without lifting a finger to do so. And when it was over, the experience left her system so gracefully, like... like an escalator neatly depositing her at the next floor. Feeling refreshed, looking great. None of those sloppy, lingering effects, no nausea, no puking, no circles under her eyes.

She saw him again several weeks later at another house, another party. Foregoing her usual aloofness, she flopped down in a chair opposite the one where he was sitting, mirroring the way he'd first presented himself to her.

"Hey," she said. He looked up at her. "All right. I've become a fan."

He squinted at her for a few seconds before responding. "Of what?"

"Your recommendation. I figured you were an asshole—and maybe you are, how should I know?—but you know your shit."

"That's what they tell me." His voice was different. Lower. And he spoke more slowly. "What... what shit are we talking about in this particular instance?"

For the first time it occurred to her that he wasn't remembering her. He was struggling to sit up in his chair, and as she watched this, she realized something else. He was sort of a mess, a far cry from how he'd looked that other time. His jacket, the same one he'd been wearing before, was creased and dingy. Actually, even his face seemed creased and dingy as he leaned forward into the light. His tongue swiped the corners of his mouth and he made a smacking sound. She was about to say *never mind* when his eyebrows lifted.

"Oh," he said. "You're... you're that girl." For a minute, it appeared he was going to leave it at that, but then he concluded, "The one from some other place. The butter-wouldn't-melt chick."

"The what?"

He smiled and blinked lazily, as if lifting his eyelids required a supreme effort. "You've never heard the expression? Means *too cool for the room*. There are a lot of you around."

"I'm not—"

"—I know you're not." He raised one finger, cutting her off. "It's just the way you like to start off. Establishing the ground rules. That life is too short for bullshit."

Bertie had been so put off by his new appearance that she'd been about to get up and walk away. But, underneath the grime and the impaired speech, she saw he was exactly the same person she'd met before. An asshole, definitely, but a sharp one. A takes-one-to-know-one, and unashamed of it. The first really interesting person she'd met in a long time.

"You're kind of a mess," she informed him. "What's happened to you since the last time I saw you?"

"Well…," he said, drawing out the word and giving the matter serious consideration, "I haven't been following my own rules. And that is never a good thing. But you know that, don't you?"

She did, but before she could think of what she actually wanted to say in response, he asked:

"You still haven't explained. What is it you've become a fan of? Of me, I hope."

His eyebrows arched and the smiled widened as she explained that she'd now experienced the revelatory effects of a speedball. A few times.

"Well, well. You gotta be careful, though," he admonished. "Remember they're just a chemically enhanced form of bullshit. And we know how you feel about *that*."

They did know. Yet, she let it happen anyway.

And now she was impersonating Sky and borrowing her money, and Derek was waiting on the sidewalk outside, so excited when she walked out of the bank, cash in hand, he actually began to tremble. He pushed his hair back from his shiny forehead.

"Sweet," he said. "Let's go see a guy."

"I need to swing by the house first," Bertie told him. "My sister is only home for the weekend, and I need to get her license back into her wallet before she realizes it's missing."

"Screw that. Let her think she lost it someplace."

"I can't..."

"How about this? How about we get the stuff—it'll only take twenty minutes—and then you can get the license back to her? She isn't leaving right this minute, is she?"

In truth, Bertie shared Derek's urgency. She was salivating so much she had to swallow every few seconds.

"All right," she said.

It had been a mistake to ever let Derek know about the whole swiping-money-from-Sky's-account thing, Bertie realized that. What did he bring to it, except, maybe, some moral support? A sense that somebody had her back. But in truth, if something went wrong, what could he do? No, his participation only meant that they blew through the money twice as fast as if she'd been doing all of this by herself.

Also, Sky had already discovered her license was missing before Bertie made it home.

"I don't understand it. It's got to be here somewhere."

"Well, think, sweetheart." Their mother stood by the counter while Sky, seated at the kitchen table, tore through her purse, searching. "Where did you have it last?"

"If I knew that, Mom, don't you think I'd know where it is?"

"I'm only trying to help."

"Well, that's not helping, can't you see?"

Bertie stood by silently, having walked in just seconds earlier. She was much later arriving home than she'd originally planned. Once she and Derek had secured all the ingredients for the cocktail, the urge to share one right then had been too difficult to resist.

Sky looked up from the contents of her bag strewn across the table and saw her.

"Berts... I can't find my driver's license. Have you seen it?"

"Why would I have seen it?" Bertie shot back, even as her fingers traced its outline in her pocket. *Damn.* She couldn't very well slip it back into her sister's bag now, now that the entire thing had been dumped out. She was pondering what other spot she might be able to leave it when Sky abruptly slapped the edge of the table. Bertie jumped.

"I just thought of something," her sister declared, sitting back in her chair. "I had to show it when I picked up a concert ticket last week. Maybe… Maybe I left it there at the window. Or I dropped it while I thought I was putting it away. Crap! What am I going to do now?"

"You call the ticket window," their mother advised. "See if anybody turned it in. And if not, well, it's not the end of the world. You go to the driver's license bureau and they issue you a new one."

Which was how Bertie was able to keep the original license permanently. Not that she planned to use it again. She'd already withdrawn seven hundred and fifty dollars from Sky's account and hadn't replaced a penny yet. But it might come in handy when she rounded up the money, in order to put it back again.

She wasn't going to tell Derek about this, though. The look in his eyes when she'd walked out of the bank, cash in hand, and the way his shaking hands could barely hold the steering wheel as they drove to make the deal made her realize that he was poised on the brink of irrationality. His own sources of income, whatever they might have been to start with, had dried up. Friends—Bertie, mostly—were his only access to speedballs and to anything else. Worse, the landings he'd raved about were becoming bumpy. These days, he was injecting rather than puffing. The results were much better, much faster, he'd been telling her, and he encouraged her to go that route as well. She'd refused. Her own landings, if not bumpy, weren't quite as satisfying as they'd been at first, but she wasn't to the point yet where she wanted to start poking a needle in her arm. That would come later.

In any event, she knew that as soon as the five hundred bucks was gone, he'd begin pestering her, asking when she could get hold of Sky's license again to make another withdrawal. Let him tap into some other friendship from now on.

Oddly, though, she only saw him a couple more times before he just vanished. Bertie was both relieved and angry. It wasn't like she hadn't figured out he was using her, but at least he could have come up with a few lies, made some outlandish excuses about why he wasn't showing up anymore. She wouldn't have believed any of it for a second, but that wasn't the point. After all they'd been through together, after she'd been so generous with her sister's possessions, he at least owed her that.

The relief and the anger were enough to make her vow to go clean, and to finally figure out a way to start putting back the money. School would be out in a month, so now was the time to try and line up a summer job.

She skipped her afternoon classes to head to the mall and put in applications in as many of the least-sucky places she could find. Afterward, she headed home gloomily contemplating an interminable existence spent refolding sweaters a thousand women had tried on, or pushing cinnamon buns on already overweight customers, all for minimum wage and possibly for the rest of her life. Somehow, despite any real effort, it looked like she was going to graduate after all, but college was out of the question.

The house was in a state of flux when she arrived.

"Guess what?" Quince greeted her. "Somebody's been stealing money out of Sky's savings account!"

"They... who... what? What are you talking about?" Bile rose in Bertie's throat as she stared at her kid brother. She could feel her legs growing numb and she gripped the side of a chair.

"It's been going on for weeks, I guess." Quince was too excited to notice anything unusual about her response, or her suddenly ashen face. "In chunks, the bank says. Dad already headed down there, to talk with the bank people. And the cops."

"The... cops? The police? They're involved?"

Quince's head bobbed up and down. "Mom's on the phone talking to Sky right now. She's really upset—Sky is, I mean—and she wants to come home, even though she's got finals this week. Mom's telling her not to. But you know Sky."

Bertie swallowed hard. "How... How do they think it happened?"

"Whoever it was used her driver's license. Remember how Sky hasn't been able to find it? Well, we know why now!"

"Yeah," she said faintly, her mind racing. Quince obviously was still in the dark, but bank people and the police—oh, God, the police!—were probably explaining it all to their father right now. They'd be headed back here soon, Dad looking stunned and crushed, the police dangling a pair of handcuffs for her. How had she not seen this coming? Why had she waited so long to try to fix it?

"...nobody we know."

"What?" she said again.

"They think he found her license somewhere. Maybe even lifted it out of her bag when she wasn't looking. In a store, or a restaurant or someplace."

"*He?* What are you talking about?"

"The guy!" Now Quince was becoming annoyed. "Why don't you listen? The guy they caught in the bank, trying to make another withdrawal from her savings account. He told them he was her brother, or something, and that he was there because she was sick, and that she'd sent him in with her license to get some money."

Quince had lots more to share, but Bertie more or less stopped listening at this point. She was still looking at him and even nodding as he rattled on, but her hand had made its way to her back pocket. It squeezed her wallet. More than anything, she wanted to dash upstairs, dig out her billfold and pour through its contents. But because she couldn't, instead she tried to remember the details of the last time she and Derek had gotten together. Some apartment, some place he was crashing with a buddy, since he'd been kicked out of his own place. The buddy wasn't home; it had been only the two of them. Late afternoon, shades drawn, only a little light filtering through. She was stretched out on a grimy sofa. Derek was lying on the floor. Both of them fully tweaked. Both talking, half-listening to each other, staring at the ceiling.

Did she... ? Had she brought... ?

Yeah, she was pretty sure she'd had her bag that afternoon. She'd come directly from school, so yes. Where had she dropped it? Somewhere in that apartment. Plenty of time, while she'd been lying there staring overhead, eyes half-closed. Probably he'd been faking it, at least faking he was as buzzed as all that, quietly going through her bag, pulling out her wallet while she rambled on about one thing or another.

It made perfect sense. Why he hadn't been around in a while. She'd told him that she'd put the license back in Sky's purse, so maybe he wasn't specifically looking for that. Maybe he was just seeing if she had any cash left that he could boost, and found it by accident.

Was that what had happened? It seemed the only logical explanation. Was Derek really that big a douche, that big an idiot, to try and pull off something like this? He would have had to be pretty desperate.

Her fear had subsided just a little, but then it came back on a fresh wave. If it was Derek the police were holding, then the trail back to her was pretty direct and obvious. All she had to do was to walk back into the bank, and at least two tellers would be able to identify her.

"I have to go to the bathroom," she announced, cutting Quince off mid-sentence. Upstairs, she sat on the edge of the tub holding her billfold. Yeah, Sky's license was missing.

"Asshole," she murmured, referring not to Derek but to herself. She fell to her knees and wretched, vomiting into the toilet. She heaved several more times, then curled into a fetal position on the floor. Here was where she would stay until the police came.

But instead, it was Trace, more than an hour later, knocking on the door. "Hey! Other people need to use the bathroom, you know!"

Bertie did not move.

More pounding. "I mean it, Berts! You've been in there forever."

"Yeah," she retorted finally. "So go find some other place to jack off for once!"

There was a final, furious slam against the door, and then he was gone.

After a bit, she crawled to her feet, swished some water in her mouth, and unlocked the door.

Life seemed unchanged on the other side of it. She ventured downstairs, expecting that a trap of some sort had been laid for her. Aria was there, but that was hardly surprising. Even though she was married and lived someplace else, she was over visiting way more often than seemed necessary. She was sitting in the kitchen, chatting with their mother.

"You look horrible," she greeted Bertie. "You look like you've been sleeping on the floor, or something."

Bertie didn't tell her how close to the mark her guess was. She didn't say anything at all, but shuffled to the refrigerator to get a carton of orange juice. She poured herself a glass and sat at the table drinking it, waiting for whatever might come next.

Her sister was droning on and on about some boring remodeling thing that she and her husband Pete wanted to do to their living room. Their mother was making a series of noncommittal noises during all of this, which likely meant she was only half-listening while she prepared dinner. Finally, when Bertie couldn't stand it any longer, she blurted:

"So, what's this about somebody stealing some money from Sky?"

The other women looked at her.

"That's what Quince told me when I got home, anyway," she added.

Her mother shrugged.

"It was some vagrant or transient, or something. They have him in custody."

Bertie's fingers gripped the juice glass tightly.

"How... How did he do it? Did he say?"

"We don't know all of the specifics, dear. The entire thing was over nearly as quickly as we knew it had even happened. Your father talked to the bank manager. They're very apologetic, and apparently they've promised to make good on the loss. Sky has nothing to worry about."

"As well they should, Mom," Aria snorted. "It really doesn't matter whether this thief had Sky's driver's license or not. How lax are their security procedures that this guy was able to make multiple withdrawals from an account that clearly wasn't his? Sky should take her money to another bank. And so should you and Dad, if you have any accounts there!"

"Oh, I'm sure everything is fine now," their mother said mildly. "They're going to be much more vigilant than before, after what happened."

As with most arguments in which she engaged, Aria was not about to concede an inch. "Fine, lose all your money, then. And, as far as that thief goes, there's something fishy about his ridiculous story. The police are going to find out more. Wait and see."

The story Derek gave the police was simple and to the point, and no matter what pressure was applied, he refused to waver from it. He told the police he'd walked past an outdoor café where a woman sitting at a table had reached down for something in a shopping bag by her feet. He'd used that split second to lean across the railing and snatch the wallet she'd left sitting next to her latte, and then he had taken off running. The woman shouted after him, but he'd ducked around a corner, up a side street, and into a library. There, in a quiet alcove, he'd looked inside it. No cash, no credit cards, but there were a whole handful of driver's licenses all issued to various women. And a handful of bank withdrawal slips, each with a name and an account number written on it. Clearly, this was a woman pulling some kind of a scam, so he was confident she wasn't going to call the police to report the theft. Instead, he figured he'd give her routine a shot. He'd picked a license at random from the stack and the corresponding withdrawal slip… Sky's. He walked into her bank, tried to withdraw some cash, and bam… he got caught. He knew nothing about the earlier withdrawals. The woman whose wallet he'd stolen must have been responsible for those, he insisted.

What did that woman at the table look like, the police wanted to know. Derek couldn't give a good description. She had been wearing a floppy hat and dark glasses.

What had he done with the wallet and all the other driver's licenses? He'd dropped them in the bottom of a waste bin at the library, figuring he could come back for them later. Now it was too late. They'd probably been thrown away. At any rate, a search of all the library's trash cans yielded nothing.

Aria was right; it was a ridiculous story, but equally ridiculous to try to refute. No woman had come forward to report having her purse stolen from a coffee shop. No other banks and no other women reported any unauthorized withdrawals from any accounts. In the end, all Derek could be charged with was attempted fraud, attempted forgery, and attempted theft of one hundred and fifty dollars, the amount he'd entered on the bank slip.

The judge sentenced him to sixty days, less time served.

Through it all, he hadn't implicated Bertie.

Smooth landing, indeed.

For a week or so afterward, she stayed clean, frightened by the close call, but the old cravings began nagging at her. *Really,* she rationalized as the itch grew stronger, *as long as she wasn't stealing, nobody was getting hurt. Nobody but herself, and that was her own business, after all.*

And so began the cycle that would follow her the rest of her days: in control for a while, then not. Clean, then not. Employed, then not.

One morning she found herself in the back seat of a trashed-out car she didn't recognize, in a neighborhood she'd never seen before, with bruises and a black eye she couldn't remember acquiring. That was just enough of a wake-up call to cause her to actually seek out and enroll in a rehab program.

That was where she met the guy.

Beau Callenforth.

And for nearly a year, for him, she managed to stay straight.

Chapter Nineteen

Eighteen year-old Sarah Bannerly squinted as the slanting rays of the sun caught her full in the face. It was another glorious October morning beneath another deep blue sky, yet today felt different. Other recent mornings had been cold, but today's chill was more insistent; summer was definitely yielding to autumn. And that was fine, so far as she was concerned. Time for more change, time to see what waited around yet another corner.

Sarah had thoroughly embraced college life, relishing each new experience and challenge almost as much as being away from her parents and her brother Jack. Not that she didn't love them, but she was definitely ready to love them from a distance for a while.

She didn't have class for almost two hours, but she had gotten into the habit of frequenting a nearby coffee shop, sometimes to study, but mostly to escape the lamentations of her homesick roommate, who spouted a ceaseless litany of everything wrong with her classes, her professors, the other students, and anything else that came to mind. Sarah had already put in a request for a transfer to another room—any other room—since her patience was at an end, and if she didn't get out soon, she was going say something that would make her the next thing added to that long, long list.

The earthy smell of espresso mixed with that of fresh pastries greeted her as she tugged open the glass door. She dropped her bag on an empty table by way of claiming it before heading up to the counter to order her drink. When she returned, coffee in hand, someone was occupying one of the chairs.

"Excuse me," she informed him, standing behind him. "But I'm sitting there."

"In both seats?" he demanded. He smirked at her over his shoulder. Sarah hesitated just a second, recognizing the man and the smirk. It was her dorm floor's resident advisor, Russ. She bunched her lips and moved around to the other side of the table setting down her cup and regarding him coolly.

"Of course not. But maybe I'm meeting someone."

He nodded, absorbing this information, and then smacked both hands on his side of the table. He rose. "In that case, I'll just stay until he or she gets here. Hold my place while I go get a cinnamon roll."

Sarah was rarely at a loss for a comeback, but he'd moved out of earshot before she could think of one. That was all right. She'd have something prepared when he got back. Unfortunately, he beat her to the punch.

"So, I hear you've put in for a transfer to another room," he said, plopping down opposite her. He set a paper plate containing one of the largest cinnamon buns she'd ever seen on the table. "Not even three weeks into the semester. Something you'd like to talk about?"

The words "Not with you" hovered on her lips, but she thought better of it. She might very well need an RA in her corner to make the change.

"Not much to say," she said offhandedly. "Personality conflict in the current living arrangement, is all."

Russ lifted the bun and took an enormous bite, leaving a strand of greasy, uncoiled pastry dangling below his chin. He prodded it into his mouth with a single finger, rendering him unable to speak for several seconds while he chewed. But he nodded vigorously as a way of letting her know he'd have something to say once he'd swallowed. Sarah watched, fascinated by his utter lack of self-consciousness.

When his mouth was empty, he reached across the table to take the napkin from beneath her cup, and swiped it across his face.

"Okay," he managed at last. "Are you just wanting a different room, or off my floor entirely?"

She watched him crumple the napkin and drop it on the table before meeting his gaze. "I don't really care. But you don't need to take it personally, if that's what you're worried about."

"I'm not. We're losing Jenny Hookstratten in 414. She told me last night that she's moving out this week. You could have her spot if you wanted it. Provided her roommate Melissa Carlson is cool with it."

Sarah had gotten to know both Jenny and Melissa a little in the past few weeks, and liked them both. "Yeah, maybe. Did... Did she say why she's leaving?"

"Something about waking up finding Melissa trying to smother her in her sleep a couple of times, I think."

She couldn't see his expression because he'd lowered his head and was concentrating on pressing his thumb into the remnants of icing and crumbs on the plate and lifting them to his mouth, but she had no doubt he was enormously pleased with himself.

She refused to give him the satisfaction of any kind of reaction. "When do I have to let you know?"

"The sooner the better. You won't be the only person wanting to move when they hear there's a vacancy. There are a lot of people who don't like their roommates." He leaned back in his chair, licking his thumb. "Let's say by five tonight. After that, I gotta offer it to somebody else."

"All right. By five," Sarah agreed. But as Russ pushed back his chair and got to his feet, she blurted, "You know what? I'll take it."

Apart from a slight elevation of the eyebrows, he registered no surprise at her abrupt decision.

"Stop by and see me after class, and we'll make it official. I'm at the front desk all evening. And let your roomie know. How's she going to take it?"

"She'll be pissed," Sarah predicted. "She shouldn't be, but she will."

"HE'S CUTE, DON'T you think?"

Sarah paused in transferring items from her bag into the dresser to look at her new roommate, Melissa, sitting cross-legged on her bed, watching the unpacking.

"Who?"

"Who do you think? Who else has been in our room in the last ten minutes?"

Sarah fingered a pair of socks before setting them in the drawer. "The RA, you mean? Russ?"

He had knocked at their door moments earlier, checking to see how her relocation was coming.

"Yes, the RA, Russ," Melissa mimicked her. "Don't play dumb."

"I wasn't—"

"—Half the women in the dorm have a crush on him, and a few of the guys probably do, too."

"Yeah, so?"

"It's you he likes."

"Oh, please." Sarah didn't even bother looking up from her unpacking. "He doesn't, and even if he did…"

"What? You wouldn't go out with him? I would."

"I thought you were already seeing someone."

Melissa flicked the air with one hand. "Oh, that. Well, it's not like Russ is going to ask me, anyway, but… you know…" She let the unfinished thought speak for itself.

"Then ask him."

"Why aren't you interested?" her roommate retorted, dodging the suggestion.

Sarah stopped placing shirts on hangers for a moment to consider this. An image of the man attempting to shovel the better part of an entire cinnamon roll into his mouth presented itself once more.

"He thinks he's too cool for the room," she said finally.

"Well, that's because he is."

"Not any room I care to be a part of. And…" she paused, frowning. "He reminds me of somebody. I can't think of who."

"Somebody from your high school, maybe?"

"Possibly."

"Somebody you dated?" her roommate persisted.

"Definitely not that. Probably just some doofus I met at a party one time, or something."

"Fine," Melissa tossed her hands in exasperation. "But can we at least agree he's good looking?"

"Fine," Sarah echoed sarcastically. "He's the best-looking thing ever."

"Okay, then." Satisfied with even a desultory concession, Melissa was willing to let the matter drop. She uncrossed her legs and slid off her bed to examine a blouse Sarah had just pulled out of her bag.

"Oh, this is cute," she declared, holding it in front of her. "Can I borrow it sometime?"

Chapter Twenty

And what if it hadn't been a dream?

What if Katie, the young woman on whose couch Bertie had crashed the last few weeks of her life really had come to see Trace in the hospital that day? What if she really had given him a note with a name on it, a name somehow linked to his sister? Purely for conjecture's sake, let's say that when the paper slipped from his fingers, it had become lodged in the sheets until the bed was stripped later, or perhaps it had fallen to the floor and was swept away as a bit of trash, no one recognizing it as anything important.

What if it hadn't been lost?

Well, probably without having to do much research, he might have located the owner of that name. "Beau Callenforth" is not a particularly common one, after all. Trace might have learned that he was now living in Scottsdale. Of course, it's anybody's guess as to how he would have reacted if Trace had reached out to him, or what information, if any, he'd have been willing to share about his life or his past association with Bertie.

But it is in the realm of possibility Beau might have told Trace that he and Bertie met in a rehab facility a few years earlier. And that they'd formed a connection based on their unique senses of humor, their weakness for controlled substances, and their skepticism as to whether the program was doing them any good.

If so inclined, Beau could've explained that against the advice of the counselors and the rules of the program, they'd hooked up both before and after leaving the facility. And that for a while, things had been good. Really good. They'd managed to stay clean, get jobs, begun to build a life together.

He might have told Trace that he'd even wanted to meet Bertie's family, but she'd discouraged the idea. *They won't approve*, she'd said. *They'll think this is just another bad hookup. What we have already is working so well. I don't want anybody telling us otherwise.*

So when the baby came, none of them knew about that, either. He was healthy, happy, and perfect in every way, Beau could have assured Trace. All during her pregnancy, Bertie had insisted, *We're gonna do this one thing right.* And they had. It was only afterward that things began to crumble.

While she was carrying their son, she was living for somebody else, putting someone else's welfare first. At least that was the best explanation Beau could have offered. But once the baby was out, breathing on his own, circulating his own blood, her system was her own once more; what she did with it wasn't going to affect anyone else. Maybe that's what she told herself. Maybe that's why there were days Beau would come home to find her by turns edgy, effusive, furtive, animated, sweaty, affectionate, sullen. She denied what was happening, and, for a while, he did too, but he'd been down that road too many times himself, and eventually it became impossible to ignore.

What was I supposed to do, he might have demanded of Trace. *If I could only save one of them, was there even a choice?*

Of course not. Even Bertie had understood that, at least one time, when she was in the grip of a particularly giddy high, and ironically when her judgment should have been at its worst. All pretense had fallen away, finally, when with maniacal intensity, she'd told him, *Give up this feeling? Are you fucking crazy? Just take the kid and go if this bothers you so much!*

So he had.

She'd regretted it later, burning up his phone with rambling incoherent tearful angry threats and pleas, promises to find them wherever they'd gone. By that time, he and the baby they'd named Russ were a thousand miles away, in a city where he had no connections, and where he knew no one, which made it more difficult for her to track them, even if she'd been in any condition to do so.

Sometimes I think she saved me, Beau could have told Trace. *I wasn't any stronger than she was, at least not back then. But one of us had to hold on. Maybe I should have thanked her for that...*

His son was two, and eventually Beau had begun a relationship with someone else, someone Russ was even calling "Mama," when Beau finally went back, papers in hand, to find Bertie, hoping to convince her to relinquish all claims. And if not amicably, well, he was prepared to take her to court.

But it wasn't necessary, because...

Well, you know, Beau would probably have concluded delicately. If he and Trace had ever actually spoken, that is.

But they hadn't. They never would.

Because, after all, it had just been a dream that day in the hospital.

Chapter Twenty-One

Bertie's post-death visits to Trace continued through the years, as capricious and unannounced as ever. The last one was on their shared fifty-ninth birthday.

"Well," she greeted him. "Happy birthday."

"Happy birthday," he returned.

Her eyes swept the room, noting the closed blinds, the people seated quietly on either side of a small table, the vase of flowers between them, the IV drip alongside the bed, and finally back to Trace himself.

"Seems like a funeral parlor in here," she observed.

"Go figure."

"So…" she rested her fingers on the edge of the bed. "Doesn't look like either of us is going to make it to sixty, then."

"I guess not."

She caught him scrutinizing her. "What is it? A booger sticking out of my nose, or something?"

He managed a grin. "I've never seen you like this. Well, not for a long time, anyway."

"Really? How do I look?"

"Young. Really young. Six or eight, maybe."

Bertie considered this for a few seconds. "You're probably remembering one of our birthday parties from when we were kids. Seems logical, given what day it is. I'm glad, I guess. Before things all went to hell. Or I did, anyway."

"I wish…" Trace began, and then he faltered for a second. "I wish you could tell me what dying is like. So I could… I don't know… be prepared."

She grinned, one of her malevolent, relishing-someone-else's-discomfort grins. "Even if I could, I wouldn't. Everyone should get to enjoy it without any spoilers."

"I bet you don't remember," he challenged. "I bet you never even knew because you were probably unconscious when it happened."

Bertie didn't rise to his taunt. "You could be right," she said thoughtfully. "A little bitty heroin train, chugging through my veins, derailing just as it got to my heart. While I was probably face down on a filthy floor somewhere, in a puddle of my own piss, unable to fully embrace the experience."

Trace sighed, a soft throaty moan that caused the people in the chairs on the other side of the bed to look up, alert. But when he made no other noise and none of the machinery attached to him reflected any change, they settled back in their seats.

"Don't take this the wrong way," he told Bertie, "But when it finally happened, when we got the news of your overdose, it was almost a relief. I don't think I quite realized until then how much I'd been waiting. Wondering."

"Oh, I get it," she said. "By that time, it wasn't a matter of *if*. Just *when*. And then, once it was done, you could get on with your lives."

They didn't meet one another's gaze. Trace, at least, was thinking about the people on the other side of the room.

QUINCE PRESSED HIS HANDS against the armrests, sliding up from the slouching position he'd been in for several minutes. Marla glanced across the table at him.

"You should go home," she told him.

"My butt's gone numb, that's all," he told her.

She persisted. "Jodi's got to be wondering where you are."

"She's fine. She understands this is where I need to be right now."

He set his jaw in that stubborn way that all of the Bannerly clan did when there was no budging them, her own two children included. Marla studied his profile, noting how much the silver hairs had overtaken the brown ones at his temples, as well as how very much a younger version of his brother he looked. She wondered suddenly whether it would be a comfort or a challenge in the coming years: looking at Quince, but seeing Trace, the Trace who might have been, if he'd only been allowed to grow older.

"How about you?" Quince demanded, interrupting her thoughts. "Have you left this room in the past three days?"

She saw no point in responding, because they both already knew the answer. The rest of the family came and went at regular intervals, but for these two, the ones bound for a lifetime to the man in the bed, this was the only place that seemed real just now.

The door opened then, and they looked up to see a slender woman with wide eyes and long straight chestnut hair step into the room, carrying an overnight bag.

"Emily, sweetheart," Marla struggled to her feet, her legs wobbly from having been seated in one position so long. She moved to hug her niece.

"Hi," Emily returned. "I brought you some stuff. Mom stopped by your place and packed more things for you." She set the bag under the table and moved to embrace her uncle, who had also risen. "Oh, Quince! I didn't even think; I should have brought you some stuff, too."

"Don't worry about it," he said. "So, where is Sky, anyway?"

"Mom's on her way to the airport to pick up Sarah and Paul and Jack."

"Jeez, is it that late already?" Quince glanced at his watch. "What time do they land?"

"Sarah and Paul get in at about five-ten," Marla said, answering for Emily. "Jack is supposed to touch down at about a quarter to six. If he makes his connection in Atlanta, that is. He has a layover of about sixty minutes, but coming from Italy, he's got to go through customs, as well. It's going to be tight."

She picked up her phone, which had just buzzed, and studied the screen for a few seconds. "Oh, good," she reported. "He just texted. He made it, barely. He's in the air now." Returning her phone to the table, she touched Emily's arm and gestured to the chair she'd just vacated.

"Sit, sit."

"I'm fine," her niece began, but Marla shook her head. "You might as well. I'm going into the bathroom. I'm going to splash some water on my face and maybe change into something else." She leaned down to unzip the bag and poke through its contents. "Oh, bless Sky. She put in my slippers! Your mom's an angel."

Quince and Emily watched her step into the other room and close the door. Then they faced one another, exchanging weary smiles.

"How's he doing?" she asked. They turned toward the bed.

"The same. So far as anybody can tell."

"Do… do they think the stroke might have anything to do with the brain tumor or the surgery he had all those years ago?"

Quince shrugged.

"Nobody seems to know. Or wants to say. Maybe, but probably not. Not that it makes much difference. Not to him, anyway." He sighed. "So hard to believe. Four days ago, he was walking around, talking, just living life. And then this."

He crossed to the bed, looking down at the gray figure whose face was mostly obscured by an oxygen mask. The blanket covering his brother's chest remained still. The only indication that life still existed beneath it came from the beeps and hisses of the machines surrounding them.

Quince clenched and unclenched his jaw for several seconds. His voice was rusty when he spoke again.

"I guess I'm looking at this all wrong. Given how close we came to losing him back then, I should be grateful that I—that *we*—got to have him for thirty more years. Maybe… maybe, one day, I can see it that way. But I don't right now."

Behind him, Emily watched as his shoulders began to shake. She resisted the impulse to move forward and wrap her arms around him. Even now, as a thirty-six-year-old woman, she knew he wanted her to see him the way she had when she was a child, impervious and brave, the uncle who could unflinchingly meet all challenges. If nothing else, she could give him that.

So instead, she shifted her gaze to the opposite side of the bed and lifted her fingers in a small wave. Her Aunt Bertie smiled and waved in return.

"So. I guess this is actually it, then," Emily thought.

"THEY'RE ALL SAD for you," Bertie informed Trace.

"Yeah, well, I'm sad for me, too. I had plans, you know." He was quiet for a few seconds before adding, "Look at Quince. He'd be mortified if he knew I can see him, see those sloppy tears rolling down his face. Hey, but maybe I'll be like you: Maybe I'll get to come back and tell him."

"Maybe."

Another silence.

"Do you want to know something?" he asked.

"Sure. What?"

"It isn't too bad. This."

"Dying, you mean."

"If that's what this is. Yeah. I mean, I'd still take living, if given the choice. But this isn't a bad jumping-off point."

"Yeah?"

"I mean, Marla and I have a trip planned to Hawaii this winter. Moloka'i, this time. The condo's reserved, the plane tickets already bought. So that's too bad. But she could still go. Take her sister, instead, after a little time has passed."

"Or her new husband," Bertie suggested helpfully. "When a little more time has passed."

Underneath his oxygen mask, Trace smiled.

"And naturally I'm going to miss Sarah's and Paul's little boy Trevor. It would have been fun watching him grow up. And any other grandchildren that come along. And then there's Jack. He's studying architecture in Italy, did I tell you that?"

Bertie merely smiled.

"I hate that he's flying all the way back for this," Trace continued. "To watch me lying here. That's not the final image I want him—or any of them—to have of me."

"Hey!" Bertie stabbed a finger in the center of her seven year-old self's party dress. "They're going to remember you all kinds of ways. You won't have any say in which ones, so don't worry about it."

WITH THAT, THEY SEEMED to have run out of things to say to one another. Trace was aware that Bertie continued to hover, pushed into a corner or someplace by the influx of bodies—real bodies—nurses, siblings, doctors, spouses of siblings, technicians, his children, everyone who came and went over the next day or so, some visiting for just moments, some staying much longer, some moist-eyed, some business-like, all speaking softly as if they might otherwise disturb his important rest. Trace himself drifted, vaguely aware of the activity around him, but mostly he was off exploring unfamiliar landscapes and curious realms far removed from his bed. He returned periodically to the hospital room, but each time it seemed less interesting and more out of focus, and he struggled to recall what business he had there.

Until the moment when he abruptly awoke an hour or so before dawn, fully aware, his senses as sharp as they had ever been. The room was dark, the bedclothes pressed against him. Oxygen rushed into his nose and open mouth over a withered and useless tongue. His right arm lay exposed, chilled, connecting him to an IV drip. Despite the mask covering most of his face, he could smell the flowers in the vase across the room. Carnations. And roses.

The chairs were occupied, like always. Marla was turned slightly to one side, folded into herself, a blanket covering her from neck to knees. Quince's arms were crossed over his chest, his head slumped forward. Both of them had surrendered at last to utter exhaustion.

Finally he could do what he had come here for.

Trace looked around for Bertie, but she was gone. Dying, after all, is a private moment.

He exhaled one last time, and felt himself falling backward into a warm abyss. As he left, he was aware that the machine by his head was beeping more frantically. The overhead light had come on, and people were approaching the bed.

Go home, he called out to his wife and his brother as he fell. *Go home and pick up your lives again. For me.*

He hoped they could hear him.

Acknowledgments

I'm grateful for the friendships and contributions of those people who have given of their time and talents to shape this story.

Davis Bennett, proofreader extraordinaire, who has laboriously plowed through just about everything I've ever written, finding errors miniscule and huge alike. Davis, thank goodness numbers are your friend, because they certainly have never been mine.

Kim Elliott, a tireless supporter and cheerleader of my writings, who read through earlier drafts of this book, as she has many of my other literary efforts.

Karen Winter, who did likewise, and finally said to me, "Don't you think you've written just about enough on this one? I don't think there's any more story to tell." (Thank you, Karen… you were right!)

Beth Foster, my editor and publisher all rolled into one. Even after the manuscript had passed beneath more sets of eyes than I can begin to recall, she still found glaring things that needed correcting.

And finally, to Ann Davis, to whom this novel is dedicated, for the number of times I interrupted her work to ask about medical conditions, symptoms, procedures, and treatments, and who gave generously of her time and expertise (at no charge!) every time. Let it be known that everything I got right is owing to her, and everything I got wrong is where I "went rogue" in the name of artistic license.

I'm sure I'll wake up in a cold sweat one of these nights long after this book's publication, abruptly remembering the person whose name was inadvertently left off this list. If it was you, I'm sincerely sorry, and I promise to catch you the next time around!

About the Author

Colorado native Scott Gibson is an award-winning playwright and the author of six novels. Gibson's plays have been performed from New York to Los Angeles and filmed for television. He particularly focuses on lifelike characters and plots that touch on the humorous and dramatic. Gibson earned a BA in English from the University of Northern Colorado and has worked as a technical editor and blogger. When he's not working on his next novel, he volunteers with animal shelters and enjoys Colorado's beautiful outdoors by jogging, hiking and cycling.

www.ingramcontent.com/pod-product-compliance
Lightning Source LLC
Chambersburg PA
CBHW050724180626
46814CB00002B/589